to

from your big fan,
Antonin Felix

FATAL REMEDY

Also by the Author:

Sonia Sotomayor: The True American Dream

Some Kind of Genius: The Extraordinary Journey of Musical Savant Tony DeBlois (with Janice DeBlois)

Wesley K. Clark: A Biography

Condi: The Condoleezza Rice Story

Silent Soul: The Miracles and Mysteries of Audrey Santo

Andrea Bocelli: A Celebration

Laura: America's First Lady, First Mother

Christie Todd Whitman

Wild About Harry: The Illustrated Biography of Harry Connick, Jr.

John MacNally: A Life in Song

FATAL REMEDY

A Novel

Antonia Felix

WINNERS BOOKS

A heartfelt word of thanks to my agent, Lois de la Haba,
for her unfailing encouragement and support.

ISBN: 0615538711
ISBN: 9780615538716

© Winners Books 2012. All rights reserved.

This is a work of fiction. Names, characters, places and incidents
either are products of the author's imagination or are used fictitiously.
Any resemblance to actual events or locales or persons, living
or dead, is entirely coincidental.

To T.S., healer of writers and other fragile souls

"If someone has committed a crime and is caught, he suffers judicial punishment. If he had done it secretly . . . and remains undiscovered, the punishment can nevertheless be visited upon him . . . for one who commits such a crime destroys his own soul."

—C.G. Jung, *Memories, Dreams, Reflections*

FATAL REMEDY

ONE

The body lay parallel to the walking path, pale as a worm. The bus driver who spotted it while pulling up to her first pre-dawn stop along Loring Park told an officer that at first glance it looked like a pile of rags. Only when she rolled the bus around a bend that curved closer to the path did she make out the contours of a body. She had called her dispatcher while staring out her open window, sending puffs of vapor into the chilled November air to float above the bare ground. Within fifteen minutes, a cluster of police cruisers and unmarked cars from Minneapolis' First Precinct had appeared along the winding drive, their blue and white lights flashing onto the condominiums and ivy-covered Women's Club facing the park. After signing a statement, the bus driver made her usual stops around the periphery and then turned toward central downtown, her well-dressed passengers straining to see a detail worth remembering.

The officers and detectives meandering inside the circle of yellow tape that cordoned off the scene kept a respectful distance from Bo Williams, the senior detective on duty.

Sporting a red knit cap with earflaps over his gray crew cut, Williams studied the position of the body and scribbled into a small notebook. He stared at the transparent plastic tarp and finally crouched down and pulled it away.

"Strangulation," he said to no one in particular, eyeing the bruising on the neck. He slipped on a pair of latex gloves and gently picked up the head. "Looks like a metal wire. Practically took off his head." He scanned the rest of the body. Muscular but not bulky, a smooth face that looked about forty, curly blond hair with coppery streaks, faint indentations along the nose from wearing glasses, manicured nails.

The medical examiner, a woman named Carlson, observed from the other side of the body. "A strong guy like that must have been taken by surprise," she said. On the way to the scene she had glanced at a report about the dozens of assaults that occurred in the park every year, most of which were committed by young males from the suburbs who drove in to get an eyeful of male prostitutes strolling brazenly along the sidewalks. They'd yell at them from their SUVs or pickup trucks until they worked themselves into enough of a pack-crazed frenzy to jump out and beat someone up.

She agreed with Williams that the width and depth of the gash on the neck indicated a wire garrote, an unusual weapon in these parts, something you'd be more likely to see in an old horror film in which the villain slips the wire connected to two wooden handles around an unsuspecting neck and twists the poor sap into oblivion. She stepped aside as the police photographer took close-ups of the flaps of skin on the fingertips that, according to Carlson, showed he had tried to pull on the wire.

"A garrote," said Williams. "That's one for the books."

"Doesn't look like your typical gay-bashing," said Carlson.

"No. More like a straight homicide—no pun intended."

Carlson winced at him and headed back to her van, but was intercepted by another detective who held out a wallet and pair of men's socks.

"We found these behind the bushes," he told her, nodding to a stand of bare lilacs a few yards away. "Business card says he was a doctor who lived across the street." He pointed to the tallest building facing the south side of the park.

Williams thumbed through the wallet. "Clayton Shepherd," he said. "I've heard of him, the psychiatrist with the radio show. Looks like he had an office at the Pembroke Clinic."

"High-end clientele," said Carlson. "Hard to imagine a Pembroke outpatient resorting to something like this because he wasn't thrilled with his therapy." She crouched by the body again and lifted Shepherd's left hand. "No wedding ring."

Williams stepped out of the way so that the photographer could zoom in on Shepherd's neck. "He talked about his divorce on the show a while back," he said.

"Shepherd was investigated for sexual misconduct by the state medical board last year," Carlson said, reading the screen on her cell phone. "Nine women testified against him. At the same time, a couple sued him for malpractice after their teenage son committed suicide."

"What did the board do?" asked Williams.

Carlson scrolled the glass with her thumb. "Suspended his license."

"How long?"

"Three months."

"He talked about those cases on his show, too," said Williams. "Claimed they were all dreamed up by another doctor who was trying to ruin his reputation."

The photographer took his last shot, a wide angle from the south, and Williams pulled the tarp back over the body.

Carlson continued reading, and then stood up to face Williams. "His show was about sports psychology," she said. "Last I checked, you're not much of a sports fan."

"It's better than late-night TV."

"Trouble sleeping?"

"Once in awhile."

Carlson stared at the blood that darkened the grass beyond the edge of the tarp. "Stuff like this could keep you awake, I suppose. If you let it." She snapped off her gloves and shoved her notebook into her coat pocket.

Williams shook his head at her and smiled. He stepped away from the body and walked toward his car. His movement stirred up a cloud of flies that had been feeding at the dark spot. By the time he reached his sedan, the flies had settled back onto the sticky ground.

TWO

Two months earlier, Clayton Shepherd's sixteen-year-old patient Mike McCarthy woke from a metallic-smelling dream, the third that had bludgeoned him awake that week. He slammed the top of his radio to disengage the alarm, which was set to go off five minutes later. A white spot on top of his dresser drew his attention with its gauzy, shifting light. He stared at the blot until recognizing it as the label on his pill bottle. More distracting was the memory of the sound that had shaken him from his nightmare. Someone had just closed his bedroom door. He was sure of it, even though in his dream the noise was made by the clamp of a steel vest locking into place around his torso and squeezing him breathless. He crawled out of bed, opened his window and inhaled air thick with the scent of spruce. Turning to his dresser, he came eye level with a glass of water, the medicine bottle and a single green pill placed beside it. He read the label aloud in a whisper, slowing down to sound out the unfamiliar words: "Michael McCarthy, Prozor (fluoxetine hydrochloride), ten milligrams, take one pill by mouth once a day, Clayton Shepherd, MD."

"Number seventeen," Mike said, squeezing the tablet between his fingers. He popped the pill into his mouth and bit down hard to crush it. The pressure he had felt in the dream returned, as if an actual steel vest was flattening his ribs and spine. Standing at the mirror on his closet door, he pulled off his T-shirt and slid his hands over his bare skin. The tightness crept up his neck just as it had the day before, gripping his head like the hose clamps in the science lab at school. He wondered if this would be the morning that his skull exploded as he bent forward to tie his shoes or pick up his backpack, actions that ramped up the pressure until it crackled and pumped red behind his eyes. If his friends had noticed his pant-like breathing or bulging forehead veins, it would be news to him. They hadn't said anything all week.

•

Later that morning, Mike lasted ten minutes in first-hour English class before Mr. Patterson threw him out for kicking the student's chair in front of him so hard that the girl bit her tongue and was sent to the nurse's office with blood smearing her chin. Mike stood in the hall and slammed his backpack against the wall again and again, bobbing freakishly and birdlike between each impact. He breathed in shallow gasps as the force around his torso increased its pressure. The principal wasn't in, so Patterson sent him to band, his regular class for second hour. He strode in late during the warm-ups, stood behind the director and glared at the empty chair in the second row, third from the left, his chair, which shouted his inadequacy because he should have moved in the other direction to principal clarinet after his biggest rival graduated. But his audition was a disaster; the mouthpiece burned like a hunk of charcoal between his lips and his fingers froze in place over their holes until, by some freakish force of will, he managed to move them like a dumb-ass who had picked up the instrument for the first time in his life. At first he was grateful to get third chair, but the more he thought about it, the more his band director, Mrs. Jensen, seemed like a hag bent on humiliating him in front of the whole school. After glancing at Jensen's back, he threw his clarinet case across the room to crash against the wall and stormed out. He glanced behind him as he jogged down the empty hall but no one followed him, no one called out to ask what was going on, no one shouted at him to stop.

He slipped into the gym and ran toward the cushioned wall on the other side of the room at full speed, slamming into it with his right shoulder. He backed up and barreled into it again, and then jumped up to grab the basketball hoop, yanking as hard as he could as he dangled in the air. He gritted his teeth and yelled as if someone were pulling on his legs, tearing apart his backbone one disk at a time. The noise bounced off the wooden floor and rolled-up stands. He released his grip, fell onto the floor and lay on his side, staring at one half of his face reflected in the polished surface. He closed his eyes and did not know how long he had slept before being jolted awake by the gym doors crashing open to let in a class of eighth-grade girls in basketball uniforms.

He scrambled to his feet and ran out to the hall, where he pinned himself into a corner to wait out the stream of students rushing to their next classes. After the bell rang and the hall emptied he walked toward the east wing, shrinking between rows of lockers on each side that frowned in agony with black, slit-like mouths. They shifted against the walls like robots inching their way to an underground vat where they would be melted alive. Their horrified, bolted eyes—why hadn't he noticed them before?

Despair oozed from their metal bodies in waves that

throttled the air and pushed him to his knees. He slid forward, pushing off with his hands from time to time until he turned to the adjoining hall, which was lined with bulletin boards and display cases instead of lockers. Rushing ahead on his feet, he came to the next set of lockers and focused on number four-thirty-seven, about one-third the way down the wall, repeating the number in his head to block out the silent but pounding grief emanating from the tragic metal faces along the walls.

When he reached his locker, he rested his forehead on the door and tried to push down the sob thrusting its way up his throat. He pressed his face into the cold metal until his nose was a flat slab.

"Mike."

When he turned to face his best friends—Nira and Carl, whom everyone called CJ—the metal faces behind them shuddered with anguish and he shifted his gaze to his friends' feet.

"We can walk you home, if you want," said CJ. "Do you want to go home?"

Mike gripped his arms around his chest to fend off the pressure that had stifled his breathing ever since he woke from his dream that morning.

"We got permission to take you," said Nira. "It's OK."

Mike glanced up at her brown eyes and long black hair. The kindest eyes. His hands shook where they grasped his arms.

"She's right," said CJ. "We won't get in trouble for leaving early." He clutched Mike's dented clarinet case in one hand.

Mike stifled the knot creeping up his throat and coughed. "They're so sad," he said.

"Who?" asked Nira.

Mike looked up and gazed at the lockers behind her left shoulder. The black slats above the steel-bolt eyes were dark eyebrows casting shadows on the glossy metal faces.

"Them," he said.

She and CJ turned around and then looked at each other.

"Let's go home, Mike," said CJ.

"I'll go," said Mike. "By myself. I need to be by myself." He pulled his messenger bag out of his locker and headed for the door at the end of the hall. CJ caught up to him, but Mike shook him off.

"Call me later," CJ called out.

"Sure."

•

Ellen McCarthy answered a call from Mike's principal, his third call in five days, as she loaded her groceries into her car. Mike had been seen leaving school early again, and two teachers were in his office, baffled and insistent that he call the boy's mother to find out what was happening at home. Over the years, they had witnessed countless sixteen year olds suffer through hormonally induced mood swings and recklessness, but no one had shifted as abruptly as Mike McCarthy. Until recently he had been an average student with close friends, a polite and seemingly well-adjusted kid, inconsistent with his grades now and then, but far from the morose loner type they had been taught to recognize after the Columbine shooting. There had to be an explanation for what was happening with Mike.

As she drove home, Ellen told the principal that she and her husband, Daniel, had scheduled a phone call with Mike's doctor for that evening because Mike was obviously reacting badly to his antidepressant medication. They had sent him to a psychiatrist, she explained, hoping that his falling grades could be explained by something he just needed to get off his chest. The psychiatrist, who had been recommended by a friend from their church, had sent them home from that first visit with a week's supply of Prozor. At the end of that first week, Mike told them that he didn't feel any different. He said the same after the second week. But a day after starting his third week's supply, Mike changed.

"He was suddenly angry and aggressive," she told him, "like a completely different kid." She confided that the doctor described Mike's condition as severe depression, far more serious than anything that could be brought on by a case of teenage rejection. During Mike's short diagnostic visit, she and Daniel figured, he must have told Dr. Shepherd about his breakup with his girlfriend, a new student in the freshman class whose family had moved from California over the summer. They had gone to the pool and the movies with some of Mike's friends and spent a few Saturday afternoons on their own at the Mall of America, but just as suddenly as they got together, they broke up.

Dr. Shepherd told her and Daniel that the breakup was the trigger, the final straw that aggravated his abnormal psychochemical condition and sent him over the brink. His lack of motivation in the new school year would deteriorate into a lack of appetite, weight loss, further withdrawal, inability to keep up his classes, estrangement from friends and family, and possibly a psychotic break if he was not treated. Thankfully, he said, a drug like Prozor would bring him back to normal just like it did a million other kids.

"I'm going to talk to Dan about taking away Mike's medication tonight. I'm sure he'll agree with me." She said she hoped that Dr. Shepherd would recommend another therapy, but if not, they'd let Mike get some rest, take a couples days off from school, or however long it took for the drug to get out of his system, and let nature take its course. If he still felt bad, they would seek out another kind of help, maybe the school counselor, whom he seemed to like—but no more drugs.

The principal, who had known the family for years, told her that he and Mike's teachers all hoped for the best. She and Dan could count on their support.

•

Ellen waited in the driveway for the garage door to open. Once inside, she gathered up the grocery bag, brought it into the kitchen and called out to Mike. She walked to the bottom of the stairs in the other room and called out again, but finding his messenger bag hanging in its usual place on the banister, she figured he was in his room with his headphones on. The unpacked bag nagged at her and she went back to the kitchen to put the groceries away. She took a six-pack of beer out to the extra fridge in the garage and made room by removing the bottle of champagne that had been there since New Year's Eve. Carrying the bottle around the corner to the storage area behind the refrigerator, she walked into Mike's legs. They gently bumped into her face as she looked up at his limp body. His head leaned over the edge of a black belt looped around a two-by-four on the ceiling.

The champagne bottle shattered at her feet. Before she could lift her fingertips to Mike's shoes, her knees gave out and she dropped to the floor. Gazing up, she saw the overturned canoe floating above him with arched, wooden ribs.

"Jesus!"

Unaware of the cuts on her arms and hands, she pulled her leg away from a stepladder that lay on its side and recoiled at the thought that Mike had kicked it away. She tried to sit up, but fell back down, knocking her head on the cement floor. Her hand shook as she reached toward a string of spit dropping from above, which slowed and hovered before succumbing to a pulse of gravity and pooling on her shirt. She pulled herself to her feet and reached up to grab Mike's wrist. The flesh was cold and hard and her knees buckled again. She crawled toward the corner from which she had come, leaving two tracks of blood as she dragged herself around to the front of the refrigerator. She rolled over on her back, the heat from the SUV's engine hitting her face as she opened her phone and dialed 911.

The operator asked for her name and she strained to speak but nothing came out. She closed her eyes to concentrate on the buzzing that seemed to start deep within her sinuses and spread across her face, but a ping from the cooling car engine jolted her back to reality. She whispered her name to the operator and watched her free arm jerk crazily upon the fog-colored floor.

THREE

A light rain dampened the windows behind the fourth-floor nurse's station at Hennepin Metro as Clayton Shepherd typed notes into his tablet computer. Squinting and holding a stylus between his teeth, he tapped the screen with his index fingers.

"Wouldn't your glasses help with the small print?" asked the nurse behind the counter, the central hub of the mental health ward. "Why don't you put them on your nose where they belong?"

"They look better up here," Clayton said, touching the tortoise-shell frames nearly hidden in his curly hair.

"I see," she said. "You're accessorizing."

"No, Carolyn. I use them when I have to, but I don't go out of my way to look old like some people on this floor."

She shot him a glance over the wire-rimmed reading glasses perched on the end of her nose.

"I understand," he said, "that a head nurse needs to look mature to demand respect, but you don't need to go overboard." He smiled at her and then continued typing.

"I've got orders for room four-sixteen," he finally said.

The patient, he noted in the chart that Carolyn brought up on her screen, a sixty-three-year-old white male with chronic alcoholism, had been brought in by his wife, son and daughter-in-law earlier that evening because he had been screaming at a creature that he claimed was sitting on the dining room table. He told it to get out of his house, threw a chair at it that shattered a crystal bowl, then lashed at the phantom with a meat cleaver. The wife told Shepherd that over the years her husband had done a lot of rambling at invisible people when he was drinking, but nothing like this. Clayton's notes included his observation that she was dressed in a floor-length apricot gown, her daughter in a red cocktail dress and the husband and the son in tuxedoes. They had been at a "dry" wedding reception with a conservative branch of the wife's family and the husband, who promised to show up sober, had not had a drop for nearly forty-eight hours.

"A withdrawal like that can set off a kick-ass psychotic episode," Shepherd told Carolyn as he aimed his tablet at a Bluetooth device near her computer monitor. "He's lucky no one got hurt." His order for one milligram of lorazepam blinked onto the main screen, and Carolyn used the intercom to alert the shift nurse in the drug dispensary down the hall.

That nurse, a young woman in a multi-colored smock and white tennis shoes, filled the medication order and stepped into the patient's room. Clayton followed her in, watched her give the injection and then asked her to help him loosen the restraints on the man's ankles and wrists. "I'm sure you've got lots of practice doing this," he said to her. She didn't catch the innuendo, and Clayton laughed as he left the room and walked down the hall to the waiting area.

All three family members sat upright on a sleek modern couch across from the flat screen television that stood on a low cabinet. He pulled up a leather side chair and, directing most of his words to the wife, assured them that the patient's condition was not permanent but directly related to long-term alcohol abuse. "If things have progressed this far," he added, "there is a very good chance that he may have other problems also caused by the drinking that would require a thorough set of tests."

Clayton leaned toward the daughter and added, quietly, "It's too bad he spoiled your night. You look beautiful."

Holding her tissue to her nose, she shifted uncomfortably against the gray wool sofa. Her husband raised his eyebrows and stared at the doctor.

Clayton sprang up. "There's nothing more you can do tonight. We'll take good care of him. Tomorrow morning he'll probably be ready to go home." He smiled and extended his hand to the son, who paused before shaking it.

After the doctor left, the daughter looked at her mother and said, "Did you hear that?" She turned to her husband. "I've never seen that guy before in my life. Why did he come on to me like that?"

Her husband put his arm around her shoulders. "He's a jerk," he said. "You've got to be a little off to be in his line of work. Goes with the territory."

•

Returning to the nurse's station, Clayton swung the monitor around and checked his patient list. Regan Moyers, a registered nurse on the ward, smiled at him as she walked into the supply room without being detected by Carolyn. Clayton returned the monitor to its former position and quickly went in after Regan. Realizing they were alone, he locked the door behind him and grabbed her wrists, holding them behind her back. He pressed her against the metal shelves and kissed her. She wriggled her hands free without releasing from the kiss and put her arms around his shoulders.

"How's your mental health today, Nurse Moyers?" Clayton said as he pulled a long strand of red hair out of the way.

"Just fine, doctor. Thank you for asking." She kissed him and he slid his hands up and down her sides, pressing along her ribs, her waist, her hips.

"I've missed you," he said. "Why don't you call me anymore?" He pulled her white tunic over her head and unclasped her bra.

"Stop it," she said, grabbing his hands. "I've got to go. I just finished my shift."

"So why haven't you called me?" he said.

"I thought we agreed that you've got your hands full," she said, smiling. "Not that I had any claim on you, but you do keep yourself busy. I'm not the type to be just one of the pack."

"Are you saying you're not a bitch?" he said as he turned her around and held her against him. "You'd be such a good one, lording your sweet ass over the rest of them."

She laughed and closed her eyes as he kissed her on the neck.

"Let me think about it." She pulled away, turned around to face him and slipped her scrubs over her head. "You," she said, placing her index finger on his lower lip, "are a naughty, naughty doctor." She put her hands inside her tunic and fastened her bra.

He grabbed her again and snapped off the light. "Remember how nice it is in here in the dark? I'll let you go this time, but only because I've got four patients to see in the next fifteen minutes." He kissed her on the forehead and flicked on the light.

•

After the commotion of the shift change tapered off, the only sign of life at the nurse's station was Carolyn's purse, which she had left on her chair. She emerged from a dark hallway with two cups of coffee and tisked herself for leaving it. Clayton appeared from the north hallway, his face glowing blue from the reflection of his computer screen and dissolving into white as he neared the desk. He leaned over the counter and aimed his handheld at the Bluetooth control for a moment. He thanked Carolyn for the coffee and straightened up.

"I'd like to download tomorrow's schedule," he said, tapping the tablet on the counter like a pack of cigarettes.

"Look at this," said Carolyn, motioning him to come behind the counter to read a suicide DOA report on her monitor. "Wasn't this one of your patients?"

•

Padmini Dalmia walked toward the station from the south hallway and stopped abruptly before the light could illuminate more than her feet. From the back she recognized Shepherd's hair and glint of a gold stud in his right ear. She moved toward the wall to ensure Shepherd wouldn't see her if he turned around. Then she heard the inappropriately loud, self-conscious laugh. She stepped back, slipped through the stairwell door and walked down to the next floor. Her steps were light and fast, even in the two-inch heels that accentuated her delicate ankles and the hem of her turquoise silk pants. After nearly twenty years in this country, she still preferred an Indian-inspired wardrobe of long tunics and slender trousers. She also wore a long white jacket to work rather than the print smocks that so many of the other nurses chose. Her gold bracelets chinked against the steel hand railings like bells on a cat collar.

The light coming through the window of the third-floor break room shot a white ray across the hall. Padmini found Karen Madden inside, sitting at a table with her phone.

"I'm glad to see you," Padmini said. "Can I get you a coffee?"

Karen stood up and kissed her on the cheek. "What are you doing down here? Is the fancy new roof above your remodeled ward leaking already?"

"I'm avoiding someone," Padmini said as she placed a small porcelain cup beneath the nozzle of the cappuccino machine. "I'm much more surprised to see you. Can I get you one of these?"

"No, thank you." Karen brushed something from the embroidered name on her white jacket. The youngest cardiologist in the hospital, she worked two days per week in the rehabilitation services unit. "I got called in to see a stroke patient and I'm waiting for Jim to pick me up. We're going to make a night of it and stroll the carpeted aisles of Binghamton's."

"Grocery shopping at midnight?" Padmini asked.

"They have a wine bar."

"I love this country," Padmini said, laughing as she sat down on a silver stool.

"Who are you running away from?" Karen asked.

Padmini dissolved a packet of sugar in her cup. "How long has Clayton Shepherd been working at Metro?" Padmini said.

"The psychiatrist?"

"Yes. He's got a private practice in South Minneapolis and I thought all of his privileges were out in the southern suburbs, but I just saw him upstairs with Carolyn."

"Just a second," Karen said, and began typing a message into her phone. "Sorry. Yes, I know he's been here for at least three or four months because he was in a patient conference with me about three months ago. I remember thinking he looked a lot different than the last time I had seen him. His hair was lighter, bleached maybe, and he had an earring. He looked thinner. The first time I met him he had a full beard, straight Ken-boy hair and a little paunch. I almost didn't recognize him. Not that I run into him that much."

"I had no idea he worked here when I joined the unit. I can't believe his name never came up."

"Maybe he just has one or two patients come through here every month. He may not have full privileges," said Karen as she tossed her phone into her purse and reached for her coat.

"Can you please stay for a minute?" Padmini said. "I really need to talk to you."

Karen dropped her coat back on the stool and reached over the table to hold both of Padmini's hands. "Of course. Just let me tell Jim I'll be a few more minutes." She recovered her phone and typed a quick message, then placed it back in her purse. She crossed her arms and leaned them on the table. "All right."

"Clayton Shepherd and I have a history," Padmini said, twisting the Ganesha charm on her necklace.

"After you and Gage separated?"

A blue vein appeared on Padmini's forehead. "He caused our separation. We had an affair while I was working at Fairview and Gage found out about it. It felt like a relief at first because leading that double life was a nightmare, but when I found out that Clayton was seeing other women, a lot of other women, I finally came to my senses."

"My God, I can't believe it. I thought you left *Gage*."

"No, he had very good reason to leave, and it ripped him up. It ripped up all of us. Nira hasn't been the same, she's very angry."

"At her dad?"

"No, she loves her dad and they see each other a lot. She's furious with Clayton for tearing her family apart. Nira is a very compassionate girl, very wise for her age. When I told her why her father was leaving, that I had betrayed him by getting involved with Dr. Shepherd, she asked me how it could be possible that my doctor would put me in that situation."

"Your doctor? Shepherd was treating you?"

"Yes. While we were chatting one day about teenagers—Nira was arguing with me at the time about not being allowed to go to a concert—I got worked up and started crying. The tears just burst from me. I knew I was overreacting, but I couldn't help it. Clayton acted deeply concerned and offered to treat me. We set up an appointment for the next day and he gave me a prescription for Prozor and Wellbotra."

"Selective serotonin . . . reuputake inhibitors?" asked Karen. "Two antidepressants at once?"

"Prozor is an SSRI," said Padmini, "but Wellbotra is an NDRI. It acts on the neurotransmitters norepinephrine and dopamine. I questioned why he wanted me to take both kinds at the same time, too. But he told me that as a psychiatric nurse I must be aware that many of our patients eventually move on to a dual prescription after failing to get good results from a single medication. I didn't know that it was usual practice for a doctor to skip the initial single-drug treatment, but I took his word for it. I was a mess then. I wasn't even aware of how much I wanted help. He made it sound like he was doing me a personal favor to combine the two right from the start, and I was grateful for his concern and his professional courtesy. What an idiot."

"You were vulnerable. It's not easy to make decisions in a state like that."

"That's just it. When I went to see him for the drug monitoring sessions, he sat across from me, knee to knee, held my hands and told me how beautiful and exotic I was. He went on and on about how glad he was to be able to help me pull myself together and get strong again. But I wasn't feeling stronger. In those first three weeks I felt as if I were hanging on to everything by sheer force of will. When I sat in his office, so close to him, I felt safe enough to let go. At the end of the third week, I was carried away by that extraordinary feeling of relief and safety, and his face was right in front of me. I looked into his eyes and let my thoughts bleed through them. He was right there, right in my head. He held my head in his hands and kissed me."

Karen rested her elbows on the table and cupped her hands over her mouth.

"It was wonderful, Karen. For the next few weeks I lived for those sessions. We turned his office into our rendezvous, lights out, the whole thing. It was a thrill to run into him in the hallway. If there weren't many people around, he would squeeze my arm or whisper something in my ear. After the second month I changed, though. I woke up stressed and barked at Gage and Nira all the time. Clayton told me that my mind was clearing and that I was finally seeing the light. He said I was in a stifling marriage and needed to get out."

"He knew Gage?"

"No, but I was so stupid that I somehow believed the few things I told him about my marriage in those later weeks, when I was angry all the time, were enough for him to be enlightened about my husband and my eighteen-year marriage."

"How did Gage finally find out?"

"That was easy. I blurted out during a quarrel that Clayton had him all figured out. He asked me who Clayton was, and I said, 'Dr. Shepherd.' He asked me why I called my psychiatrist by his first name, and from my silence and the defiant look I must have had on my face, he figured it out. We argued about it for almost another hour, and I finally told him I didn't love him anymore. He left that night."

"Doctors can't sleep with their patients, Padmini," Karen said quietly. "That's a felony in this state. You have to go after him."

"Right. And drag Nira into the black hole of this thing all over again when it gets in the newspapers? No way. She's determined to get her dad and I back together, and God willing, it could happen. I won't do anything to jeopardize that."

"What can I do?"

"I'm fine now. All that matters is Nira. Seeing Clayton just now shook me up. I'll find out when he's scheduled here and I'll work around it."

"Are you seeing another psychiatrist?"

"No, and I'm not taking any more medication, either. This crisis actually did me a lot of good. My priorities are back in line and I have a true focus. My life is for Nira, her future. Once I realized that everything else fell into place. If I'm lucky, I'll get Gage back, even though I don't deserve him."

Karen's phone hummed loudly on the table. She stood up and hugged Padmini, then stood back and looked at her for a moment. "I have to go, but we aren't done talking about this." She picked up her coat and headed for the door.

"Karen, one thing."

"What's that?" she said, turning around.

"Steer clear of the fourth floor."

FOUR

Nira moved closer to CJ as a flurry of orange and yellow leaves swept around the curves of Mike's coffin. They both looked up to watch the sparrows and chickadees that made a bright racket in the sun above the small crowd. CJ's dad, Anthony Robson, and Nira's mother, Padmini, also stood in the front row near Ellen McCarthy, who was barely recognizable behind enormous sunglasses and wide-rimmed black hat. CJ held himself together through the closing prayer and did not begin to cry until he followed Nira's lead and placed a rose on top of the coffin. Anthony put his arm around his son's shoulder as the minister opened his prayer book. "As we read in the gospel of John, our Lord said: 'Do not let your hearts be troubled. Trust in God; trust also in me. In my Father's house are many rooms; if it were not so, I would have told you. I am going there to prepare a place for you . . .'"

After another reading by Mike's older sister, Jaclyn, the minister gave the blessing and everyone turned and walked slowly to their cars. Padmini lifted the hem of her brown sari above the leaf-covered ground with one hand and held her daughter's hand with the other. The cars winded their way out of the cemetery, and just as Anthony was about to drive beneath the wrought-iron arch of Lakewood Cemetery onto 36th Street, he stopped to let CJ jump out and jog over to Padmini and Nira's car.

"My dad said it's OK if Nira and I walk along the lake for a while," CJ said through Nira's open window. "He'll park and wait for us and bring us over to the McCarthy's. Is that OK, Mrs. Dalmia?"

"Of course. I'll see you both later."

Anthony dropped them off five blocks away at Lake Calhoun. "Take your time," he said. The two teenagers walked across the boulevard to the pedestrian path that hugged the circumference of the lake while Anthony sat on a bench and watched them until they were out of sight. He rested his head on the back of the bench and closed his eyes. A few minutes later, Padmini gently shook his shoulder.

"Would you mind some company?" she asked, offering him a coffee from a cardboard holder.

"Not at all," said Anthony.

"It is really too horrible for me to even comprehend yet," said Padmini. "CJ is lucky to have a psychologist for a father to help him get through a time like this."

"Nira is probably in better hands," he said. "Psychiatric nurses deal with much more severe trauma than I do. Most of my patients are just trying to shave a few seconds off their breaststroke time." He pointed at a moving spot a quarter way around the lake. "There they are." He squinted into the sun. "CJ was numb for a couple of days, but he's mostly angry now. Very angry."

"That's understandable," she said. "His best friend is gone forever."

"It's more focused than that," said Anthony. "He's mad as hell at Mike's psychiatrist, Clayton Shepherd."

"Mike was seeing Shepherd?"

"Yes. It's a small world, isn't it?"

"Very small," she said. "Shepherd and I used to work at the same hospital. Last year, CJ told me how angry he was with Shepherd for stealing his mother away, as he put it. It's no wonder Mike didn't tell him that he was seeing the doctor that broke up his family."

"On top of that, CJ's visit with Mike's parents last week was enough to put him over the edge. CJ grew up with Mike, as you know, and Dan and Ellen treat him like a son. Maybe they shouldn't have opened up with him this much, but they told him that they learned that two other teenage patients of Shepherd's had also committed suicide in the last couple of years. Now CJ is convinced that Shepherd is evil, an even bigger monster than he had already figured him out to be. Yesterday I found a cartoon that CJ had made on his computer, a picture of Shepherd with an axe stuck in his chest."

"Multiple suicides," said Padmini. "I hadn't heard about that." She drew her shawl more tightly around her shoulders. "If I may ask, are they still together, Shepherd and your ex-wife?"

Anthony squeezed his empty paper cup. "Yes. He set a trap for Marie at her first appointment and has never let go. She needed a prescription for her PMS mood swings, a mild antidepressant that women take like candy these days, but he started pumping her full of drugs and a lot of lies about me and our marriage." He stared at the far shore of the lake where the shadows of the pine trees cast a dark edge across the water. "I've learned that that's his pattern. He seduces women—including the mothers of his child and adolescent patients—who are already vulnerable and exploits that vulnerability with medication." He turned to Padmini. "How else can you explain the radical transformation that would make a woman like Marie abandon her son, no questions asked? Marie and CJ were very close, but once Shepherd got his hooks into her nothing else mattered."

Padmini shook her head. "How do you know all this?"

"I've been asking some questions around town. Shepherd has burned a lot of bridges and it hasn't been hard to find people dying for a chance to vent about him. One woman, the mother of one of Shepherd's teenage patients, told me a very bizarre story a couple of months ago. A few weeks earlier, she and Shepherd had been necking in his car and my show came on the radio. He shoved her back into her seat, turned up the volume and made her listen as he made a running commentary on everything I said. She said it seemed like he was taking notes in his head, which he verified when he said he was going to have his own radio show soon, a call-in show that would make mine sound like an amateur hour."

"But you do a sports psychology show," Padmini said. "He doesn't specialize in that, does he?"

"No, but according to this woman he does specialize in trying to either imitate or outdo me. I don't know why he wants to take what's mine, but he's done a pretty good job of it so far."

"He's disturbed," said Padmini. "You're not the only one who realizes that."

Anthony looked over his shoulder as if making sure no one would overhear. "Marie wasn't the first of his conquests, and she's certainly not going to be the last," he said. "It's been such a pattern that the state medical board is running a sexual misconduct investigation on him based on the complaints that several women have brought forward. Some of the women on his office staff claim they've been harassed, and I hear that they've even got complaints from a couple of his women patients who say he's had sex with them. His only criteria are that the women be beautiful, ripe for a depression or anxiety diagnosis and preferably rich. But that's another story."

He began to tear up his plastic coffee lid and drop the pieces into Padmini's empty cup. "I want to learn more about Shepherd's history with suicides," he said. "I've been so focused on CJ that I haven't given a lot of thought to the odds of the numbers that the McCarthy's uncovered. Does that amount sound realistic to you, three young suicides in two years, under the care of the same doctor?"

"Unfortunately, even though the teen suicide rate has fallen gradually over the past few years, it's still much higher than it was when we were CJ and Nira's age," said Padmini. "This is the state of things, Anthony. Every day I tell parents visiting their kids on our ward that about two million young people attempt suicide every year, and about two thousand of them succeed. That's triple the number from forty years ago."

"So the suicides on Shepherd's watch shouldn't raise any red flags?" he asked. "His practice can't be that huge that these numbers fit into normal statistical ranges."

"It's a good question, because the official word is that about two to three percent of kids taking antidepressants have increased suicidal thoughts and actions. That may not sound like a lot, but don't tell that to the parents of the two out of one hundred kids who try to kill themselves."

A flock of ducks landed near the shore of the lake and

ambled onto the grass in front of them. Padmini pulled a package of sunflower nuts from her purse and threw some on the ground. "CJ will be all right, Anthony." You're doing a marvelous job with him. He's a good student, a good athlete. He's a very good boy."

"You deserve the same credit. Nira had a hard time with your divorce at first, too, but she's a great kid. I think their friendship has had a lot to do with how well both of them are turning out."

"It's funny," said Padmini, "Nira isn't really a tomboy, but she doesn't seem to have romantic feelings for CJ. She loves him like a brother, I think."

"I think so, too. But who knows. That may change. A tragedy like this might bring them even closer."

Padmini squeezed Anthony's shoulder. "I have a casserole in the car for the McCarthy's reception," she said, "so I better go. I'll see you there."

As she turned away, Anthony grasped her arm. "Thank you for tracking me down," he said. "I needed this."

"I know you will take good care of him," she said, patting his hand. She tossed their two empty cups into a wastebasket on the way to her car.

FIVE

Anthony flashed his ID card at the back door lock of the Lowden Building on University Avenue, halfway between downtown Minneapolis and St. Paul. The windowless building, topped by a cluster of satellite dishes that sent and received programs across eighty square miles, stretched along half a city block. He waved at the news anchors as he passed the open double doors of the television studio and stopped in the green room on the opposite side of the hallway to pick up a cup of coffee, then he made his way to the KJOK radio studio at the far end of the building.

Stepping quietly into the control room, he stood behind Jack, the engineer, who was queuing up the next four minutes of advertisements on a touch-screen computer monitor. Through the window that separated the control room from the studio, Anthony watched Aaron and Susie Bradley, hosts of "The Bradley Buzz," wrap up their show. At ten seconds before the end of their time slot, Jack pointed at the clock on their wall, and Aaron closed his program with a lead-in:

It's Friday, and Dr. A-Rob is in the house! Stay tuned for Dr. Anthony Robson, host of 'The Mind of Sports,' the

FATAL REMEDY

award-winning sports psychology show. This is Aaron and Susie Bradley of 'The Bradley Buzz' for KJOK—the Twin Cities' only twenty-four-hour all-sports station. Have a great weekend, everybody.

Anthony joined them in the studio and placed his coffee and a set of index cards next to one of the microphones. The white walls were covered with framed photographs of radio personalities from KJOK, including a shot of Anthony standing between Aaron and Susie, both dressed in white warm-up suits with Olympic gold medals around their necks. Behind them a banner read: U.S. OLYMPIC SWIM TEAM GOLD MEDALISTS 1984. Another photo was a close-up of Anthony with his arm around Tiger Woods' shoulders, autographed by Woods with a note that read: "To Anthony, with many thanks for your work with the Healthy Kids Foundation." Next to that hung a larger photo of Anthony accepting an award from the president of the National Sports Broadcasters Association.

Aaron and Susie removed their headphones, and Susie handed Anthony a small square envelope.

"What's this?" he asked.

"An invitation to a barbeque we're having in a couple of weeks," she said. "The new deck and landscaping will be done by then, and we want to celebrate."

"Pretty fancy," said Anthony, opening the invitation.

"CJ's invited too, of course," said Aaron. "And if he wants to bring a friend, that's fine."

"How's he doing since his friend's funeral a couple days ago?" asked Susie.

"He's holding up."

"He's a great kid," said Aaron. "It's a shame he has to deal with this on top of everything else."

"You'll call us if he needs anything, won't you?" asked Susie.

"Thanks," said Anthony, reaching for his KJOK baseball cap that hung on the door. He slipped it on backwards and picked up a set of headphones. "And thanks for the invitation. We'll both really look forward to it." He lifted his hand and Aaron squeezed it on his way out.

Jack spoke up on the intercom. "Do you have a guest today?"

Anthony adjusted his headphones more snugly around his ears. "Yes, a phoner who's calling in at quarter past."

"Great," said Jack. "Ten seconds." He pushed the button on his board to turn on Anthony's mike, paused, then held up five fingers and counted down.

Good afternoon! This is Dr. Anthony Robson with 'The Mind of Sports,' glad to be with you on this beautiful Friday. Today we're going to talk about an issue that came up last weekend during the all-city high school swim meet in Edina. If any of you were there, you know what I'm talking about. And if any of you watched the local news this week, you've heard the gist of it. For everyone else, there was an incident after the meet in the parking lot, where one parent confronted another. Evidently he wasn't happy with how the other man's son performed in the relay, and he wanted him to know that the boy's 'sloppiness,' as he called it, was not acceptable. This whole thing escalated to a shouting match, and then the first dad shoved the other one against a car. All of us have probably seen an aggressive parent or two at the softball field, but witnessing this after a swim meet was a first for me. Why do some parents invest so much of their emotional lives in their kids' sports activities? That's what we're going to discuss today.

Jack began to play the bumper music for the first break and gradually increased the volume. He held up five fingers.

It's time to break for the weather, but we'll open up the phone lines when we come back, and I'll introduce my special guest. I'm Dr. Anthony Robson and this is 'The Mind of Sports.'

Anthony pulled his headphones down to rest on his neck and checked the notes on his cards. Two blinking white lights lit up on the console and he hit the intercom button. "We've got callers already?" he asked Jack.

Jack was busy typing in the current caller's name and location into the computer system. Five names appeared in the list on the monitor, and three more lights began to blink on Anthony's console. Jack finished his call and spun around to check the digital announcements queue on another monitor. He pulled off his headphones and hit the button to speak to Anthony. "Five callers. They were all at the meet."

"I knew this hit a nerve," said Anthony. He drank his coffee and eyed the second hand on the clock until the break was nearly over. Then he slipped on his headphones as Jack counted down the seconds and drove up the bumper music.

Welcome back to the 'Mind of Sports.' I'm Dr. Anthony Robson and today we're talking about parents who cross the line. Before I bring on my guest, let's go to our first caller, who I understand was at the meet in Edina on Wednesday night. Hello, Glen, you're on 'The Mind of Sports.'

Thanks for taking my call. My daughter was in that meet and we both saw the fight in the parking lot . . .

Jack looked at Anthony with a concerned expression, but didn't disconnect the call.

. . . my take on all this is that Anthony Robson is a stupid son of a—

Jack cut the line and shook his head angrily. Anthony jumped in:

Sounds like some overgrown kids are having fun messing around on their cell phones today—sorry about that. My expert screener and boy genius engineer Jack is giving me a very apologetic look.

Jack flashed an instant message onto Anthony's monitor to alert him that his guest was on the line and ready to go.

We'll take more calls in a minute, but now I'd like to introduce my guest, one of the coaches from that meet who spent some time talking to all four of the parents who faced off in the parking lot that night . . .

At the next break, Anthony went into the control room to hear Jack's story. "I'm sorry about that, Anthony. When I screened him, he had an English accent and he said he was going to tell you about what his daughter and her friends had to say about the fight. As soon as he got on the air and dropped the accent, I knew something was up."

Anthony laughed. "If we had a nickel for every time a lunatic called in . . ." said Anthony. "Is there a way to find out where he called from, at least?"

"I already dialed the number back, but it was a pay phone outside a convenience store in Wayzata. The clerk answered, and he said he couldn't describe the caller because he can't see the phone from behind the counter."

"Smart. But we both have a pretty good idea, don't we."

"Shepherd is still pulling this kind of shit on you?" asked Jack.

"You'd think he'd have better things to do."

"Faking an accent—that's something you'd expect from a kid, not a shrink." Jack swung around to look at the side console. "Geez, look at all these calls. I've got to line them up." He pulled on his headphones and pushed the button that linked him into the phone system. "KJOK. Your name, please?"

Anthony returned to the studio and shuffled through his cards until he found the one containing a list of key points to draw from when introducing the swim coach. His cell phone suddenly lit up with an alert that he had a new text message. He hit a key and read the text, which was from Aaron: "We're listening in the car. Can't believe he's still pulling that crap!" Anthony smiled and put his phone in his shirt pocket. He looked up at the muted television attached to the wall near the ceiling and watched the two news anchors from down the hall exchange a few words, then cut to footage from the recent swim meet altercation. The camera closed in on a man pushing another man against a parked car. The man who was pushed strode toward his attacker and shoved him to the pavement.

Anthony buzzed Jack and nodded to the TV screen. "Therapy," he said. "What this town needs is a lot more therapy."

SIX

The cedars lining the driveway to Pembroke Medical Center in South Minneapolis threw shadows across the dashboard as Anthony neared the meticulously landscaped front lawn. Just an eighth of a mile off sooty West Lake Street, the grounds and their ivy-covered manor did their best to hide the fact that a medical clinic and all the discomfort and vulnerability it entails waited inside. Anthony didn't know any of the doctors at Pembroke, but had heard all the legendary stories about the place, such as the customer service training taught by a consultant from a five-star hotel in New York that every doctor, nurse and staff person had to undergo. The staff catered to a clientele that had become accustomed to valet service, a uniformed doorman at the entry and waiting rooms with espresso machines and flat screen televisions.

Anthony stopped along the circular drive to get a full view of the building, which the website had stated was inspired by a sixteenth-century English estate. The limestone structure was flanked on all four corners by round towers topped with flags representing the State of Minnesota, the

City of Minneapolis, the American Medical Association and Pembroke. A stone marker to the right of the building pointed to a dark, round opening in the trees that was actually the entrance to the underground parking garage. The combined effect of the architecture, gravel driveway and absence of cars gave Pembroke an air of timelessness, and Anthony couldn't help but marvel that such an oasis lay less than a hundred yards from one of the most bustling sections of the city. Pembroke looked like a piece of history around which the entire city had grown over hundreds of years, but in reality, as Anthony had read, it was the newest structure in town.

The contractor had purchased eight city blocks, courtesy of a water main break that destroyed the basements and foundations of most of the 160 homes in the area. The company survived a fight with City Hall and two neighborhood associations, ultimately convincing them that the price it would pay each homeowner—and the city—more than compensated for the razing of a small parcel of South Minneapolis. One year after the groundbreaking ceremony, Pembroke opened for business and was recognized in construction and architectural circles as a miracle of inner city development. Patients came from around the world for all types of therapies, surgeries and treatments. Some of the doctors, especially surgeons who did gastric bypass and plastic surgery, had waiting lists more than a year long.

Anthony pulled a business card out of his pocket and glanced at the upper floor of the building as he drove toward the parking entrance.

•

Bill Olson, MD, one of two psychiatrists who made up Psychiatric Partners with an office on the top floor of Pembroke, wasn't hurting for new patients. The majority of them received therapy in the form of medication management sessions, usually lasting about fifteen minutes each, but he also had a handful of patients undergoing long-term talk therapy whom he saw in fifty-minute sessions once or twice a week.

The Psychiatric Partners suite included a waiting room with French doors leading out to a balcony. Bill's office, as well as that of his partner, Clayton Shepherd, faced the front of the building, and the entire staff had quick access to the patio and swimming pool on the roof. In good weather, patients could enjoy coffee and snacks at the little café tables on the balcony or, in the winter, be served by the receptionist indoors. Unlike many of the other practices in the building, the Psychiatric Partners' waiting room did not have a TV—patients did not need the anxiety of the news or the noise of game shows, Bill thought—but was instead wired with a stereo system that played classical music.

Built-in bookcases covered two walls of Bill's private office, and before a patient arrived he tucked away his laptop and papers in the antique roll-top desk by the door. Two matching, overstuffed chairs faced each other in the center of the room, separated by a small round table holding a box of tissues. A pile of journals on the floor next to the desk and an overloaded coat stand in one corner added to the cozy, lived-in atmosphere of the room.

Bill was finishing a sandwich at his desk when the receptionist buzzed his intercom phone. "Your next appointment would like to meet you in the Quiet Room on the third floor," she said. "He doesn't want to risk running into Dr. Shepherd here in the office."

"Dr. Robson," said Bill. "Tell him I'll meet him there in five minutes."

Bill tossed his paper lunch bag in the wastebasket, slipped a business card in his wallet and told the nurse in the outer office that he would be back within a half hour. He found Anthony seated in a white leather sofa facing a window with a view of the Minneapolis skyline.

Anthony shook his hand and introduced himself. "I'm sorry to take you away from your office," he said, "but after you hear what I've got to say, I think you'll agree it was necessary."

"You're the sports psychologist," said Bill. "With the radio show."

"Right."

"I can't say I've heard it. I'm afraid I don't listen to a lot of sports radio."

"That's all right."

"It's an interesting field, I would think, sports psychology."

"It is. But that's not why I'm here. It's not about me or my practice."

Olson nodded.

"I didn't want to bring you into this, but now I don't have any choice. A recent tragedy is deeply affecting my son, and I need your help."

"Would you like me to see him?" asked Bill. "You could have made that appointment over the phone."

"No, it's not about that, either. I've got that covered. It's about your partner, Clayton Shepherd."

"Oh?"

"You probably know that Clayton has been dating a woman named Marie for quite some time, and that they're getting serious. He met her a year ago when she started treatment with him for her PMS mood swings. She visits him at the office a lot, so if he hasn't introduced you to her you've probably seen her, anyway—long brown hair, petite, about five-two, very beautiful."

"Yes, I think I know who you're talking about. I've seen her talking to our head nurse a few times, and I just saw her and Clayton together in a restaurant a couple of weeks ago. He didn't see me, so I didn't have a chance to meet her."

"Marie is my ex-wife," said Anthony. "We were happily married until she started seeing Shepherd. He prescribed her a cocktail of psychotropics in the first couple of weeks of her treatment and convinced her that her marriage was a failure. A month later she declared that Clayton—she referred to him by his first name from the beginning—was her soul mate and she didn't have any time for me or our son, CJ. He's sixteen now, and he doesn't see his mother very much."

"Is that the tragedy you're talking about?" asked Bill.

"That's one, but it's not the trauma that concerns me right now. Last week, CJ and I went to the funeral of his best friend, Mike McCarthy."

Bill recognized the name and squinted his eyes. "Oh."

"When CJ found out that Shepherd had been treating Mike, he went ballistic. The news reignited his rage over the divorce, rage that's been focused on Shepherd personally and that he's been working hard to process. At the same time, CJ learned that Mike was the third suicide among Shepherd's patients in the last two years. In CJ's eyes, Shepherd is a murderer, and he's obsessed about getting revenge for his friend."

"I see."

"I'd like to know if those suicides have raised any flags around here, especially in light of the sexual misconduct investigation that the state is pursuing on Shepherd. It looks to me like the guy is a loose cannon."

"I'm very sorry to hear about your wife and your son," said Bill. He stood up and walked to the window. "I am aware of the suicides, of course, but I have read those patients' charts and they each exhibited suicidal ideation before they went into treatment with Clayton. The parents were well aware that in the first weeks of treatment the antidepressant medication can exacerbate those feelings."

"I can't speak for the first two kids," said Anthony, "but Mike was like a son to me and there is no way he was contemplating suicide. He was having some problems at school and had broken up with his girlfriend, but he had certainly not spiraled down that far."

"How can you be sure?" asked Bill. "You just told me that you didn't learn that Mike was under Clayton's care until after he died. How can you determine when his suicidal thoughts began?"

"I was with him the weekend after he and his parents returned from a short vacation. He stayed over with CJ on Saturday and Sunday night before going back to school. We watched movies and played board games and basketball and had a great time. He confided in me that he was angry about things happening at school and that he'd been sent home a few times, but he said his parents had really helped him when they were up at the lake because they listened to his complaints about the homework his teachers overloaded him with. He knew that they were going to make him follow through with his first psychiatric appointment when they got back, but he felt better about everything when he got home and wasn't resisting as much. I'm still kicking myself for not asking him which doctor he was going to see."

Anthony stood up and joined Bill at the window. "I *knew* that kid," he said. "He was not suicidal. I now know that he started his medication the following day, on a Monday, and sixteen days later he hung himself in his garage."

"There is a small percentage of young patients who suddenly have severe suicidal ideation when they begin an SSRI, you must know that," said Bill.

"But three of a doctor's young patients in two years? Does that sound reasonable?" He took his keys out of his pocket. "I'm sorry. I didn't mean to put you on the defensive. I just wanted to let you know how concerned I am about Clayton's history, and to ask if there's anything you can tell me about him that may help me calm down my son. God knows I don't have anything good to say about him myself. I already sued him for breaking up my marriage. But maybe there's something redeeming about him that will make him appear less evil in CJ's eyes. Maybe there's an angle here somewhere I've missed."

Olson watched a taxi wind its way around the circular drive.

"How long have you and Shepherd shared a practice?"

"A few years."

"Does he do any pro bono work? Anything I could point out to my son?"

Olson gazed down at the top of the taxi.

"I thought so."

"I've got concerns about Clayton, too," said Bill. "I'm cooperating with the Minnesota Medical Board in its investigation of sexual harassment and misconduct charges that have been filed against him. But there is more going on than that, and it's significant enough that there may be some changes here soon."

"There will definitely be some changes if the board takes away his medical license," said Anthony. "That would be very good for CJ, too. If Clayton lost his license, or better yet went to prison, my son would feel that some justice had been done." He looked at his watch. "I've taken up enough of your time."

"I see what you're trying to do for your son, and I'll give it some thought. But his therapist must have a strategy for dealing with his anger and other affects related to the maternal abandonment and grief over his friend's death."

"Yes, she has a strategy. And a good track record. I trust her."

"But?"

"My son is coming close to the edge. I feel it. I talk to him as much as I can, but I'm still too angry at Shepherd myself to try to help CJ look at him objectively. And I'm not about to send him to a psychiatrist for medication."

"I understand," said Bill.

They walked away from the window and toward the grand staircase that led down to the first floor. Before reaching the first red-carpeted step, Anthony faced Olson and asked, "Do you treat adolescents with antidepressants?"

"I have only had a handful of child and adolescent patients over the years. It's not my specialty."

"But it *is* Shepherd's specialty," Anthony said. "Your business partner spends ninety-five percent of his time dispensing drugs to kids, drugs that have not been studied for their long-term effects on developing brains. You must have an opinion on this." He was relieved to see Olson's eyes remain calm, his large pupils revealing empathy rather than defensiveness.

"I'm glad you came to me," said Olson. "When some legal issues are cleared up, which I expect to happen soon, I'll be able to talk to you more about Shepherd. And my perspective on the value and efficacy of clinical psychopharmacology will also have to be a conversation for another day." He extended his hand. "All right?"

Anthony shook it. "All right." Olson's eyes were a darker blue than that of the stiff blue shirt collar rising out of his pullover sweater.

As Anthony made his way down the center of the staircase, the deep carpeting seemed to sigh beneath his feet. The doorman opened the massive oak door to the left and Anthony walked through to a lobby where a fortyish man and a boy, about eight, stood waiting for the elevator. An orchestral version of a Beatles song played softly as they each stared at their blurry reflections in the elevator doors.

SEVEN

CJ and Nira ate their sandwiches by the railing overlooking the lower level of the mall, where store windows were crammed with Halloween and Christmas items. A line of shoppers and their children winded around the kiosks and benches, waiting for a ride on the carousel.

"My mom used to say that it was weird to have a carousel ride inside," CJ said. "Every time we came here, she said a carousel belongs outside in a park, like the one she used to ride as a kid at Excelsior."

"My mom remembers that carousel, too," said Nira.

"How old was she when she came here?"

"She was just a little girl, about five, I think," said Nira. "My grandfather got a job at Honeywell, so they all moved from India, even my great-grandmother." She told him about the relatives she'd meet when she finally got to travel to India, the aunts and uncles and cousins spread out from one end of the country to another, and the trains that connect them all.

"Maybe you'll find a boyfriend like one of the guys on Slumdog, with no front teeth and a tattoo on his skinny—"

Nira leaned over and grabbed CJ's neck in a mock strangle hold. He laughed and made choking noises until Nira suddenly froze. She stared at his neck. "Shit. I wasn't thinking," she said.

CJ straightened his T-shirt and looked down at the crowd. No matter how far away he got from school or the neighborhood, it was only a matter of time until a memory of Mike crashed in. Once again the dream flooded his head, the one that he'd had three times since the funeral, in which his mom and Mike are sitting on a black couch in Dr. Shepherd's office and lightning is crackling down from the ceiling. Sometimes he's looking at them, and sometimes he's Mike. When he's Mike, the lightning burns his face and hands as if someone were putting out cigarettes all over his skin, but Shepherd isn't touched. His mom's dress is covered in burn marks and her bangs and the tips of her long black hair are on fire. Shepherd sits at the desk laughing and slapping his knees like he's watching the funniest movie in the world.

Nira kicked the table leg. "Hey, CJ, are you listening to me?"

"Sorry," he said, wiping beads of sweat from his forehead. "What?"

She opened her compact and freshened up the black eyeliner on her bottom eyelid. "You're always so mad," she said.

He wanted to tell her that everything he looked at was poisoned by Shepherd, as if he had sprayed a toxic film over the whole city. He wanted to explain that he was just as sad as she was, but his hatred for Shepherd drowned that out like it had a life of its own. That snake stole his mom, killed Mike, broke down his dad, ruined everything.

He stood up and cleared away both trays. Nira joined him and they strolled along the periphery of the second level, passing elaborate window displays without a glance. When they reached the entrance of the bookstore, CJ led her into the back of the store and moved two large upholstered chairs together.

"It's all that bastard's fault," he said, leaning his head close to hers and looking straight ahead at the wall of books facing their chairs. "I want to tell you what he did to us."

"Who?"

"Dr. Shepherd."

Nira handed him a book to keep open in case a clerk came by. "The doctor Mike was seeing," she said.

"The doctor who killed him."

She nodded while keeping her eyes on the magazine in her lap.

"One morning I heard my parents arguing," said CJ. "It was very early. My dad was still getting ready for work and my alarm wouldn't go off for another half hour. But I heard them and I went to their bedroom door and listened. Dad was almost yelling, asking her why she was washing her face after she had put on her makeup only an hour earlier. It seems she had already gone out that morning for an appointment with Shepherd and came back in less than hour. Dad asked her what kind of psychiatrist makes appointments for seven o'clock in the morning and what kind of appointments make her come home to wash her face. I had never heard him use that tone of voice with Mom before, and she was mad, too. She said she didn't have to tell Dad anything. When she started to come to the door, I didn't have time to run back to my room so I stepped back into the hall. She went through the door and completely ignored me, like I wasn't even there. She went into the den and slammed the door behind her."

"What did your dad do?"

"I went into the bedroom and asked him if everything was OK. He looked surprised to see me and put on a cheery voice. 'You're up early,' he said, and he kissed me on top of the head like he used to when I was a kid."

"So she was going to Shepherd, too, like Mike?"

"Dad told me later that she needed help back then, some medication for her cramps or something, so he sent her to Shepherd. He didn't know he was an asshole who would seduce her and give her drugs to mess her up. What kind of doctor is that? How can he get away with drugging up a patient and making her hate her family?"

"Jesus."

"Dad blames himself, which is making him crazy, too."

Nira gasped with a sob that she muffled with the back of her hand.

"It's OK," said CJ. "I didn't mean to get you all upset."

"It's not that," she said. "I'm sorry about what happened to your mom and dad, but it's not just that." She starting picking at the loose threads around the hole in the knee of her jeans. "I've got a story about Shepherd, too."

"What do you mean?"

"I never told you this before because you've had plenty of your own stuff to deal with, but he did the same thing to us. My mom and dad's separation was all Shepherd's fault."

"You're kidding me."

"One night last summer my parents were fighting, so I went around to close the windows so that the neighbors wouldn't hear. I was freaked out because they had never fought before, at least not in front of me. I listened from the hallway. Mom told Dad that she had finally seen the light, thanks to Dr. Shepherd, and she wasn't going to be held back any longer. They really got into it, blaming each other for working too much and not caring enough about their marriage or me. Then Dad finally said, 'You've made your choice, and I hope to God you can live with it.' He stomped his feet so hard going upstairs that the floor shook. Fifteen minutes later he called for me and told me that he was leaving for a while but that he would make arrangements to see me almost every day. He hugged me and cried like somebody had died."

Nira curled her legs beneath her and turned toward CJ. "I really hated Mom for that for a long time."

"It wasn't her fault," said CJ. "Shepherd got to her just like he got to my mom."

"If you're right, it explains a lot. She seemed like another person. Didn't you notice?"

"I guess. But I probably wasn't paying much attention."

"She's better now. Dad left a year ago, but they've been talking normal to each other on the phone lately. I really think they might get back together."

"Your dad should talk to my dad," said CJ.

Nira read a text on her phone and tossed it back into her purse. "Time to go," she said. "My dad's going to pick us up at the main door."

They walked toward the store entrance, and CJ held up the paperback novel he had been holding during their talk. "If this was a book about Shepherd, I wonder how it would end," he said. He flung the book on a nearby chair.

EIGHT

The dozens of men, women and children waiting in line stared at the faded lettering on the school's canvas sign as it rippled with each gust of wind. The words MINNESOTA AIR NATIONAL GUARD flipped around as the workers inside rearranged the tables to make room for the crowd. None of the patients needed to look to the sky to know that the downpour was minutes away. At the beginning of the wet season in northeastern Peru, the faintest change in daylight signaled heavy rain that could fall for hours on end. Master Sergeant, LPN and military med technician Camilla Black helped set up plastic folding chairs and instructed the patients already inside to move into one section so the others could easily find empty seats. She applied a Band-Aid to the cut on an eight-year-old girl's finger and set her in her mother's lap.

Philip, a nurse and med tech who also worked as a translator, continued writing patients' names on pill bottles. "Do you remember what Nurse Camilla said about taking these?" he asked a young woman in Yaguan. "One pill once a week, and one-half pill for the baby," he said. The woman smiled and nodded as her baby grabbed the pill bottle from Philip's hand and shook it. He placed another bottle, filled with a three-month supply of malaria-preventing chloroquine, in her other hand and shook it with her. Two other babies seated in their mother's laps nearby reached toward Philip and laughed, opening and closing their hands.

Camilla opened the door and signaled for the guard to let the people in just as the first sheets of rain slammed across the clearing. A six-foot chain-link fence topped with barbed wire surrounded the school grounds, and two armed guards stood at the gate to control the flow of patients. The two hundred or so people waiting outside the gate scattered for shelter in the jungle. Inside, Philip told everyone to sit in the chairs and asked the parents to hold their children so they would not knock over any of the supplies on the folding table in the center of the room. After everyone was settled, Camilla began swabbing hydrogen peroxide onto a man's infected toenail and gasped out loud at the sound of a drawn-out crack of thunder. The children found this very funny, and she suddenly realized she was squeezing her patient's ankle with both hands. He feigned pain and jumped around on one foot, sending the children into hysterical laughter.

"Let Nurse Camilla finish her work, Maras," Philip said pleasantly. The man returned to his chair and delicately put his foot back into Camilla's hand, smiling and speaking to her in his native tongue.

"What did he say?" Camilla asked.

"He said they all love to see you laugh. Don't let his palm skirt deceive you, Camilla. I learned earlier today that Maras is a successful businessman in this little corner of the Amazon. He walks several miles every day to bring fruit to the market at Iquitos. He's been walking on that sore toe for a week, and his wife insisted that he stay in the village today to have you take a look at it." He winked at Maras, who knew Philip was talking about him.

"Tell him I'll have to drain it and that it will heal up quickly. I'll give him a couple weeks worth of waterproof bandages." She took a lancet out of its plastic wrapper, slipped on the eyeglasses that hung by a chain around her neck, and focused on Maras's big toe. Suddenly a young mother began screaming at Philip, squeezing her one-year-old boy to her chest and holding up an empty pill bottle. Philip rushed over and found several pills lying around the woman. "He's eaten half a bottle of chloroquine," he said as he grabbed the child and thrust his finger in his mouth. The mother continued yelling and grabbed a pill bottle from the woman next to her, screwed off the cap and thrust it in Philip's face. The baby's face was red. "He's choking on the cap!" Philip shouted. Camilla rushed over and positioned the baby on Philip's lap so that he could perform the Heimlich maneuver. Philip gently but firmly squeezed as the baby's mother kneeled before them. Camilla put one hand on the woman's shoulder and the other on Philip's knee. "He's turning blue," she said firmly.

Camilla stood up and motioned everyone back to their chairs. Another woman's voice broke through from outside the building, and without looking away from the child in his lap Philip called out to Maras to open the door. The woman clung to the gate and yelled, gasping for breath and wiping the rain from her eyes. Maras relayed her words to Philip, who translated them to Camilla. "It's Anta. Her son, the boy we treated for his fever this morning, ran out of the hut and into the jungle," he said as he continued to rhythmically squeeze the baby. "She's been searching for him but she needs help, and a flashlight, because she thinks she heard him crying up in a tree. She won't let anyone help her but you."

Camilla remembered the woman from that morning. She was so grateful for Camilla's treatment of her son that she gave her the beaded necklace she had been wearing. Camilla tried to refuse, but the woman would not leave until she allowed her to put it over her head. The yellow and red strand of beads still shone against Camilla's sweaty neck.

"Maras could have left to help her a minute ago," said Camilla, "but I just lanced his toe and he's bleeding. And I can't leave you alone with this baby and all these patients. We've still got to dispense all the de-worming meds and vitamin packs."

With one more thrust, a white plastic lid shot out of the baby's mouth and hit his mother on the forehead. The baby screamed and kicked in terror. "And I've got to make sure he didn't swallow any pills," said Philip.

The woman continued screaming outside the gate. "She won't take help from anyone but you," said Philip. "Wake up one of the other techs and go."

Camilla stepped into an adjacent room, a porch that had been covered up with metal sheeting, to find her two fellow Guard members sound asleep in their camouflage uniforms despite the deafening noise of the rain against the walls. When she shook the shoulder of the sergeant, Barry, he slowly sat up and looked at his watch. She explained the situation and apologized for waking him up. None of them had gotten much sleep in the freezing, cramped KC-135 that had flown them ten hours straight from the base in Minneapolis, but Barry came to quickly.

Camilla pulled a flashlight from a box beneath the table

in the other room, slid on her backpack and rushed out of the building. The Pervian Army guards let her through, and Anta immediately took her hand and started running toward the jungle. The narrow beam of the flashlight illuminated more rain than turf, but Anta seemed to know exactly where she was going. Camilla kept up a jogger's pace behind her, and once they left the clearing and began weaving their way through the forest Anta kept up her speed. The rain fell more lightly, slowed down by layers of foliage, and most of the water that drenched them came from the leaves they slapped aside. "Shit," Camilla said aloud, realizing that she had not sprayed on leech repellant. Anta made a gradual curve northward and slowed. She stopped and reached out for Camilla's hand. They both looked upward, listening. "Roca!" Anta shouted. "Roca!"

"Mama!"

They snapped their heads to the right. "Roca!" Anta called again.

"Mama!" *Arriba aquí!*

Following his voice, they ran a few yards and aimed the flashlight skyward. "*Allí,*" Anta yelled, pointing. Camilla moved the beam a couple of inches and found him. Thirty feet above ground, he sat with his back pressed against the trunk of the tree and his knees hugged to his chest. He did not look down at Camilla and his mother but was staring straight ahead. "*Mama, ayúdeme,*" he said.

Camilla slowly moved the beam along the limb in the direction of his stare. About four feet away from the boy, the light suddenly struck a long white object, a vertical line that created a shocking contrast to the outstretched branches. Camilla slowly followed the line of the creature up to the branch above from which it hung. Stretching what looked to be eight feet, the snake had the size and white-orange belly of a Bushmaster. When it twisted slightly, Camilla recognized the telltale diamond-shaped splotches along the top of its body. She turned to watch Anta reach around her back and pull out a pouch from her skirt. She slowly turned out the flap and pulled out a two-foot-long blowpipe and curare-tipped dart. Camilla put her hand on Anta's arm to stop her. "You can't risk it," she said in English, shaking her head. "If you miss and just disturb the snake it will strike, and Roca will die." Determined that the intent of her words would get through, Camilla put her hands on Anta's shoulders. "Wait," she said quietly. "Stay here and wait."

Camilla took off her backpack and dug inside for a brown nylon rope. Her eyes had adjusted to the darkness enough for her to choose her target, a nearly unobstructed limb behind and just below the boy. She pulled off her shirt and wiped the sweat from her neck with her sleeveless T-shirt. After giving a reassuring glance to Anta, she flung the rope up to the branch and watched it drop down the other side. She knotted the two ends together and began climbing, quickly and nimbly, her muscular arms doing most of the work while her feet grabbed the rope. When she reached a point about one foot below the branch, she reached up with one hand and, feeling secure, let go of the rope with the other and pulled herself up. In one swift move she was straddling the branch two feet below and behind the boy.

"*Escuche mí, Roca*," she said, hoping that the boy understood Spanish as well as Yaguan. "*Venido a mí, lentamente. Muy lentamente.*" She reached up with one hand and touched his leg. He turned his head and looked down at her, keeping the rest of his body rigid; then looked back at the snake. "*No puedo*," he whispered.

"Yes you can, Roca" Camilla whispered back to him. She stood up on the limb, grasped the tree and leaned around to get as close to him as possible. The boy was shuddering with fever, transfixed by the snake that hung before him a few feet away. Camilla squeezed his shoulder. "*Ahora, Roca.* Grab my arm. It's going to be okay." Roca shook his head. "Please, Roca, you can trust me." He turned to look at her and she squeezed his shoulder again. He pulled away, and with that flinching movement his eyes rolled up and his body went limp. Camilla watched him lean sideways like a diver in the tuck position, his arms unlocking from around his knees. She reached down and grabbed one of his wrists, swung him toward her and slipped down to once again straddle her branch. Anta screamed from below, but Camilla had a strong hold and used both arms to pull Anta up and into her arms. She drew a knife from her ankle strap, lifted up the rope and cut it. Shifting Roca from arm to arm, she wrapped the rope around his chest and beneath his arms, then carefully turned herself around to tie him to her back, wrapping more of the rope securely around her waist. With no rope on which to climb down, she pressed herself against the trunk to begin her descent.

Camilla leaned her head around the tree and did not see the snake. Peering carefully down the branch that Roca had been on, she saw two coils about three feet away from the trunk. The snake had dropped down and wrapped itself on the new branch. She looked down at her right foot, which was grasping the trunk. The Bushmaster's diamond-shaped head was six inches beneath her shoe, its neck puffing out in the strike attitude. The potential disaster flashed before her eyes: if the pain of the bite from its one-and-one-half-inch fangs didn't make her fall, the venom eventually would.

She slowly slid her foot up the trunk and placed it on her branch. Surveying the branches above her and the closest tree to her left, she quickly drew her other leg up onto the branch, bent her knees slightly and jumped up to grab the branch above. She shimmied away from the trunk along the branch, Roca's dead weight bouncing on her back. The branch bent beneath their weight as she moved several feet away from the tree. She stopped, looked straight down to confirm her plan and let go. Eight feet down, she grabbed a branch from the neighboring tree and held tight. This time her feet made contact with the branch below, and she easily pulled herself toward the tree trunk. A sudden itch made her grimace, and she looked up at her forearm to find a black, glistening, four-inch-long leech planted there. Unable to hold on with just one arm, she couldn't rip it off, so she kept moving. The thought of the leech made her entire body itch, and she groaned through clenched teeth.

Once she reached the trunk, Camilla wrapped her arms and legs around it and inched her way down. About ten feet from the ground, Roca woke up and grasped her legs. "Good boy, Roca, we're almost there," she said. Camilla did not dare jump the last few feet, but carefully continued her descent. When her feet touched ground, she cut the rope from her waist and Roca's torso. Anta held up her son and tried to make him walk, but his legs would not hold him. Camilla picked him up in her arms and nodded to Anta, instructing her to lead them back.

The rain had weakened to a soft shower by the time they stepped out into the clearing, and Philip and the Yaguan patients were waiting for them there. Philip took Roca from Camilla and brought him into the school. "He stopped taking his pills long enough to get infected," he said to Camilla as he lowered the boy onto a cot and covered him with a blanket. "I wish we could get this message through—Malaria is entirely avoidable, but only if you take your medication." Camilla began to set up an IV.

"Where did you find him?" Philip asked.

"About thirty feet up in the canopy."

"How did you convince him to climb down?"

Camilla just looked at him.

"How the hell did you climb thirty feet?"

"A rope and a lot of practice. Some of us in the Guard take our workouts seriously."

"I see that," Philip said, looking at her bare, muscular arms. "Hey, you're bleeding."

"Leech," said Camilla. "Shit!" Grabbing Barry, who was squeezing Roca's IV bag, she led him into the other room, slammed the door and began peeling off her clothes. Stripped down to her underwear, she faced Barry and raised her arms in the air. "Get them off me!"

He slowly circled her. "How many?" she asked.

"Looks bad," he said. "One on the back of your left leg, one on the front of your right, and one right here." He touched her with his index finger just above the navel and she opened her eyes and pushed him away. "That's not fair, Philip. Quit fooling around and get these things off of me."

"You're fine," he said, "I don't see any. But you better check between your toes." Camilla dropped to the floor and inspected her feet. "I got lucky," she said. "The jungle gods must be watching over me." She got dressed, and when they returned to the main room Barry cleaned and bandaged her wounds. After inserting and taping down the IV needle in Roca's arm, Camilla gave Anta a clean towel and pointed to a basin of fresh water. Philip told her she could cool her son's head. He and Camilla walked outside into the humid evening air.

"I finished dispensing the medication, but we have a lot of people yet to see," said Philip. "I told them to come back in the morning. Two med techs from the one-thirty-third are joining us tomorrow, thank God. They're flying in to Iquitos tonight."

They sat down in folding chairs and looked into the campfire that one of the guards had made. "I can't wait to hit the waterfall in the morning," Camilla said, rubbing her grimy neck. "I wish it wasn't already getting dark so I could go right now."

"You could use the shower in the Peruvian Army base down the road," said Phillip.

"How often do I get a chance to stand under a waterfall?" she said. "That base is creepy, anyway."

Philip handed her a stick and they both leaned in and poked at the fire.

"How's Maggie?" asked Camilla.

"I don't see much of Dr. Reyes these days," he said. "She works double shifts in the pediatrics ward at least three times a week, volunteers at a research clinic twice a week and ships out on medical missions with the Guard like us as often as she can. I had hoped she'd be assigned to this trip. I want you two to meet. You're a lot alike."

"I investigate doctors when I'm not on a med mission," said Camilla. "That doesn't make me terribly popular with a lot of them."

"Doctors are very supportive of the medical board's work," Philip said, tossing a shiny leaf into the fire. "They want the bad guys out more than anyone."

"They can't help being paranoid around me, though,"

said Camilla. "They think I'm checking them out, taking notes. It's tough on a person's social life."

"You're looking for love at doctor's cocktail parties? You'd have a better chance at a *barra local* in Trujillo."

Philip's satellite phone buzzed in his pocket.

"There's Maggie now," said Camilla, "wondering how much I've asked you about her."

"Maggie doesn't have time to be paranoid," Philip said. Seconds later he handed the phone to her. "It's for you."

Camilla jogged over to the school building and leaned against the wall. "This is Sergeant Black."

Five minutes later she returned to the campfire. "What do they want now?" asked Philip. "Another keg of manioc beer lugged home on the flight back?"

"An investigation I began just before I came here has gone critical," Camilla said. "Louise, my boss at the investigative unit, says I've got to get back right away and work on it full-time. She cleared my release with Colonel Dickinson. I'm flying out tomorrow on the KC-135 that's bringing in those two med techs tonight."

"How much do you know about this case?"

"I haven't read all the complaints yet. All I know is that the guy is a child psychiatrist and that three kids have committed suicide under his care in the last twenty-four months."

"Sounds like a dangerous man. Have you investigated many shrinks?"

"No. Most of my cases have been about fraud, like doctors who use false advertising to attract patients." She picked up her stick and began pushing around a glowing piece of wood. "One time, for example, a surgeon from a town north of Minneapolis was advertising that he performed laparoscopic appendectomies but was actually using the old, much more invasive procedure. Those complaints, I found out, were just the tip of the iceberg. We learned that he had a serious drinking problem, and God knows how much more damage he would have done if we hadn't taken away his license. He was old, too. He should have retired years ago, but doctors are scarce in those small towns."

"Sounds like your new guy might be as bad, or worse," said Philip.

Camilla threw a gum wrapper into the fire. "Three kids, Philip. Who keeps practicing when their patients keep killing themselves, one after another? What kind of a person does that?"

"You'll soon find out."

Camilla glanced at her watch. "I've got to get on the boat that brings those two techs here in about four hours. I don't think I'll bother trying to sleep. I'll ask Anta to take me to the waterfall tonight so I can get cleaned up."

"I'm dirty, too," Philip called out to her as she walked toward the school entrance. "Can we play Tarzan and Jane?"

Camilla tossed him his phone without turning around, then disappeared through the door.

NINE

Clayton unlocked the middle drawer of his desk and pulled out a worn leather envelope. He placed the contents—a bank deposit slip and three checks from Brown-Dixon Labs in the amount of one thousand dollars each—onto the top of the desk. Glancing at the clock, he endorsed the checks and filled out the deposit slip.

"Not bad for three hours' work," he said aloud as he stood up and slipped the checks into his wallet. He opened the closet door and looked in the mirror, smoothing his hair and checking his teeth for bits of parsley from lunch. Staring into his eyes, he gently pulled back his skin from his temples to see the lifting effect. He fingered the two small rings in his left earlobe, gave his mouth a shot of breath freshener and closed the door.

The speaker phone buzzed. "Mrs. Doyle is here for her two o'clock," said Cindy from the front desk.

"Tell her to come in," he said. He turned on two floor lamps and switched off the overhead light before opening the door to watch Leslie Doyle walk toward him in the hallway. She met his eyes as she delicately approached in three-inch heels and listened, a bit self-consciously, to the satin lining of her tight Dior skirt rub against her thighs.

"Good to see you, Leslie," Clayton said as he gestured her toward the chair in front of his desk. He held the back of the chair as she sat in it. She tugged on her skirt, but it was too short to pull near her knees. She crossed her legs and folded her hands on top of her handbag.

Clayton sat down behind his desk. "What a beautiful suit. Just look at you." Leslie smiled and looked at her hands.

Clayton opened the folder on his desk. "It's been three weeks since we increased the Wellbotra to three hundred milligrams. How do you feel today?"

"Much better," Leslie said, looking at the folder. "I'm so relaxed. I think it's finally working."

"How are you sleeping?"

"A lot more than I'm used to. I've been dead to the world for eight hours every night this week."

"Do you feel refreshed when you get up?"

"It takes awhile to get going, but yes, I feel good in the morning." She glanced up at him and quickly turned her eyes back to his desk.

"It seems like there's something on your mind today, Leslie. What would you like to tell me?" He leaned forward, stretched both arms across his desk and clasped his hands together. More quietly, he said, "What is it?"

She looked up at him.

Clayton got up and dragged a matching wingback chair across the carpet and placed it next to hers. "You are much too pretty to be sad. Tell me what's going on." He enclosed her clasped hands in his.

"I feel good, I really do," she said, "but there's still something missing. I can't explain it. I should be ashamed of myself because I've got everything I need, I'm very lucky.

But ever since our first session, when you told me to respect all of my feelings, I've been trying to pay attention to this nagging little thing. I'm probably just a spoiled brat." She pulled back one hand to draw a long strand of her black hair behind her ear.

Clayton grabbed her free hand. "No way, Leslie. That's actually excellent! It's wonderful that you're so aware of that feeling. It's very important. You're starting to open up to yourself, and you'll be discovering a lot more soon. I knew from the first minute you stepped in this office that you are a deeply passionate woman with a lot going on inside you. There are parts of you that are waiting to come to life. And we're going to help that happen."

"What kind of parts of me?"

"You mentioned last week that you don't think Jack pays enough attention to you. You realize now, I'll bet, that he probably isn't able to appreciate your sensuality because he doesn't have the same level of sensuality himself. He can't recognize what he doesn't own."

"I don't think it's that," she said, looking down at her purse. "Jack's very comfortable with his sexuality. I think I just expect too much sometimes."

"Don't sell yourself short. Women like you need to be able to find a way to express their sensuality at the deepest, most profound level instead of compromising and settling for less. There are men out there who are capable of that, but I don't think Jack is one of them. You know what I'm talking about."

Clayton moved one hand up her wrist and along her sleeve. "You deserve to live out your most honest feelings. You're such an exceptional woman, with such good taste, and so beautiful. I'd like to help you. Really help you."

He let the words sink in for a minute, then gently put

his hand on her crossed leg. He opened up his hand and slid it up her calf, then squeezed. After another long pause, he said, "Let me help you."

Leslie leaned forward and Clayton met her halfway. He kissed her and quickly moved his lips to her cheek, reveling in the moment of victory that he had been so carefully working toward for weeks. He put his arms around her and kept his mouth close to her cheek. "So soft, so beautiful."

Leslie shifted her head to kiss him, and they sat there for five minutes until the phone softly beeped once.

"Your next patient is here," said Leslie. "These medication follow-up sessions are so short."

Clayton slid her over to his lap and put his arms around her waist. "I think it would be good to start therapy sessions. Fifty-minute appointments, as a compliment to the drug therapy. You told me that you feel better but that there is still a problem, and we need to do therapy to work that out."

"How soon can we start?"

"Next week. Tell Cindy you need to schedule a session on Monday. We'll set them up for twice a week."

Leslie stood up and smoothed her short suit jacket. She looked at the door and said, "I'll see you in a few days, then."

Clayton embraced her and said, "I'm so glad you're here. I'm not going to get any sleep tonight." He held her hand, walked her to the door and opened it. "I'll see you Monday." He leaned against the doorframe with his arms crossed against his chest and watched her walk away. Before stepping around the corner, she turned around to see him smiling at her.

Clayton walked back to his desk and pressed a button on his phone. "Who's waiting for me?"

"Mrs. Lyon, Jimmy Lyon's mom."

"Send her back in two minutes."

He moved the wingback chair back to its place, pulled a folder from the wooden file cabinet next to the closet and turned on the overhead lights. After spending a minute looking over the file, he switched off the lights again and opened the vertical window blinds halfway. He checked his face in the mirror, wiped off a smudge of pink lip gloss from his chin, and popped a breath mint into his mouth.

Standing at the open door, he recalled his first meeting with Jessica, her husband and their son, Jimmy. The kid was hyperactive eleven-year-old boy with no extracurricular interests but an obsession with gory video games. Mr. Lyon wore four-hundred-dollar shirts and a Bluetooth receiver in his ear and never glanced at the art on the walls. But Mrs. Lyon . . . *oh, my*. Sexy short blond hair, Italian eyeglasses, some kind of accent. He had asked her to make an appointment on her own so they could discuss the family dynamic. As she walked down the hallway toward him, he smiled and stretched out his arm, gesturing her in.

"Jessica Lyon," he said. "Look at you—what a beautiful suit."

TEN

Cheryl cleared a space on her desk for Ted Elliot, the accountant who reviewed the books at Psychiatric Partners once a month, and placed a red file folder next to the coffee she always had ready for him. As he waited in her office doorway, she logged in the records he would need to access and tilted her computer monitor slightly to avoid the glare of the overhead lights. Ted made himself comfortable in her chair and frowned at the stacks of papers lying on the desk.

"I know," said Cheryl. "I'll finish keying in by the end of the day. Then it will all go in the shredder." She patted the back of her newly permed hairdo.

"But this office creates too much paper in the first place," he said. The staff at his firm competed over who could produce the faintest footprint, and his insistence on reading financial logs on his monitor rather from bulky printouts was responsible for the squint he had developed at the ripe age of twenty-eight. "You're one of the only practices at Pembroke without a full electronic charting and accounting system."

"I told the doctors we can afford it," said Cheryl. "I explained that it would pay for itself in less than two years and that in a couple of weeks after starting to use it they would be kicking themselves for not installing it years ago, just like you said."

"Keep working on them. It will make your job easier, too."

Cheryl straightened her blue medical smock, slipped off her reading glasses and slid a thick folder labeled "September" toward him. "I appreciate your concern for my quality of life." She smiled and picked up the red folder. "I really do. You set a high standard for all of us, and that's why I need to talk to you about this before you leave."

Ted stared at the folder in her hands. The bright color stood out from the standard manila used for every other file in the office. She couldn't have been any more obvious about waving a red flag. He admired Cheryl's meticulous organization and the ease with which she performed her double duty as nurse and office manager. He had fantasized more than once about flirting with her when she gushed over him during these visits, and if she weren't married with a teenage daughter, he would loosen up and play along.

"Let me know when you're done," she said, "and I'll only keep you a few more minutes. Is there anything else you need?"

Ted turned to the computer. "No. Looks good."

•

A half hour later, Ted poured himself another coffee at the front desk and told Cheryl he was ready to talk. Back at her desk, he pulled up a second chair and propped up his computer tablet.

"Before you tell me what's in the red file," he said, "I need to go over something about Dr. Shepherd's paperwork."

Cheryl sat close enough to catch a whiff of his cologne. She patted the back of her freshly permed hair.

"Three months ago," Ted said, "he deposited nine checks from Brown-Dixon Labs that are listed as speaker's fees. These checks lined up with nine speaking events on his calendar from the three months before that." Ted pointed at two documents on his tablet showing a schedule and a bank deposit record. "Those events and deposits are highlighted."

"I see," said Cheryl. She wondered if the elegant scent was aftershave, or if he had daubed a fingertip of cologne behind his ear that morning.

"Have you changed your system for gathering together and depositing his checks?" asked Ted.

"No, not at all. Why?"

"There are deposits missing over the last three months," Ted said. "Look." He flipped to another document. "His schedule shows eleven speeches for Brown-Dixon, but only five checks from that company were deposited during those three months."

"Maybe he just forgot," said Cheryl. "He can be a little scattered at times."

"Can you ask him?"

"I'd like to know something else, Ted," Cheryl said. "Have you looked any further into this? Maybe nine, twelve, or fifteen months back?"

"Not yet. I noticed the discrepancy in the past three months and thought I'd check the previous three-month time frame for a comparison. Do you think there's a reason to look further back?"

"I think it would be a good idea," she said. "How soon can you do it?"

"I can work on it this weekend from my office. All the

records I need are online." He glanced at the folder on her lap. "If you're suspicious of Shepherd, you should tell me everything. We need to address whatever's out of line."

Cheryl stepped to the doorway, glanced down the hall and closed the door. "I just started writing up a memo to Dr. Olson about several calls we've gotten from Shepherd's patients about billing problems." She returned to her chair and opened the red folder. "Eight of his patients claim they've received bills for unscheduled sessions. Each of them said that it's happened not just once, but at least three times. They refuse to pay for sessions that they did not even know about, of course, and they're getting irate about it, which I can perfectly understand. I marked down the false appointment times they got billed for, and when I checked the calendar I saw that Shepherd was out of town during every one of them."

"How did phony bills get sent out?" asked Ted. "I thought you did all the billing from right here at your desk."

"I *did* send out those bills, based on the paperwork Shepherd gave me. I didn't notice the discrepancies over the dates because I do stacks of these every week. When the patients started calling, I looked it up." She sat up straight and swiveled her chair toward him. "Dr. Shepherd has been writing up fraudulent bills and asking me, right to my face, to process them. To do an illegal act."

"That takes guts," said Ted.

Cheryl reached into her purse for her cigarettes. "I'm going to hold off on that memo to Dr. Olson until I hear from you. You can take this." She handed him the red file and said she'd walk out with him.

"If this is all true," Ted said, pulling on his sport jacket, "Dr. Shepherd is in some serious trouble."

"Which means we all are. Have you come across this sort of thing with other medical clients?"

"It shouldn't come as a surprise that there are dishonest people everywhere, Cheryl," he said.

"Unfortunately," she said, "for his patients, dishonesty may be the least of it."

She followed him out of the office, and he said they could take the long way to the parking garage. She stopped to light a cigarette when they reached the gravel drive in front of the building. "We can only smoke over there," she said, pointing to a cast iron café table and chairs beneath a willow tree near the side of the building. "They don't want us to stink up the fancy shrubbery in the entryway. I heard that these potted shrubs cost two thousand dollars apiece."

"What do you do in the middle of the winter?" asked Ted.

"I drag out my fur coat," Cheryl said. "Almost all of the women on staff here who smoke do. After lunch on any given weekday in January, it looks like a bus stop for millionaires' wives."

Ted laughed. "I'll call you on Monday."

She walked beside him toward the parking entrance carved out of the stands of spruce and birch. "They're going to move the smoking area to the back of the building," she said. "Some designer said we're messing up the feng shui, but we know it's because the patients who drive up can't stand looking at us freezing our behinds off."

Ted shook her hand and told her, as he always did, that she should quit smoking. She watched him walk briskly toward the cave-like entry, sending puffs of vapor into the chilly October air.

"You really do care about my quality of life, don't you?" she called out.

He waved her off without turning around and disappeared into the dark oval in the trees. Cheryl strolled across the lawn to stretch her legs and waited for Ted's car to appear. A movement at the top northeast corner of the building caught her eye, and as Ted passed by and waved she looked up to see the blinds closing in Clayton Shepherd's office window.

ELEVEN

Stopping at his neighborhood wine shop on the way home, Anthony paused in the "Italy" aisle to read a recommendation taped to the shelf. *The original Super Tuscan, a marvel of winemaking and the most bold innovation in Italian wine in the last millennium. Fifty percent off during the Uptown Wine Cellar's anniversary celebration.* "A Super Tuscan," he said to the short man with a white goatee standing nearby. "Didn't Russell Crowe play that in a movie?"

The man looked at him over his reading glasses. Anthony grabbed a bottle and picked up a six-pack of German beer on his way to the cashier.

"Hey, Tony," said the owner behind the counter.

"This looks like a good deal," said Anthony, setting down the wine bottle.

"You won't believe it. We're not even breaking even with this sale, but we want people to try this stuff. We're spreading the love this week."

"No discounts on the Pauli Girl, though," said Anthony.

"A man's gotta eat!" He bagged up the beer and gave Anthony a receipt.

"What anniversary is it, Vic?" Anthony asked.

Vic leaned on the cash register and folded his hands in a pose familiar to his regulars. "We opened up thirty years ago. This wine you just bought was making headlines back then. Italians were shooting each other over the scandal. Blending grapes like no one had ever dreamed of—you'd think they had started mating cats with dogs the way their competitors went nuts."

"So it's good?"

"Just you wait. What are you cooking? Steaks? Fettuccine carbonara from that recipe I gave you?"

"Buffalo burgers."

Vic stared at him.

"It's really rich meat," said Anthony. "And healthy."

Vic handed him the bags. "You let me know what you think."

Anthony stashed the bags in his trunk, flipped down his visor and searched through the CD holder. A loud rap by his head made him jump.

"Hey, flunkie, stocking up on your booze?" Clayton Shepherd glared at him through the driver's side window.

Anthony flipped the visor back up and started the car.

"Look at me, you son of a bitch," Clayton said.

"What do you want, Shepherd?" Anthony shouted, taking his hand off the keys.

"I've already got almost everything I want," Clayton said.

"And what is that?"

"Your wife, for one. Take a look."

Clayton slapped a photograph onto the glass. "Look at it. See what kind of fun your wife is having now."

Anthony turned to look at the five-by-seven color print

of Marie inside an SUV, blouse open, facing and straddling Clayton in the passenger seat. The photo appeared to be taken by Clayton, with his camera arm stretched over to the driver's side.

Clayton slapped a second photo in front of Anthony's face. This one showed Marie in the same position, naked from the waist up.

"Jesus," Anthony said as he flung open the door, throwing Clayton to the ground.

"You smashed my elbow, you son of a bitch!" Clayton yelled.

"You should have stayed the hell out of my way," said Anthony, standing over him.

Clayton wiped off a dribble of blood from his lip. He looked at the blood on the top of his hand and laughed.

"The big shot is going to have a fit because his wife left him."

"You're the one who's looking for a fight," said Anthony. "You came after me. Get out of here before I call the police."

"I knew you were a soft little coward," said Clayton, rubbing his elbow.

"Stand up and say that."

"Get over yourself. Go home and keep those pictures in your mind. Maybe it'll help you sleep to know that your wife is finally satisfied."

"You're going to get yourself into a lot of shit," said Anthony. He slipped back into his car and turned the key. Clayton jumped to the window and held up his phone, which showed a black-and-white photo of him and Marie kissing. "See how much she loves it?" he yelled through the glass.

Anthony used his entire body to thrust open the door again, sending Clayton back to the asphalt. He put the gear into reverse and checked the rearview mirror—Clayton's car was parked behind him, broadside, blocking his exit. Anthony shoved the gear into park, locked the doors and dialed the police on his cell phone.

"I'm just getting started!" yelled Clayton. He got up and checked out a tear in his shirtsleeve as he walked to his car.

Five minutes later, a Minneapolis Police Department cruiser arrived and the officer found Clayton in his SUV and Anthony leaning against his car talking to Vic. Anthony described the confrontation, and the officer recorded the facts on a form. When they were finished, the officer tapped on Clayton's window and asked him to roll down the window.

"Sir, move your vehicle so he can get out," he said.

Clayton rested his elbow in the open window.

"Move your vehicle to that space," said the officer, pointing to a parking spot in front of the liquor store door, "and show me your driver's license and registration."

Clayton didn't flinch.

The officer stood back. "Sir, drive over to that spot so this gentleman can move his car and we can get this sorted out."

Clayton sighed loudly, turned on his ignition and drove to the parking space as instructed.

"You're free to go, sir," the officer said to Anthony.

As he drove away, Anthony watched the officer walk over to Clayton's car, open the door, and motion for Clayton to get out. Just before driving out of view, he saw Clayton get into the officer's car. "That's right, get him off the streets," he said, looking in the side mirror. "Lock the bastard up."

TWELVE

A staffer from the Minnesota Medical Board lifted a twenty pound box labeled SHEPHERD, CLAYTON, MD, out of his trunk and lugged it onto Camilla's porch. His boss had instructed him to lock it in Camilla's garage, but he forgot the key at the office and was anxious to get to the airport to pick up his girlfriend. Feeling confident about the tall stands of grasses and flowers that hid most of the porch and the relatively long distance between the sidewalk and the house, he pushed the box into a far corner of the porch and slid a wicker chair in front of it. On the way to the airport, he called the Air Reserve Station and left a message for Camilla, telling her where she could find the box.

Ten minutes after he left, an express delivery truck parked in front of the house and the driver bounded up the porch steps with a tracking monitor. He went straight for the box in the corner and reached to pick it up when his cell phone rang. He listened to the caller, whispered, "Shit!" and sprinted back to the truck. A few seconds after he drove off, an Air Reserve jeep drove up and Camilla got out with the driver, who carried her duffel bag to the front door. She asked him to carry in the box from behind the chair, and he dropped it on her living room floor with a grunt.

"Thanks for the ride," she said.

She brought her duffel bag up to the bedroom. In spite of not having slept for twenty hours, she felt revived enough after a shower to make a sandwich and bring a glass of wine and stack of files from the box up to her room. Sitting up in bed, she spread out some of the loose papers and opened a thick folder labeled "McCarthy." She winced at the sight of the eight-by-ten evidence photo that slipped out—a full-body shot of what looked to be a teenage boy hanging from the neck by a belt. She flipped the photo around to read: "Michael S. McCarthy, DOB 02.16.88.; manner of death: suicide."

She picked up the next photo lying on the top of the file, a close-up of the boy's head and neck, still suspended by the belt. His face was blue and swollen, and Camilla looked closer to confirm the *petechiae*—small red blotches on his skin and the whites of his eyes caused by burst blood vessels—another telltale sign of asphyxiation. The tongue, protruding from the center of his mouth, was also blue and enlarged.

She picked up another photograph, a school portrait taken the previous year. The boy's shiny black hair, pale skin and bright blue eyes were all set off by a dazzling open-mouthed smile. The smile and the crinkled edges of his eyes made him appear to be laughing. She put the suicide photo next to this one—but for the hair, the boy was unrecognizable.

Camilla turned the photos over and looked at the next item in the file, a statement by the parents, Daniel and Ellen McCarthy. She flipped through the pages looking for highlighted passages, and found, on page four, an entire paragraph circled in yellow:

The second week after Mike's death, we knew we needed to throw ourselves into something that would take our minds off our grief and that would also help us follow up on our questions about the drug Mike started taking shortly before he died. Because his taking Prozor was the only variable that lined up with his sudden hostility and aggressiveness, we did a lot of research on the drug and were shocked by what we found. One Harvard Medical School study, published ten years earlier, had pointed out the possibility that Prozor could induce what they called 'suicidal ideation' in some patients. Another study, also from the early 1990s, found that some child and adolescent patients who were given Prozor suddenly became obsessed with thoughts of harming themselves, or actually did hurt themselves. None of those kids had ever had those kinds of thoughts or behavior before taking the drug.

We were upset that Dr. Shepherd hadn't mentioned any of this to us when we asked him about side-effects of the drug when he first prescribed it. When we talked to him about it on the phone about three weeks after Mike's funeral, he told us that those studies did not come up with statistically significant results, so there was no scientific credibility to them. He said that if a link had been found between the drug and child-adolescent suicide, the FDA wouldn't have approved it.

That started us on another round of research, and we've found a lot of support in a group made up of parents all over the country who had a child who committed suicide soon after taking an SSRI. Even though the FDA did approve Prozor for childhood depression, it is the only antidepressant that has been approved for juveniles among all the rest. It sounded very suspect to us.

•

Camilla took a sip of wine and looked at the photograph stapled to the back of the statement. The McCarthy's and their son—at age fifteen, according to the date on the back—were standing on a dock with a pine tree-lined lake in the background. Mike, grinning beneath a skipper's hat, was also holding up a catch of sunfish. She paged through the next document, a memo from Brown-Dixon Labs, one of the most successful drug companies in the world thanks to Prozor. The memo had evidently been requested by her boss, the board's Director of Investigations Louise Sunderland, for the McCarthy case. The memo stated that Shepherd was a long-time consultant for Brown-Dixon who spoke frequently at medical conferences and other events about the company's psychopharmaceuticals.

"Bastard!" she said, slapping the paper onto the top of the file. She picked up her cell and called Louise.

"I'm sorry to call you at home," Camilla said, "but I'm back and I just started looking over the Shepherd case."

"I knew you'd dig into that file before you got some sleep. Did you have a good trip back? How's Phillip doing there?"

"Phillip's great. According to the McCarthy file, it doesn't take much to connect the dots about his loyalty to Brown-Dixon Labs and the fact that he didn't talk to Mike McCarthy's parents about Prozor's possible side effects."

"OK," said Louise. "Good evening to you, too. I think we should start on this in the morning after you've gotten some rest."

"The suicide material in Shepherd's file really throws

me," Camilla said. "I thought this case was just about sexual misconduct, which is serious enough in itself."

"Doctor-patient sex is a felony in Minnesota, as you know," said Louise, "and I wanted to give you a felony investigation. But some new information about the suicides has put this case even higher on the list."

"Part of me doesn't want to think the suicide photos are real. When it's a kid, it just doesn't compute."

"There are more where that came from, Camilla. Two other teenagers have killed themselves in the past twenty-four months while under Shepherd's care. Mike McCarthy was number three, and we're waiting on more records to find out how many others there were before that."

Camilla listened while opening some folders at random. Stapled to the inside cover of one was a photograph of a thirteen-year-old girl hanging from a white patent-leather belt in her closet. "Jesus, here's one of them," she said.

"Put it away, close up the box, and watch some TV so that you can get to sleep," said Louise. "I'll call you tomorrow afternoon to tell you about some new statements for this case that will be coming in later this week."

Camilla wished her a good night and gathered up all the folders but one. She returned the rest to the box downstairs, locked up the house and brought the bottle of wine upstairs. Settling into bed, she turned on the TV and began reading through the first document in the folder she had kept on the bed. The tab of the folder read: ANTHONY ROBSON, COMPLAINANT.

THIRTEEN

Clayton didn't mind the traffic rushing past the glass walls of his favorite bar near Lake Calhoun. Nothing, he thought, could detract from the perfection of the place. The interior combined the mahogany coziness of the Minneapolis Club with the casual elegance of the Miami Beach Marina where he and his twin brother kept their forty-two-foot Catalina. Seated at the bar and facing the antique mirror, Clayton stared at his softened reflection in the dim light. Turning around on his barstool, he watched dog walkers and joggers move along the lake pathways in one of the most expensive neighborhoods in the city. He had several patients from this part of town, and others from around the equally upscale Lake Harriet and Lake of the Isles. Those patients, like most of the people who came to this bar, bought their clothes at designer boutiques in the western suburbs and flew to Chicago to do their Christmas shopping. A familiar voice made him swing back around to the bar.

"It's the good doctor," said the female bartender.

Clayton turned around to find Jan, his favorite, placing a cocktail napkin on the bar. "Now my day is complete," he said. "What a feast for the eyes."

"Nice to see you," the twenty-four-year-old said with an Irish accent. "The usual?"

"Yes. *Comme d'habitude.* And stir it slowly, please."

She blended a cosmopolitan in an icy shaker and poured it into a large martini glass. With pinky in the air, she stirred the drink with a shaker spoon, smiled and shook her head. "To most people, it's either shaken or stirred, not both," she said. "And a cosmo is a girl's drink." She set down the glass.

"I'm comfortable with my feminine side because I'm a real man," Clayton said. "Only a real man can drink one of these."

"There may be some kind of logic in that," she said, "but it'll take me awhile to find it."

"I'll be happy to show you what kind of man I am. You know where to find me."

She laughed and stepped away to another customer. Clayton looked around the room and set his eyes on a tall blond in a white Chanel jacket at the end of the bar with two other women. He grasped the bar and leaned back as far as possible to get a good look at her. A hand landed on his back and pushed him forward.

"You could break your neck that way," said the man. "That wouldn't make a very nice cause of death in your obituary."

"I'm very coordinated, don't worry," said Clayton. He offered the stool next to him to his friend, Terry Strick, a regional sales representative for Brown-Dixon Labs.

"You're right on time," Clayton said. "It's been awhile. Have a drink."

Terry reached into his breast pocket, pulled out a five-inch cigar and ordered a beer. Jan poured his draft into a tall glass.

"Jan," said Clayton, "do you know what I just asked

Terry? I said, 'Are you going to light that thing in here or are you just happy to see me?'"

Jan shook her head again.

"You know Jan doesn't fall for that stuff," said Terry. "She's going to put guys like you in their place after she graduates from law school." He looked at Jan. "You want to be a prosecutor, right?"

"Damn straight," she said. "Cock of the walk."

"My God, I'm in love with you," said Clayton. "I hope you come after me as judge, jury and executioner and beat me to a pulp."

"Like you said, I know where to find you," she said. Another customer called her away.

"Look at that," said Clayton, pointing his head toward the blond in the white jacket.

"Nice," said Terry. "Listen, Clay, I've come with a message. From way up."

"How far up?"

"Brown and Dixon themselves."

"Am I getting another raise in my speaker's fees?"

"Better. Tell me when you're ready for another Shirley Temple or whatever the hell you're drinking." He motioned to Jan to bring Clayton another drink.

"Here's the thing." He tapped his unlit cigar on the bar as he spoke. "They're very pleased with the progress on the final phase of the new drug trial, and they've cooked up another reward for you."

"A new speaking circuit? Or a book? I'd love to write a book. My so-called business partner may not appreciate me, but I know there's an audience out there for a book about my approach to therapy. I think I've got a responsibility to bring these ideas to the general public and—"

"Clayton, it's not a book. It's a percentage of the sales

when this new drug goes to market. And you know what that means."

Clayton downed his first drink and pushed the empty glass away. "Really?"

Terry nodded.

"What that means," said Clayton, "is that I'm going to be freakin' *rich*."

From the other end of the bar, Jan gave him one of her polite but explicit looks that said *quiet down*.

"This drug is going to make us all rich," said Terry. "The first antidepressant specifically designed for children and adolescents? There's no bigger market in the world." He clinked Clayton's glass. "They're cutting you in because they want you to help them write up the summary of the trial. They've seen what you can do with a crowd of your peers. They think you can make this study sound like Brown-Dixon drugs are the one-stop cure for everything from kids' depression to their bad taste in music. They want you to sell it."

"What's good for Brown-Dixon has always been good for me."

"With Prozor going generic in a year," said Terry, "the company is counting on the Killer-J to step in and keep up the profits that have made Brown-Dixon one of the most successful corporations on the planet."

"Killer-J?"

"That's the nickname for the drug at headquarters," said Terry. "The killer juvenile antidepressant—not a drug that kills juveniles, but a juvenile drug that will make killer profits."

"Cute," said Clayton, stirring his drink.

"I know."

Clayton watched Jan move around behind the bar.

"Thanks to you," said Terry, "we've got a couple of strong-selling SSRIs besides Prozor that are very popular in this part of the state. But now that we're at the end of the nine-year trial on the juvenile version, word is spreading that we're going to redefine the industry."

He tapped his fingers nervously on his glass as he watched Clayton stare at the bartender. "How is that situation you told me about?" he asked.

"I've got it under control," said Clayton.

"Those kind of allegations could cause you a lot of problems. The guys at Brown-Dixon weren't happy to hear about it."

"I told you, I've got it under control. I'd rather talk about how I plan to spend some of that money." He pulled his smart phone from his pocket and searched for a photo. "The women are coming out of the woodwork lately and they have very expensive taste. You should see some of my patients' mothers. They're unbelievable. Here's one who insisted she start receiving therapy herself." He flashed Terry a photo of a lipstick-smeared Jessica Lyon. "Another one took a picture of me naked from the waist up after she had massaged me with that oil I told you about. She posted it on a website so she could show me off to her girlfriends." He found the website and handed his phone to Terry. The page contained a color photograph of Clayton leaning against a tree, shirtless, jeans unbuttoned and zipper partially down. He wore a pair of sunglasses on the top of his head and a Puka shell necklace around his neck. His bare, muscular torso and arms were slick with oil and his thumbs hung through his belt loops at his hips.

"We had just had ourselves a lovely afternoon," Clayton

said, "and she insisted that I pose like that."

"This is the mother of one of your adolescent patients, you said?"

"Yes," said Clayton, "but don't worry. She's getting separated from her husband." He looked at the image with a grin and shook his head. "I've got her on three hundred milligrams of Wellbotra and she sees me for medication follow-up and therapy twice a week."

Terry pushed the phone down onto the bar. "We've been friends a long time, Clay, but I think you're being reckless. You may have friends at the medical board, but one of these days this is going to catch up with you."

"Come on, Terry. I'm giving these women real help and they love it. They're not going to complain, and even if they do, it's their word against mine."

"Some of the women you've tossed out are already talking, and eventually one of their complaints is going to get into the wrong hands at the board."

"Do you think a board member, probably a doctor himself, is going to believe the words of a hysterical, medicated woman over mine? It doesn't work that way, Terry, and you know it."

Terry ordered another beer and avoided looking Jan in the eye. "How many women are we talking about, Clay?"

"After all those years of hell with Isabel, I deserve getting back on track. I don't even have to go out looking. The women walk into my office every day or roam the halls at the hospital. They're nuts about me. It's too easy."

"You date nurses, too?" asked Terry.

"Once in a while. But the mothers of my patients are more interesting. They come in alone to talk about their marriage or ex-husband or kid who's driving them crazy, and I prescribe the perfect solution. The combination prescriptions settle them down, make then languid and even more beautiful. There's a powerful beauty in vulnerability." His first session with Marie Robson flashed into his mind, the softness of her small hand as he held it and led her to the corner of the couch. "Within a month there is nothing these women will not do for me. I have all the answers, I stop all the pain, I make them feel beautiful again, and they're just waiting for it."

Terry sighed and waved away the phone when Clayton tried to show him another picture.

"You have to remove your photo from that website," said Terry. "There's too much at stake."

Clayton pushed his empty glass away. "Jesus Christ, Terry, it's a photo of me with most of my clothes on. I'm starting to think you're pissed off because you're jealous. You can't tell me you never think about getting friendly with some of the nurses and doctors you see on the job all the time. You just don't have the balls to follow through with it."

"I'm a salesman, not a psychiatrist with a code of ethics to follow."

"Ethics! I'm doing more for these women than any therapist in this state could come close to doing. And I don't have to explain myself to anyone when the methods work."

"That's your call," said Terry, as he put two twenties down on the bar. "Forget it. I'm sure no saint." He saluted to Jan at the other end of the bar and picked up his briefcase. I've got to drive to Moorhead tonight," said Terry. "I just wanted to deliver your good news in person. The last thing I want to do is make bad blood—you're one of the best things that ever happened to my career. I've got the bonuses and a yacht on Lake Superior to show for it."

"I appreciate that you're looking out for me," said Clayton, staring at a redhead in a black cocktail dress who had just walked up to the bar. "But don't worry. I know what I'm doing. Now get out of here so I can keep doing it."

Terry slapped Clayton on the back, stuck his unlit cigar in his mouth and made his way through the crowd for the door. Before stepping out, he turned around to see Clayton gesture to the redhead to sit down in the empty barstool next to him. Terry then made eye contact with Jan, who was drying a glass. She had also just witnessed Clayton's swift move, and she shrugged at Terry. He shrugged back and turned to leave. "Oversexed bastard," he said as he pulled open the door.

FOURTEEN

The Olsen's three miniature Dachshunds yipped behind the door as Cheryl and Ted walked across the doctor's pillared front porch. Bill Olson's wife, Glenda, answered the door, holding a three-year-old girl on her hip and prancing around to block the dogs from escaping. "Bill's waiting for you out in the back, so go right through," she said.

They walked through the central hall and kitchen to the sprawling backyard deck, where Bill was seated at a glass table. Two heating towers created a bubble of warmth that allowed Bill to dress in a short-sleeved polo shirt. He set aside his newspaper and motioned at the chairs around the table. "Good morning," he said. "Take off your coats and have a seat."

"Thanks for letting us come over on a Saturday," said Cheryl. "We thought it was best to talk outside the office."

Glenda brought out coffee and a plate of doughnuts while the three-year-old waited for her by the sliding glass doors. "Is the little girl your granddaughter?" asked Cheryl.

"Our first grandchild," said Glenda. She skipped back to the girl and shut the door behind them.

"You said this is about Clayton," said Bill.

Ted drew some papers out of his portfolio, turned to Cheryl, who nodded, and handed Bill a three-page memo.

"What's this?"

"It's an outline of two very serious problems you've got with your partner," said Ted. "I found one, and Cheryl found the other. They're both about money."

"Give me the short version," said Bill.

"First," said Cheryl, "he's been billing some of his patients for unscheduled sessions. I've had dozens of calls from angry patients in the last month alone. He sends out bills for phony appointments written up for dates that he's not even in town.

"Why would he do that?"

"To make up for fees that he's not depositing," said Ted. "Speaker's fees from Brown-Dixon Labs. According to a comparison of his speaking schedule and his deposits, he's withheld about thirty thousand dollars in those fees this year."

"I've received some Brown-Dixon checks from him to deposit," said Cheryl, "but Ted found the discrepancy in his last review and I asked him to look into it further."

"Thirty thousand dollars," said Bill. "We agreed at the beginning that his speaking fees would be considered partnership earnings. Just like my book royalties, his income from the speaker's circuit is supposed to go into the general account. I know he was clear on that. We worked it out in detail with our attorney when we were setting up the practice."

"He obviously decided to keep a chunk of it for himself," said Cheryl.

"There's a word for that," said Ted.

Bill poured himself some coffee. "Embezzlement," he said.

"I've worked for you for a long time, Bill," said Cheryl,

"a long time before Clayton came into the office. Out of respect I haven't mentioned this before, but I think he's got other problems, too. You don't see him around the office as much as I do, in the break room, with the staff and out in the waiting room. He's very inappropriate with the younger women, like our new receptionist, Jean. It's only a matter of time before another one of them slaps him with a sexual harassment suit."

"I warned him about this a couple of months ago," said Bill. "Have you seen him continue this behavior yourself?"

"Many times."

Bill flipped through the pages of the memo.

"I'm not the psychiatrist here," said Cheryl, "but I have to say it. There's something wrong with this man, Bill."

Bill looked at her over the top of the memo.

"Take the stunt he pulled last week in the kitchen," she said. "He described the lurid details of one of his patient's sex fantasies to Jean while she was making tea. I came in and told him to stop."

The door slid open and the three dogs ran out into the yard.

"I'm going to call our attorney before I approach Clayton about these missing funds," Bill said. "These are serious charges, and unless he has a valid explanation, there is no way he can stay in this partnership."

"He'll owe you quite a bit of money, too," said Ted.

"I wonder what he's been spending it on," said Cheryl. "Actually, I don't think I want to know."

"Did any of his patients send in payments on those extra bills?" asked Bill.

"No," said Cheryl. "I asked all of them to mail them back, and I've collected them in my office."

"Let's send out a letter to each of them with an apology

for the mistake," said Bill. "We don't need to tell them any details. Just let them know that we fixed the problem and that we regret the inconvenience."

Cheryl took a notebook from her purse and wrote a note in it.

"I need to report my findings to my manager," said Ted. "I'm giving him a copy of that memo on Monday morning."

"I'd like to talk to Clayton, with our attorney present, before he hears about it from someone else," said Bill. "Is that possible?"

"I'm sure the firm will go along with that. I'll explain that to my boss and ask him to speak to you, and only you, if he wants to discuss it."

"Thank you."

Glenda stepped out of the kitchen with a giant platter of marinated chicken and asked if they would like to stay for barbeque.

Cheryl and Ted put on their coats. "That looks great," said Cheryl, "but we don't want to intrude on your weekend. I've got some guests coming over soon, anyway. Hope and her dad are making lunch on our grill as we speak."

"How about you, Ted?" asked Bill. "You're more than welcome."

"Thanks, but I've got to get back to the office and finish another job I'm working on this weekend. If I get done this afternoon, I can go to the Twins game tonight."

"All right," said Bill. "I'll see you Monday, Cheryl."

They made their way back through the house, and Bill and Glenda watched their cars meander around the cul-de-sac and disappear. Bill put his arm around Glenda's shoulder. "You were right," he said. "Clayton Shepherd is a lot more trouble than he's worth."

FIFTEEN

Clayton pressed another tissue into Emily Carter's hand. She wiped her eyes and stared at the mascara-smeared tissue. He had sat silently by her side for the past five minutes, letting her cry, squeezing her forearm now and then and sighing deeply to help her relax. Once her breathing was quiet, he got up and opened the office blinds halfway. Emily closed her eyes and turned her face slightly to allow the late afternoon sun to cover it, then she rested her head against the back of her chair. With hands resting loosely in her lap, she remained silent.

"You've crossed a major milestone to finally share that," said Clayton. "I'm humbled that you put so much trust in me. Things are going to move quickly now. We're getting down to the real thing, and it's all due to your work. You should be very proud of yourself."

She opened her eyes and smiled at him. "I thought I would feel more ashamed, but actually I feel incredibly good. The fact that I told you and you're not judging me or changing toward me makes me realize that I'm not a freak."

Clayton sat back down and leaned toward her to speak

more quietly. "Everything the mind does has a healing purpose, a healing directive," he said. "As odd as that might sound, your condition has played a positive role. The mind will do whatever it takes to make you feel safe and balanced."

Emily pulled up her legs and crossed them, yoga style, in her lap, smoothing out the folds of her linen pants.

"I'm not at all surprised by what you told me today. It makes perfect sense that an executive like you who assumes so much responsibility day after day, who makes million-dollar decisions and holds the careers of so many people in your hands, who is constantly in control, would need to counter that with some type of experience that would make you feel vulnerable and submissive. Otherwise, the controlling, master-of-the-world part of yourself would devour every other part of you. What you just called 'humiliating, perverted habits' are actually life-saving actions."

Emily held the tissue to her nose for a moment. "Do you really believe that?"

"Of course. You're not alone, you know. I'm sure you've become familiar with an entire community of people who do the same thing. There are many high-powered people in the world who look to this type of activity to balance out all the control they wield in their lives. They probably aren't conscious they're doing it for that reason, but they're dead serious about it, like you."

He kissed her hand and went to his desk to open the scheduling calendar on his computer. "We've been meeting once a week," he said. "I'd like to move that up to twice a week. How do you feel about that?"

"If you think it's time to speed things up, that's fine with me."

He returned to the chair next to her and took her hand.

"What a great session," he said. "You had a real breakthrough. You're a remarkable woman, a powerful, wonderful human being, and I'm grateful that you're working with me. You're an inspiration."

Emily got up and started to step into her shoes. Clayton quickly crouched down and put them on her feet.

"Thank you," she said.

"Thank you, Emily. Tell the receptionist that you need to make a therapy-hour appointment for next Wednesday." He opened the door for her, left it open and returned to his desk to check his schedule. With one hour before his next patient, he buzzed the front desk.

"Jean, is Bill with a patient right now?"

"Just a minute. No, he's eating lunch at his desk."

"Thanks."

"There's pizza in the kitchen if you want some."

Clayton jumped from his chair without responding and jogged down the hallway to Bill's office. He knocked on the door and walked in without waiting for an answer.

"You will not believe what I just heard," he said, grabbing a napkin. "You know Emily Carter, the executive who's been seeing me for over a year? I finally got her to admit that she's one perverted freak."

Bill typed a few words onto his laptop with one hand while eating a folded slice of pizza with the other. He didn't look away from his screen.

"She's a vice president at Aeromarket, and she just gave me all the details about her underground life at a bondage club. Did you know there's a bondage club in town, Bill? She's a raving masochist who can't even start to get excited unless her mouth is taped shut and she's watching her boyfriend screw somebody else."

FATAL REMEDY

Bill put down the pizza, wiped his mouth and stretched his leg to close the door with his foot. "Not the most erudite clinical description, but I get the picture."

"You should have seen her," Clayton continued, "the big executive with her Fendi bag and thousand-dollar shoes, choking on her words as she tells me how turned on she gets when another woman kicks her in the ribs in her own bed. I've seen this woman's house, Bill, on Summit Avenue, it's a mansion. She's one of the most eligible divorcees on the Twin Cities' A-list and she's a total whack job!"

"Keep it down, Clayton. I've got to finish these emails over lunch or I'm never going to get the speakers for the national conference sorted out." He returned to his one-handed typing and waved Clayton away.

"Speaking of that, I just got a call from St. Cloud State and they want me to speak to their psychology class about adolescent therapy," Clayton said. "It's a freebie, of course, but I'm going to do it." He put his hands in his pockets and stood in front of Bill's framed diploma from Harvard Medical School. "And the St. Paul paper is going to interview me next week for an article about teenage depression. That will be my fourth newspaper interview this year. I've had to cut down on my Brown-Dixon speeches because I could never fit them all in and keep up with my patient load."

Bill continued working on his laptop.

Clayton stepped over to one of the bookshelves and stood eye level with the trio of books standing upright with the front covers facing out, the books with Bill Olson's name on them. A sticker on the cover of *Straight Talk to Parents about Psychiatric Drugs* read: USA TODAY BESTSELLER. Clayton picked it up and read the biography beneath Bill's photograph on the back cover:

William E. Olsen, MD, graduated at the top of his class from Harvard Medical School and completed his residency in psychiatry at the University of Minnesota. He has special interests in child neurology and attention deficit disorders and is board certified by the American Board of Psychiatry and Neurology. A founding member of Psychiatric Partners, LLC, in Minneapolis, Minnesota, he is the author of two previous books, *Understanding Your Overactive Child* and *A Parent's Guide to Adolescent Depression*. William Olson and his wife, Glenda Clayborne Olson, MD, live in Edina, Minnesota.

•

Clayton placed his hands on the wall and began doing Achille's heel stretches.

Bill answered his phone, turned to Clayton and said, "I need to take this, do you mind?"

Clayton shook out his shoulders. "I wanted to show you something, very quickly. I'm getting ready for the Duluth marathon—"

"Clayton, I told you I need to take this call."

"Will you stop in my office when you're done?"

"Sure."

Clayton returned to his office, opened his closet and took off his shirt and undershirt, then put his shirt back on over his bare skin. He sat at his desk for ten minutes, updating his schedule and reviewing the file of his next patient, then walked back to Bill's office. The door was closed, so he walked into the kitchen to make a cup of tea. Jean and Cheryl were at the table eating sandwiches and reading the newspaper. Clayton filled a coffee cup with water and set it in the microwave. He tore open a tea bag package and waited for the water to heat. Bill walked in with his coffee mug.

"I wanted to tell you something else about Emily Carter, Bill," said Clayton.

"Sorry, I just got off the phone. I've got a minute. Just let me get a coffee."

"The details that she spilled today. It was incredible," said Clayton. Cheryl and Jean looked at each other.

Bill poured some milk into his coffee and opened a few drawers looking for a spoon. "She meets another couple, a man and woman, every Saturday night at their place, and makes the guy put black duct tape over her mouth, all the way around her head," Clayton said, dipping his tea bag into his cup.

"This isn't the place to discuss a patient," said Bill.

Clayton moved closer to Bill and continued in a lower voice. "She said she didn't start having orgasms until she saw her first bondage video when she was twenty-five years old. But that wasn't good enough. She wanted the real thing, so she hooked up with a group of other masochistic freaks and started living this stuff out like her life depended on it."

Cheryl slammed her paper down and looked at Bill.

"What's the matter, Cheryl," said Clayton, "never heard anything kinky before?"

"Clayton, that's enough," said Bill. He led him to his office and shut the door.

"That was uncalled for," said Bill. "You can't talk about patients in front of the staff. I wanted to talk to you about this before, but—" His cell phone rang and he answered it. "I'll call you back in five minutes." He put the phone in his front shirt pocket. "I've got a patient coming in two minutes. I can't talk about this now."

"There's just one more thing," said Clayton. "I started to tell you that I'm running the Duluth marathon next weekend. I wanted to show you how much I've been working out. My trainer thinks I'm going to be among the top twenty finishers." Clayton unbuttoned his shirt and spread it open. "Look at those abs!"

Bill looked up at him briefly and turned back to his computer monitor.

"My legs are really hard now, too," he said, moving close to Bill's chair. "Feel this." He took Bill's hand and slapped it down on his thigh. "Like my grandmother would say, ' Dr. Clayton, strong as bull!' Isn't that something?"

Bill drew his hand away. "Get away from me—I almost spilled my coffee. Grow up and get back to work." Clayton was accustomed to Bill's gruff tone, which was so consistent that he, like the nurses and staff, could rarely tell if Bill was angry or making a joke. Clayton made a habit of believing the latter. He buttoned his shirt as he walked back to his office.

•

Cheryl knocked on Bill's door and he reached to open it slightly without getting out of his chair.

"Can I talk to you about what just happened in there?" she asked.

"Not now," Bill said. "I've got a patient waiting, but I realize he was completely out of line and I promise I will talk to him about it. I'm sorry you had to hear it."

"The thing is," she continued, "it's not the first time. Like I told you last weekend, he's blabbed about his patients in front of us before, and sometimes I think people out in the waiting room can hear him."

"I'll handle it," Bill said. He smiled at her and closed the door.

Cheryl went back to her office, unlocked her desk drawer and pulled out a notebook. She jotted down the date, summarized what Clayton had said in the kitchen, and tossed the notebook back in the drawer.

SIXTEEN

CJ stopped his bicycle in front of a Vietnamese restaurant on Hennepin Avenue, just south of Lake Street. His cell phone at his ear, he shifted his gaze back and forth between a black SUV parked across the street and the streams of people going in and out of the multi-level Uptown Mall on the corner. People sat at sidewalk tables eating lunch, and a steady flow of traffic rushed along the avenue. Two Minneapolis police officers in navy blue shorts pedaled by on bike patrol.

Clayton walked out of the mall entrance, and CJ straightened up. "I see him," he said into his phone. "I'm going to follow him this time."

"I covered for you today," said Nira, "but if you cut class again you're probably going to get caught."

"I'll call you back," said CJ. He dropped his phone into his pocket and stepped out into the street, straddling his bike. Clayton got into the driver's seat of his SUV, and a man in a gray suit stepped into the passenger side. CJ followed them as they turned west onto Lake Street, then right into the grocery store parking lot one block away. He watched as Clayton parked on the far end of a full row of cars. He had been following Clayton around the Uptown neighborhood for the past five days, riding his bike to the entryway of Pembroke Medical Center at five o'clock where he hid behind a wide tree trunk until Clayton's car drove out.

So far, CJ discovered, Clayton's afternoons followed a regular pattern: his first ritual after leaving the center just after five was to drive to the Uptown parking ramp a few blocks away and have a quick drink during happy hour at the bar in the mall. He always sat at the bar in the center of the room, never at one of the long counters that stretched along the windows and looked out to the street. After about a half hour he would walk to the grocery store, come out with a bag or two, get back in his car and drive off. Every time CJ saw him leave the parking ramp, Clayton was talking on his cell phone—usually with a big smile on his face. CJ had not followed him any further than that because the traffic was too fast farther west where Lake Street turned into Minnetonka Boulevard.

This afternoon, CJ decided to track Clayton down after lunch in order to put a wrench in his precious routine. The previous evening, while following Clayton around the grocery store aisles, he overheard him talking about a lunch meeting the next day at a restaurant in the Uptown mall. He skipped school after his last morning class in order to find Clayton and his car.

CJ set his bike in the rack next to the store entrance and crouched by the row of cars where Clayton was parked. He walked slowly behind the cars, keeping his head below window level, and stopped behind Clayton's SUV. Clayton and the other man were talking loudly enough that CJ could hear them through their open windows. The day before, he had rushed out of the store after hearing Clayton's lunch plans, ridden his bike to Clayton's car in the ramp and broke out the driver's side mirror. As a result, Clayton couldn't see someone creep along that side of the car. CJ's heart pounded as he slid his back along the side of the car and stopped midway.

"The trial data from my practice looks good, for the most part," Clayton said. "It's almost ready to submit."

"You don't sound very enthusiastic."

"I'm concerned about the strange curve the data falls into. Most of the patients' responses are either excellent, with few side effects, or very bad, with pronounced suicidal thoughts. I've had three suicides on the drug since I came on board with this study. There's very little response in between, so the data looks skewed.

"When your results are combined with the nine years of data the company has already gathered, won't they spread out and basically disappear?"

"Nothing disappears from a clinical drug trial. The FDA reads every line, every number, every asterisk."

"You're forgetting about Prozor's side effects," said Terry. "They didn't stop the FDA from letting us put it on the market."

"The FDA didn't know it would be prescribed to kids at the rate it has."

"They could have taken it off the shelves, but they haven't."

"Not yet," said Clayton. He rummaged through the storage compartment in the middle of the front seat. "You think I live on the edge. Brown-Dixon is so fixated on the fortune they're going to make that they're willing to pay me to run a secret trial that they'll incorporate into their own data just to get the numbers."

"You told me it was the sweetest deal that ever came your way," said Terry.

"It's sweet, but it's also dangerous. My patients think they're getting Prozor, and they're getting something that hasn't even been approved yet, let alone named."

"That's true," said Terry. "But you know better than anyone that the market has been screaming for an antidepressant designed for children and teens. And with the absence of significant side effects, which you have so clearly reported so far, this drug might make Brown-Dixon the top drug company in the world."

CJ kept his hands on his knees, careful not to lean against the car too heavily. He heard the click of a cigarette lighter and a few seconds later caught a whiff of marijuana.

"The agitation I'm seeing in the early phases of the drug is more profound in almost all the cases," said Clayton, "but after the first four weeks that behavior settles down and the drug is effective. At least it hasn't been any worse than the drugs everyone's prescribing already."

"Except for the three suicides?"

"Except for those," Clayton said, trying to stifle a cough. "And the suicidal attempts that didn't succeed. I couldn't believe that boy from Maplewood—remember him? The kid who tried to off himself by punching a dart into his wrists. What a mess to have to crawl out of bed for in the middle of the night."

CJ listened to the pause as they passed the joint back and forth.

"I've only reported eleven of the attempted suicides, as you know," said Clayton, "and I only included those because there were hospital admissions involved and it would be impossible to make that paperwork go away. All the other reports disappeared into never-never land, as far as my data is concerned."

"The suicide ideation is alarming, I agree," said Terry, "but the frequency is much less than it was with the original compound they worked on before this study. That's what gives the guys at the top so much confidence in this product."

"How do you know all this?" asked Clayton.

"Brown and Dixon bring the top regional managers to the private session of the annual meeting where they lay out the progress of the trial. I probably shouldn't tell you this, but the drug you've been testing is the result of a breakthrough they had been waiting for for twenty years."

CJ covered his mouth so his breath wouldn't float up in the cold air.

"Some whiz kid chemist they hired," said Terry, "was able to minimize the molecular element that they believe causes the aggressiveness and suicidal ideation. It's still there, but it's much less than it had been when the lab came up with the first formula. For the past nine years, they've been calling that molecular tweak 'the miracle.'"

Clayton crossed himself piously and they both laughed hard enough to ignite a coughing fit. Then they passed the joint again.

"Suicide ideation," said Clayton. "I knew that McCarthy kid was going to be a pain in the ass the first time he stepped in my office. He had an answer for everything. He hated my guts, the little shit. And he's still trying to make things difficult."

"I don't think he killed himself just to make you look bad," said Terry.

"I wouldn't put it past the little prick," said Clayton.

He slammed the cover of the storage box between the seats. "Let's get out of here. I've got a dinner date with the mother of another little shit." They burst out laughing again, and Clayton started up the car. He flicked the remainder of the joint, a half-inch wad of cigarette paper, out of the window and instinctively looked into what should have been the mirror on the side of the car. "I've got to get this damn mirror fixed tomorrow," he said.

By this time CJ had slipped behind another car. He watched them go and then ran back to his bike. As he moved things from his back pockets to the front ones for the ride home, he found his pocketknife and cursed himself for forgetting about it. Slitting Clayton's tires would have to wait.

SEVENTEEN

Clayton buttered his bagel and turned on the radio before settling onto a stool at his kitchen counter. The reflection of his laptop shone on the black marble countertop. He clicked open his pen and set it on top of his open stenographer's notebook. At one o'clock, he turned up the volume with a remote control device.

Welcome to 'The Mind of Sports.' I'm Dr. Anthony Robson. It's a beautiful autumn Friday in the Twin Cities, and whether you're having lunch or headed up to the lake, thanks for tuning in.

Clayton stared out the window to watch a pair of young women walking their dogs in Loring Park.

Today we're going to start out with a topic that is controversial among not only school coaches and school psychologists but parents as well. It's about the amount of anxiety kids experience in competitive sports. I've read studies that say student sports anxiety is acceptable because it's a normal byproduct of any kind of performance activity, like a classroom presentation or a test or a band concert. And I've read other studies that say that kids up to the age of about sixteen are not yet capable of handling the type of performance anxiety that comes with the heavily competitive sports programs that are becoming more and more typical in our schools. I'll be back in a minute with Dr. Adele Mortensen of the Minnetonka Public School System. She recently published an article on this, and we're going to hear where she stands on the issue. But first, here's Mike with the news break.

After jotting a note, Clayton went to the front closet to pull out a shoebox-size metal box hidden on the floor behind a stack of medical journals. He brought the box to the kitchen counter, unlocked it and began taking out the contents. Among the cut-out newspaper and magazine articles was an interview with Anthony that included a photograph of him with the star shortstop from the New York Yankees. In another article, a photo showed Anthony standing between two swimmers with Olympic medals around their necks. Clayton pulled out a glossy publicity photo with a red KJOK logo in the corner that showed Anthony in the radio studio, reaching over the console to shake hands with George Foreman. He then lifted out a glass paperweight inscribed with gold-filled etching that read: TO ANTHONY ROBSON, PHD, WITH GRATITUDE FROM THE UNIVERSITY OF MINNESOTA HOCKEY CHAMPIONS, 2004. He set the paperweight on the counter and pulled out a framed photograph of Anthony shaking hands with L.A. Lakers Coach Pat Riley. The bottom half of the photo was covered with a hand-written dedication from Riley.

Welcome back to 'The Mind of Sports' on KJOK. I'm Dr. Anthony Robson. My guest today, Dr. Adele Mortensen, has a lot to say about sports anxiety in elementary-aged kids. Thanks for coming to the show, Adele. So, what do you think? Are kids getting a healthy amount of competition in our schools or are they forced to deal with too much?

My research in my district shows that they're dealing with too much, too soon, and that it's taking a toll on everything from their grades to the amount of sleep they're getting at night. And with children, lack of sleep can lead to a lot of health problems.

How much is too much? How far over the limit have we been putting our kids?

The shocking thing is, Anthony, that the amount of performance anxiety shown in my study group is equal to the anxiety that comes with professional athletes.

You mean, they're working at the same level as professionals?

No, but the anxiety registers at that level because a child's system is not set up to handle the amount of stress he's being exposed to.

Clayton made another note, refilled his coffee and then returned to the metal box. He pulled out a creased program booklet that was folded to a page containing Anthony's photograph above a caption that read: *As the 2002 recipient of the Sports Broadcasting Excellence in Programming Award, Anthony Robson will be presented with a check for $50,000 from the National Sports Broadcasters Association at this evening's banquet. Governor Jessie Ventura will present live remarks via satellite at the beginning of the program.*

He returned the paper to the box, pressing it and the various clippings down with the glass paperweight. Taking a scissors from the drawer beneath the bar, he then cut out an article from the morning paper's sports section that began with the headline, SPORTS PSYCH ROBSON SIGNED WITH

U.S. Cycling Team. He glanced over the article and slipped it into the pile.

"He wouldn't know the Tour de France from a soapbox race," Clayton said aloud, rolling the combination to lock the box.

I've read your article, and I've got to agree with the last caller that in the past few years the demands we've been putting on young children in team sports has gotten out of hand—

Clayton used the remote control to switch to satellite radio and tune in to the club mix channel. He turned up the volume and danced across the room to return the box to the closet.

EIGHTEEN

Camilla scheduled her first meeting with Anthony to take place after his radio show on a Friday afternoon at a coffee shop near the studio. When she called to introduce herself, she explained that she was the lead investigator on the Shepherd case and would appreciate any insights he could offer based on his previous experiences with him. She was surprised at his upbeat attitude in light of all he had gone through in the past year. Arriving at the coffee shop fifteen minutes early, she ordered a cappuccino, plugged in her portable digital player, which included a radio, and listened to the end of Anthony's show. She had heard a minute or two of the show in the past when dialing around the radio, but hadn't stopped to listen.

Throughout my career in sports psychology, I have learned many things about the winning attitudes of great athletes and coaches. They all hate to lose because they are highly competitive people, but they also value their failures because of what they learn from them. Every lost game or match is a reality check that teaches them something about their commitment, their drive and their confidence. With-

out those losses, they would not forge themselves into the high-performing people they ultimately become. The winners teach us that it's all in our attitude—rather than feeling defeated after losing a tennis match or golf game, demand more of yourself and work out ten minutes longer or practice your putt an extra half hour. It's been great being with you today. This is Dr. Anthony Robson. I'll see you next week.

Camilla recalled hearing that same voice on her phone recently and smiled. She put her player in her purse and pulled out a pen and a legal pad. She would be able to recognize Anthony, she figured, by his picture on the radio station website. Less than ten minutes later, he walked in, looking younger than his picture: dark, wavy hair; brown eyes; and lithe and quick on his feet like a runner. She waved him over.

"I just listened to the end of your show," she said. "Learning from our failures. That's good advice."

"Easier said than done, usually," said Anthony, "but it works. Do you catch the show often?"

"I have to admit, this is the first time I listened to it," she said. "I'm more into the gym than team sports."

Anthony noticed her well-toned arms and trim physique, set off by her tight, black sleeveless shirt. "Where do you go?" he asked.

"The Bridgeside Gym in Dinkytown."

Anthony laughed in admiration. "That's a serious crowd! And no frills, either. I'll bet there aren't many other women who work out there."

"A few cops and firefighters," Camilla said.

"Do you play any sports at all?" asked Anthony.

"I do Kendo and run marathons when I've got time to train."

"Wow," he said. "An athletic medical investigator. How in the world did you come to your job?"

"I've got a background in both medicine and law enforcement," she said, "so when I discovered this work at the medical board I thought I would be a good fit. I'm a registered nurse, I used to serve with the State Patrol Capitol Security Force, and I'm on active duty in the Minnesota National Guard."

"Is the capitol force the outfit that guards the governor?"

"Right. I used to be one of Jesse Ventura's bodyguards."

"Amazing!" said Anthony. He excused himself and returned a couple minutes later with two cappuccinos.

"Thank you," said Camilla. "Now, if you don't mind getting right down to it, what is your professional opinion of Clayton Shepherd? Is he just a dishonest, oversexed doctor or does he have an even more serious problem?"

"You're asking if he's dangerous," said Anthony. "My answer is, absolutely."

"What do you base that on?"

"I've witnessed his effect on someone very close to me. He destroyed her right before my eyes. I caught him in so many lies, manipulations, and destructive acts with people—all done without a tinge of remorse and done with such cold-hearted cruelty—that I have no doubt he's a sociopath. Hell yes, he's dangerous."

Camilla stirred a packet of sweetener into her cappuccino. "I know about your wife. I read your file that my boss put together for this case. I'm sorry about your family."

"Thanks. I just didn't see it coming. Shepherd and I had been referring patients back and forth to each other for years, and I had no idea there was anything out of the ordinary about him until I sent Marie to him. But she changed and turned on me and CJ so quickly, it's as if he brainwashed her in their second session. She suddenly began ranting that our marriage was a horrible sham, that she had never loved me. She left the house at seven in the morning for sessions with 'Clayton,' as she called him, and came back with her makeup smeared and her clothes all messed up. He called her at all hours and was obsessed—" He sat back in his chair. "I'm sorry—I'm getting carried away, as usual. I didn't mean to recite my life history."

"No," said Camilla, "tell me the rest. That's why I wanted us to meet."

Anthony rubbed his hands across his face and continued. "The third week of her sessions, Marie told me she was leaving because Clayton told her that our marriage was not healthy for her. This, after ten years of a wonderful life together and no sign of any problems. No big problems, anyway—every couple goes through their ups and downs, but we were happy. She had been a fantastic mother to our son, but that disappeared in a matter of weeks through a combination of pills and sexual and emotional coercion from Shepherd. She yelled and fought with me in front of CJ with no regard for his feelings, and I refused to let her destroy him, too. She left, and I didn't stop her."

"It's hard to understand how a woman could turn her back on her child, even if she's having an affair," said Camilla. "A lot of women have affairs, but not many of them abandon their families."

"Shepherd is a seducer, a predator who isn't satisfied until he's made a total conquest, and he relies on prescription drugs to make his vulnerable victims even more pliable. It's the combination of his ability to manipulate and to dispense antidepressants that makes him such a menace.

As you know, the city is littered with his prey. He's got to be stopped."

They watched the foot traffic on University Avenue for a minute. "I'm not the only one who witnessed the sudden turnaround in my wife's behavior," said Anthony. "Her parents, sisters, cousins—her entire family has distanced itself from her because they hate the fact that she abandoned CJ. They haven't changed their feelings toward me at all. They've actually been wonderfully supportive. They're committed to helping CJ get through it, and I'm glad they're there for him. He's turned most of his pain into anger, but he's working on it."

"Anger is certainly a part of grieving," said Camilla.

"Have you lost someone?" asked Anthony.

Camilla pulled out a set of dog tags hanging from her neck. "My husband, Nick. He was killed in Iraq two years ago."

"I'm very sorry," said Anthony. He watched her brush her thumb across the lettering on the tag. "What branch of the service was he in?" he asked.

"Army. He was killed by a roadside bomb in Falluja. Eight of his buddies were killed that day, too." She slipped the tag back beneath her blouse.

"Do you have children?" asked Anthony.

"I lost our baby when I got the news about Nick. I was about four months along."

"I'm sorry," said Anthony. "You've had more than your share."

"I've got a lot of work to do—and I love my work—so I'm doing OK," she said. "I know that my investigations for the medical board make a difference, and that's important to me. I need to know that I'm on the right side, being part of the solution, as they say."

"I'm sure I'll sleep better now," said Anthony, "knowing that Camilla Black, ex-cop, Kendo master and soldier nurse, is out there kicking ass!" He was happy to make her laugh.

"I hate to say this, but I've got to go pick up CJ," said Anthony. "I've got a lot more to say about Clayton Shepherd, if you'd like to hear it. If you have time, I'd be happy to meet with you again."

"Definitely," said Camilla.

"Making a difference with what you do is really an understatement," Anthony said. "Shepherd has to be stopped because he's destroying his patients. He's unbalanced, and he's capable of anything. I've got selfish reasons for wanting him in jail, of course. My son is torn up with hatred for this man, and it's not pretty. I'm doing everything I can, but he's going through hell with fantasies of revenge and God knows what else. I want him to know that there's justice in the world, that men like Shepherd can't get away with what they do, and that his victims—like CJ's best friend who just committed suicide under Shepherd's care—can rest in peace. That's a tall order, but I've got to know that I'm on the right side, too."

Camilla squeezed his arm. "I understand," she said.

Anthony walked her to her car and waved her off, holding his coffee in a lidded cup for the drive to Minneapolis South Junior High.

NINETEEN

Clayton stuck a label on a medicine bottle, popped in three pills and handed it to his patient. "Here's your medication for the next three days, Steve, until I see you again," he told the thirteen-year-old.

The boy held the bottle close to his face. "It says Uptown Pharmacy, but you had the bottle in your desk."

"I worked it out with the drug store. Having the bottles and labels here saves your parents a trip."

"Oh." The boy stuck the bottle in his backpack and then continued moving the arms of the Luke Skywalker action figure he'd taken from the collection on Clayton's desk. Twice a week, when his schedule was filled with ten- to fifteen-minute medication follow-up sessions with children and teenagers, Clayton placed toys around the office and hung a framed poster over the bookcase. The current poster, which he selected from a stash he kept in his closet, featured a rapper with a bevy of nearly naked dancers crowding around him.

"Tell me more about what your parents did last week," said Clayton. "Do you think that taking away your video games for the weekend was too strong, or was it fair?"

"I don't know," he said, yanking on Skywalker's leg. "Who cares."

"They were upset that you kicked a hole in the basement door. But from what you told me, it shouldn't have been locked in the first place because you had a lot of stuff down there. I'd get mad about that, too."

"I guess they'd never seen me wreck anything like that before and they didn't like it."

"So the first time you do it, they take away all your video games. I don't know if that's really fair."

"They're making me pay for the new door out of my allowance, too," he said. "It's their stupid house. Why should I have to pay to fix it up?" He whacked the doll's head on the armrest of his chair.

"Your mom tells me that you've had some problems in school this week. What's that about?"

"Mrs. Comstock got all mad because I was making noises. But my legs kept bouncing all the time and they'd hit the bottom of my desk and bang against it. I couldn't help it. She kicked me out of class a couple of times. I don't care. It's a stupid class, anyway."

"What else happened?"

"I kicked Brad's locker door when I was walking down the hall because it was open, and it hit him in the face. He had to get stitches."

"Why did you do that?"

"It was in my way! Everybody's shoving after the bell, and I would have banged into it myself if I hadn't kicked it out of the way. Can I go now?" He dropped the doll face down on the table beside him.

Clayton rolled up the sleeves of his plaid shirt, which he wore open over a T-shirt imprinted with a picture of Napoleon Dynamite, and leaned toward his patient. Steve eyed the temporary tattoo, a yin-yang sign, on top of Clayton's right hand. "Once your medication settles in, all of this stuff is going to go away. No more tantrums, no more fights, no more being pissed off at your parents and everybody else. It's just a chemical thing, Steve, and we're going to fix it. You're going to have a great summer, and you'll be into so many new things that you won't have time to remember any of this. I promise."

Steve sat with both arms extended along the armrests and one leg crossed over his knee, jerking wildly.

"You can trust me," Clayton said. "A lot of guys your age have sat in that very chair and told me the same things about the bad rap they get at school and at home. They've told me about how they can't seem to control their temper and how no one understands what they really feel. But guess what? Every one of them has gotten better, a lot better. Every one of them has fixed the problem with this medication and with talking to me, and they're like new kids now."

Steve stared at the Hulk Hogan figure on the desk and bit his lower lip.

"One guy, in seventh grade like you over in St. Paul, had burned down his parent's garage before he came to me. He was really messed up. But now he's the number-one sprinter on his track team and he's getting straight A's. He's got a cute girlfriend, too. The girls are all over him."

"He's just like me? Did his sister get killed in a car crash, too? Does he have a shirt with blood all over it?"

"Look at me, buddy," said Clayton. "He lost somebody in a bad way, too, but I can't tell you about that right now. Maybe next time. But I can tell you that he emails me all the time because we're still friends, and everything good about his life is there because he sat in that chair and talked to me, just like you." Steve heaved a bored sigh and looked away.

"It's time to go," Clayton said, patting his foot. "You're doing great."

Steve bounded out, and Clayton closed the door behind him. He typed notes into his laptop, checked his schedule for his next patient and filed away Steve's sheet of labels. He pulled out a new folder and prepared another three-pill prescription bottle for his next patient, a girl. Sweeping through the office as he did a few times a day, he switched out the action figures to Barbie dolls, unicorns, horses and a Batgirl figure and flipped over the rapper poster to expose the Jewel poster on the other side.

On his way to the kitchen, Clayton found Steve sitting alone in the waiting room. "Hey, buddy, what are you still doing here?" he asked.

"My mom can't come for a half hour," he said.

"C'mere," said Clayton waving him back into the hallway. He led him into the play room and switched on the TV and video game equipment, then pointed to a shelf full of games. "Help yourself. Just put the headphones, OK? I'll tell the receptionist to come and get you when your mom gets here." Steve stood at the shelf and turned his head slightly to read the titles on the spines of the game boxes. Clayton closed the door halfway and went to the kitchen for his water, then he walked back to his office. He buzzed the receptionist and told her to get Steve from the play room when his mom arrived, and not to tell her what Steve had been doing.

"And Jean," Clayton said. "Are you going to bring me a cup of tea again this afternoon?"

She giggled. "You don't have a break. You've got patients all the way through."

"I can always make time for you," he said. "I know you liked our last little chat. A few minutes looking into your pretty face is just the break I'll need. Come in after my three o'clock."

She blushed and giggled again. "OK, Dr. Shepherd."

TWENTY

The female custodian in a black uniform and white apron wheeled her cart to the door of the Psychiatric Partners suite and put a key in the door, but the door opened on its own. She looked in and, seeing Cheryl at reception and someone sitting in the waiting room, began to back out.

"Sorry, Ginny," said Cheryl, "but we'll be out of your way soon." She came out to the room. "It's been a crazy day. I wanted to close up two hours ago. My daughter's been waiting for me to take her home since five-thirty. Say hi to Ginny, Hope."

"Hi."

"Hello, Hope," said Ginny. "It's nice to meet you. It's no problem. I'll come back later. I hope you both have a nice evening."

"We'll be gone in about a half hour," said Cheryl.

"I'm sorry about this, honey," she said to Hope after closing the door. "I'm glad you have something to read."

"It's OK. I like this couch," she said, running her hand over the charcoal gray wool fabric. "This whole room looks like it was made over by those gay guys on TV."

"Dr. Shepherd paid a small fortune for a designer to renovate," said Cheryl, "and I still can't believe Dr. Olson went along with it. The place was brand new when we moved in. You should see his office. I mean, not really, you shouldn't go in there, but you should see what he did with it. What are you reading?"

"*Heart of Darkness.* It's for English."

Cheryl sat down next to her and kissed her on the forehead. "I've got to finish up some things on my computer back in the office, and then we can go. It shouldn't take too long."

Down the hall, Clayton switched off his computer, opened his closet and unwrapped a laundered blue shirt, one of several stacked neatly on a shelf. He changed into the shirt, slipped on a black suit jacket and put his laptop in his briefcase before striding out.

"Hello there," he said, stopping in front of Hope. "Are you waiting for an appointment?"

"No, Cheryl's my mom. I'm just waiting for her."

Clayton looked into the receptionist area. "She's still working?"

"She said it's been a crazy day."

"I guess it was. We had some emergencies. I see you're reading Conrad. Are you in college?"

Hope smiled and looked down at his shoes. "No, I'm a junior in high school."

"I would have never thought that," he said. "You look like you're at least twenty years old." He sat down next to her and rested his arm on the top of the couch behind her. "I'll wait with you. I'd like to ask you something."

She looked at the cover of her book.

"Do you know any guys at your school who wear earrings?"

"Yeah, a couple, I guess." She reached behind her head to pull her long, brown braid around her neck and began to play with the end of it.

"Are they straight?"

"I don't know. I think so. A lot of guys have either earrings or piercings. The girls, too. Why do you want to know?" She kept looking at the end of her braid.

"I was just curious about what a girl like you, a very fashionable girl, thinks about it. I know that men's earrings are about a personal statement, about being an individual, but a lot of guys my age are uptight about it and assume it means you're gay. They're about twenty years behind what's going on. It's such a drag to have to explain these things all the time, you know?"

"I guess."

"Your outfit, those boots, especially—where did you learn to dress like that?"

"I just shop with my mom and I know what I like. She lets me pick out everything."

"You've got exceptional taste, really, and you're very pretty. Have you ever thought about modeling?"

Hope rolled her eyes and laughed. "No!"

"I can't believe that. You look at yourself in the mirror every day and you know what I'm talking about. Let me see that profile." He slid toward the edge of the couch and turned to look at her directly from the side, then held her chin with the tips of his fingers. "That's a beautiful, what they call classical, nose. And those cheekbones. You look like a movie star."

Hope continued fiddling with the end of her braid. "I don't think so," she said. A red blotch started blooming on the front of her neck. "I'm not interested in modeling, anyway. I want to be a chef. I'm going to do an internship at the French Culinary Arts School in Chicago this summer.

"That's fantastic," he said, taking away his hand. "What a glamorous career you'll have. I bet you plan on studying in France, too. *Parles tu francais?*"

"A little," she said. "I've taken it for three years, but I hate trying to speak it. My mom says I'll get much better at it if I go there for a while."

Clayton moved closer to her and leaned back, returning his arm to rest on the back of the couch. The blotch on her neck sent red tendrils towards her ears.

Pulling her braid out of her hands from the back, Clayton took it into his fingers. "Do you braid this yourself? Your hair must be very long." He pinched each thick segment.

"Yeah, it's easy."

Standing up suddenly, Clayton stretched his arms and rotated his head. "I've got to get to the gym. I work out every day and lift—look, thanks to my new trainer, my tennis arm is like steel." He slipped off his jacket, sat next to her and stretched out his arm to show her his bicep. "Go ahead."

Hope touched the top of the bulge lightly and moved her hand back to her book.

"The machines are doing the same thing to my abs. Look at this—" He stood up and began pulling his shirt out of his pants. At that moment, Cheryl walked into the reception area. She rushed through the door into the waiting room.

"What's going on here?"

"I was going to show Hope my abs. She doesn't believe they're as tight as my biceps."

"I didn't say that," said Hope, glaring at Clayton.

"We've got to go," said Cheryl, glancing at the reddening skin on her daughter's throat. "Hope, come back to my office with me to get our coats."

Clayton extended his hand. "I'm honored to have met you, Hope. I wish you all the best in your career and your world travels. I hope you come by again so we can talk more."

Cheryl took Hope's hand and led her back to the reception desk area. As they passed by the open window on the way to her office, she looked at Clayton, who was tucking his shirt into his pants. She slowed to make sure she saw him leave. When she got to her office, she turned Hope toward her and put her hands on her shoulders. "Are you OK? Did he do anything to you?"

"He didn't do anything. But it felt really weird to have him sit so close to me and talk to me like we were friends. He's a doctor, right?"

"What did he say to you?"

"He asked me something about men wearing earrings and told me I have good taste and should be a model. He was really nice, but it was bizarre."

"I'm sorry he made you uncomfortable. I promise I won't put you in that situation again, OK? Are you sure you're all right?"

"Yes, he just talked to me, Mom. It's no big deal."

"Good."

Cheryl said goodnight to the cleaning lady on their way out and ten minutes later they were on Lake Street headed west, listening to the local news.

"He said I was very fashionable, Mom," said Hope, turning down the volume.

"You don't need Dr. Shepherd to tell you that," said Cheryl. "You're a lovely girl in every way and you've got a lot more going for you than just being pretty and having a sense of style. But some people can't see beyond that, and they miss out on a lot. They put people into narrow little boxes."

"People like Dr. Shepherd, you mean," said Hope. "But he's a psychiatrist. I thought those kind of doctors were only interested in the deep parts of a person."

"You'd think."

They turned onto their street, and Hope switched the radio tuner to a top-forty station. "I hope you're hungry," she said to her mother.

"Are you kidding? It's eight o'clock. I'm starving."

"I'm going to experiment on you again tonight." She pulled out a piece of paper from her backpack and read, "Les Gambas à la Provençale."

"I have no idea what that means, but I bet I'll love it. Does it take a long time, though?"

"Nope. It's grilled shrimp."

"All of those words mean 'grilled shrimp'?"

"Pretty much."

"Do you have everything you need to make it?"

"I gave Dad a list this morning and he called me about an hour ago and said he got everything."

"That was nice of him," said Cheryl. As they got near the house she saw her husband's car in the driveway. "I see Dad's home, so the kitchen's all yours. I can't wait, honey. I love it when you cook."

TWENTY-ONE

CJ rode his bike home at full speed from his eavesdropping session by Clayton's car and dumped his bike by the front steps.

"Dad, I have to tell you something," he said after rushing into the kitchen.

Anthony turned off the burner on the stove. "What happened?"

"It's about Dr. Shepherd." CJ gasped for air and tried not to cry.

Anthony poured a glass of water and guided CJ by the shoulders to the living room couch. "Drink this and take a few deep breaths," he said. He patted the couch, and their Irish setter, Teddy, jumped up and sat next to CJ.

The boy drank the water and petted his dog. "He's doing a secret experiment with his patients, Dad. I heard him talk all about it to some guy in his car. I stood outside and I heard the whole thing. The guy works for the drug company and he's in on it, too."

"Wait a minute," said Anthony, "you tracked down Shepherd?"

"Dad, I've been following him around Uptown for weeks. I'm keeping an eye on him."

Anthony squinted.

"You've got to believe me. He's been giving kids a drug that's still being tested and they don't know it. They think it's a real drug. It makes some kids crazy and kill themselves, but he's covering that up in a report he has to give to the drug company. That's what killed Mike, right? That's not legal, is it, Dad, experimenting on kids like that?"

"No, it's not, unless the parents give permission."

"Mike's parents said he was on Pro-, prax-"

"Prozor."

"Right," said CJ. "But I bet he wasn't. I bet he was on the experimental pills."

Teddy shot off the couch, ran to an adjacent window and barked. He stuck his snout between the drawn curtains and the glass and steamed up the window. Anthony called to him, but the dog wouldn't stop. CJ walked over to the window, peeked through the curtains and told his dad it was just the neighbor taking his garbage can to the curb.

"It's just Mr. Lindberg, Teddy," CJ said, gently pulling the dog back to the couch.

"What exactly did Shepherd and the other man say about this drug?" asked Anthony.

"Listen for yourself," said CJ. He pulled a digital tape recorder out of his cargo pants pocket.

"You taped them?" asked Anthony.

"When you hear them coughing, that's from the pot they were smoking."

Anthony held the small silver recorder.

"CJ, you have to promise me that you won't follow Shepherd anymore. Promise me."

"OK," said CJ. "But we can nail him, now, right, Dad?"

"Are you sure he hasn't seen you?" asked Anthony. "Where were you when you heard this conversation?"

"He was parked at Lunds. He goes there all the time."

"You can't talk to anyone about this," said Anthony. "Not our family, not Nira, not anybody. I'm going to take this to the medical board and they'll deal with it as part of their investigation."

"You're just going to *give* it to them?" said CJ. "Why don't we go to the police right now, tonight, so they can arrest him? Why are you going to let him keep going?"

"We've got to do this the right way, CJ," said Anthony. "Camilla has put together a strong case against Shepherd, and this tape could become one of the most important pieces of it. Just think how bad we'd all feel if Clayton got arrested now, got out on bail—which he probably would because he's a doctor and can afford a good lawyer—and disappeared? Then we'd never have a chance to see him punished, and all the work the board has done would go up in smoke. We can't let that happen, can we?"

CJ slumped back on the couch and scratched the dog's ears. "I guess not." Without looking at his dad, he apologized for yelling at him. Anthony hugged him. "That's all right. You have every right to be mad about all this, but it's all going to be over soon. I promise."

"Something's burning," said CJ.

Anthony jumped up and ran into the kitchen. He flipped open the oven door and smoke poured out. "No garlic bread tonight."

•

The next morning, Anthony drove to an industrial park south of the city to meet an old friend who worked at BioDesk, a privately owned lab that did contract work for the Minneapolis Police Department and other law enforcement. On the way, he stopped at the McCarthy's to pick up one of the pills that Mike had been taking and explained to Ellen that it might be critical in the Shepherd investigation.

At BioDesk, he stood at the reception desk where a young receptionist in heavy makeup and goth outfit glanced up from her phone long enough to point at a clipboard. He signed in and printed the name of his contact, Peter Roland, Ph.D. A minute later his friend came through an unmarked door wearing a white lab coat and the same short ponytail he'd sported since they were in high school. Peter had been Anthony's best man at his wedding and was married to the sister of another good friend, Susie Bradley, who had a show with her husband, Aaron, at the radio station. Peter was like family, and CJ called him Uncle Pete. They went to the break room, where Peter said they'd have some privacy before lunch. Anthony filled him in on the Shepherd case and described the conversation CJ had heard.

Peter rotated his wedding ring on his finger as he listened to Anthony's story. "My first question," he said when Anthony finished, "is why don't you submit this pill to the board's investigator? Why come to me?"

"I can't wait to find out," said Anthony. "I know that sounds selfish, but when I get this back from you and turn it into the board, it's going to take several days for the bureaucracy to get an analysis report back into the hands of the lead investigator. I've got to know now if this is Prozor or not. And another reason is that I can't trust the lab that it will be sent to. Shepherd has connections everywhere, and it wouldn't surprise me a bit if he had people watching out for things like this."

"That sounds a little paranoid," said Peter.

"You wouldn't say that if you knew everything I do," said Anthony. "Shepherd is capable of anything. He's a henchman for a billion-dollar drug company that will do everything to protect its secrets." He placed the pill on the table. "Will you do it? Will you run an analysis?"

"Of course I'll do it," said Peter. "And I'll use my personal computer so that it stays out of the database."

"That's perfect," said Anthony. "How long will it take?"

"I'll call you tonight." He picked up the pill and dropped it into his pocket.

They walked across the lobby and hugged each other. Peter pressed a button to unlock the front door and Anthony walked briskly to his car, patting his arms in the cold.

The receptionist waited for Peter to disappear behind the lab door before picking up her cell phone.

TWENTY-TWO

Jan set a cosmopolitan down in front of Clayton just as he sat down. "And what would your friend like?" she asked, looking at the fiftyish-looking man in the wrinkled shirt sitting next to him.

"Charlie would like a beer, I think," said Clayton. "Wouldn't you?"

"I'll have a Southern Comfort on the rocks, please," Charlie said.

"Is she as beautiful as I told you?" asked Clayton.

Charlie glanced up briefly at Jan and shifted uncomfortably on his stool. "She sure is. And she's quick, too," he said, adding a short, pointed laugh. "I guess she's made that drink for you before."

"Jan is starting to anticipate my arrival and my every need," said Clayton. "She's perfect."

"You're my world," said Jan in her lyrical brogue as she poured two shots into a glass and gave it to Charlie.

Watching her every move, Clayton took inventory. Her starched pale yellow shirt was neatly tucked into a black pencil skirt, which was partially covered by a tightly wrapped white apron. Her hair was pulled back into a ponytail that was folded and held together in a loose bun, with shiny edges of hair sticking out in controlled messiness. Moving just as quickly behind the bar was a young man, about twenty-four years old, wearing glasses and the same yellow shirt with black dress pants. A blond waitress with French braids clinging to the sides of her head stood at the waiter's section at one end of the bar, and Clayton noticed that her pink lip gloss matched her dangling earrings.

"Minneapolis is full of women like Jan," Clayton told Charlie. "Smart, beautiful, independent. They don't need men for anything except their own pleasure. Jan, for example, is working her way through law school and doesn't take handouts from her daddy or anyone else. The only reason she'll go out with a man is because she wants to have a good time, not because she needs anything. So she can be very picky about who she takes home. She takes a guy home for only for one thing, so she makes her choice based on looks, I'm sure. Just like a man, superficial but functional. And why not? I think it makes her even more hot."

Charlie spun the liquid in his glass nervously. "How do you know all that about her?" he asked.

"I've been coming here quite awhile and we talk before it gets too busy. She's confided in me about quite a few things."

Charlie shook his head in admiration. "I could never get a woman like that to talk to me," he said. "I'm surprised she even looked at me, I'm such a sorry piece of shit." He nearly shouted the last word, which made heads turn in their direction.

Clayton hadn't expected it because Charlie had never erupted in anger with him in public before. Sitting next to a lunatic would not help his chances tonight, so he tried to dispel the mood with an upbeat tone. "Whoa there, Charlie. Let's just relax. You had a great session today and you should feel good."

Charlie knew that he was being patronized, but he appreciated the attention. "It's been three years," he said. "I should be making some progress by now."

Clayton spoke with the same emphatic tone he used on his teenage patients. "Remember how much *better* you felt a couple of months after you started your medication? I think you've forgotten how depressed you were when you first came to me. When we found the perfect balance of your meds, you were able to go back to work. You take your life for granted now, and I'm glad for that, but you need to give yourself credit for how far you've come."

Charlie sipped his drink tentatively, as if he didn't know what was in the glass. "I'm functioning," he said, "but I still don't have a girlfriend. We both know it's way too late for me. I have no idea what the point of anything is anymore." He began to breathe loudly, working himself up, and finally said, "I'm just *sick* of it!"

Jan dropped another ice cube into the glass in her hand and walked over to them. "No need to get noisy, I'm right here," she said, replacing Charlie's drink. She looked at Clayton to get an idea of his response to Charlie's outburst, but he was looking at a woman on the adjacent side of the bar. Jan wanted to roll her eyes but fought it back and looked again at Charlie. "So how do you know the good doctor?"

"He's *my* doctor. I've been going to him for years."

"Really? I didn't know that psych—" She stopped herself when a customer waved her down. "Excuse me," she said, and left.

A man in a black suit walked up to the woman Clayton

had been watching and kissed her on both cheeks. Clayton turned back to Charlie and realized that bringing him was a bad idea.

"You know, Charlie, you put yourself down, and people don't want to be around negativity. They run from it. When you described in our session today how much you complain at work, at the store, on the phone to your cousin, you took a big step toward getting out of that negative trap. Being aware of it is the first thing you have to do, and you're there."

Charlie scratched the back of his head. "I didn't used to be like that," he said. "It's just been for the past couple of months. I can't seem to help myself." He fixed his eyes on a bottle and scanned his memory for something out of the ordinary that had happened two months back. The only change in his life was Dr. Shepherd's invitation to go out for a drink after their session. He had been thrilled at the thought of being the kind of person with whom Shepherd would want to socialize. After his initial surprise, he thought the doctor was extraordinarily kind to ask him along. But soon something began to nag at him. The doctor seemed out of place. Drinking with him felt strange. He, Charlie, was the same person, but Dr. Shepherd was different. Instead of focusing on Charlie, he paid attention to everything in the room at once, the pretty bartender, the women, the TV. Shepherd wasn't a doctor anymore, he was just a *guy*. The disconnect made his stomach hurt.

A burst of loud laughter from a group near the bar jolted Charlie back, and he took a long sip of his drink. Returning to his memories of the first time he came to this bar with Shepherd, he recalled that he hadn't been drinking before then. He had never drunk too much, anyway, maybe a few beers on the weekend, but when he started taking his medication he stopped. He had read about the possible dangers of drinking while taking antidepressants, but when he tried to ask Dr. Shepherd about it, he couldn't get a straight answer. He didn't start drinking again until that first night with Shepherd. He continued to put the pieces together in his mind, recalling his first angry episode at work all those weeks ago. He was as surprised as everyone else when he swore at a secretary for not putting paper in the copy machine. He felt as if the anger had come from outside of him and that the voice he used with such mean spiritedness was not his own.

Clayton had his head turned toward Charlie, but he continued to look beyond him at the woman seated to his right. She finally glanced at Clayton and toyed with an unlit cigarette.

"I'll be right back," Clayton said to Charlie. He got up and stood behind the woman, setting his hands on her bare shoulders.

"Can I light that for you outside?" he asked, bending down to speak in her ear. "I just picked these up and I think they're meant for you." He showed her a gold-dusted matchbox imprinted with HOTEL PRINCE DE GALLES – PARIS. Clayton put his hand on the small of her back as they walked outside.

Charlie watched them wind their way through the crowd and step outside to join the other smokers standing on the patio beside the front entrance. He set down his drink, rested his elbows on the bar and tapped his balding head with his fingertips. *It started with the drinking, but Dr. Shepherd wouldn't have brought me here if he thought it would hurt me. A person can count on a lot of people to go out of their way to screw you over, but not a psychiatrist, for Christ's sake. That's just more negative thinking.*

Maybe even paranoia. It could be that the medication just isn't working anymore, and the darkness is creeping back in. It must be that.

Charlie broke from his thoughts when a man sat down on Clayton's bar stool. "That seat's taken!" he said shortly, almost shouting the last word. The man put up his hands and slipped away.

Jan saw their exchange and plunged a metal shaker into the ice cube bin. She held the shaker over Charlie's glass. "Would you like a bit more ice?"

"You probably think I'm drunk," he said. "My eyes are red, I'm too loud, Dr. Shepherd couldn't stand listening to me anymore. I don't think watering down my drink will help." He grabbed his glass and finished the drink in one swallow, then set the glass down very slowly. "There, that's better. See, I can behave myself. Problem is, who cares?"

Jan took away the glass and poured him a seltzer in a mug with a lot of ice. She looked into his eyes, smiling, and touched his arm. "I hope you have a good night." She did not take her hand away until he smiled back. When he began to reach inside his jacket for his wallet, she stopped him. "Clayton will take care of this," she said. "Forget it." A waitress called her to the other end of the bar, so she left him with his hands gripping the frosted mug.

A few minutes later, Jan stood at the cash register with John, the bar manager, their backs to the customers. A fellow law student, John worked a few shifts with her every week and was also in her Wednesday night study group. They were both accustomed to silently analyzing the cases they were studying while they poured drinks, wiped glasses, and listened to customers, and they made a game of lobbing questions at each other while they rang up bills. Jan expected John to toss her another query about the first amendment controversy in Tinker v. Des Moines, but instead he glanced over his shoulder at Charlie and asked, "Who's the guy who looks like he's about to lose it?"

"You won't believe this," Jan said. "He came in with that psychiatrist, the curly-haired guy with the earrings who comes in every week."

"So?"

"This guy's his patient."

"Really? Isn't there some kind of rule against that?"

"I've worked in a bar since I was twenty-one," said Jan, "and this is the first time I've even heard of a doctor drinking with a patient. And look at him—this guy's not stable. What if he's on medication?"

"We should talk to Professor Ames about it," said John. "You've got me curious. If this doctor is taking a patient out for drinks, knowing that the patient is taking medication that should not be mixed with alcohol, he could be breaking the law."

"We don't know if he's on medication or, if he is, what the labeling is," said Jan. "But even if medication isn't the issue, there's got to be some kind of ethical rule about socializing with patients. Maybe it's a ruling with a state licensing board or the American Medical Association."

"Remember that extra credit proposition Ames threw out at us at the beginning of the semester?" said John.

"You're right," Jan said, "this would be perfect. I'll see what I can find out from either the doctor or the patient tonight and the next few times they come in."

"I could start looking for some pharmaceutical information, but I don't know what he's being treated for," said John. He slid another credit card through the slot on the front of the cash register.

"I heard them talking about depression," said Jan.

"That narrows it down." John jotted a few words down in a notebook he kept in his back pocket.

Charlie wiped his mouth with a napkin and stumbled as he got up, grabbing the edge of the bar for support. Without looking at Jan, he began to walk away.

"Charlie," she called out.

He slowly turned around and looked at her, annoyed. She had just told him that he didn't need to pay. Or did he imagine that conversation?

"Come back soon," she said. The customers at that section of the bar, as well as those standing around behind them, turned to look at Jan. They had never heard her say that to a customer before.

The smoking crowd outside had grown, and Clayton had staked out a cozy spot partially hidden behind a potted tree. He was leaning against the building with one arm, engrossed in conversation with the woman pressed against the wall in front of him. When Charlie walked by, he turned to him and said, "Leaving already, Charlie?"

Charlie kept walking and gave him a dismissive flick of his hand.

"Is he all right?" the woman asked, running her fingers along one of his lapels.

"He'll be fine. He just really, really needs to get laid."

"Doesn't look like he had much luck tonight."

"What about me?" Clayton asked. "How am I doing?" She looked away and laughed, and he kissed her on the neck.

TWENTY-THREE

Two pots of spicy lentil soup simmered on Padmini's stove while a dozen balls of bread dough rested on the counter. The fragrance of curry and garlic brought CJ and Nira up from the family room where they had been working on a paper for their summer honors history class. Padmini stirred the second pot of dal—free of green and red chilies, which she had made especially for CJ—as Nira and CJ admired the table set with bright yellow dishes, linen napkins and a vase of autumn branches. Padmini told them she was rolling out their favorite Indian dishes to celebrate their success in being chosen for the honors class.

Nira and CJ sat down at the table and watched Padmini press the naan dough into flat, oval shapes with her palms and place the pieces on baking sheets. She slid the bread into the oven and set the timer. "When the naan is done we can eat," she said. She poured a steaming pan of chicken curry into a bowl and then heaped basmati rice onto a platter to serve with the curry. She surprised them with another platter filled with a basmati rice dish made with raisins, onions, saffron, cinnamon and cloves, all delicately fried in ghee. "Bengali pulav," she said, setting the dish on the table ceremoniously. Then she ladled dal into bowls for her and Nira and served the milder version to CJ. "Dal, a little less spicy, just the way our Minnesota boy likes it," she said.

"You made a separate one just for me?" CJ asked.

"You're very welcome," Padmini said.

Padmini removed the naan from the oven and brought it to the table in a basket. "Go ahead, dig in," she said. CJ took a piece of naan and tore it into four pieces, then dipped one into the soup. After a second dunk, he said, "You've got to teach my dad how to make this, Padmini. This is my favorite bread in the world."

"It's very simple," she said. "Nira has been helping me make naan since she was a little girl, and she makes it very well now. You just have to give yourself plenty of time because the dough must rise for a few hours."

Nira folded a piece of naan and dipped it into her soup. "We decided to do our paper on the topic you gave us, Mom," she said. "The breakup of India in 1947. We've been reading about all the deaths. How could Great Britain just leave them like that and let it turn into such a bloody mess?"

"I don't understand," said CJ, "why there are so many different numbers out there about how many people actually died. Some people say a few thousand and some say two million. Who are we supposed to believe?"

"Casualty counts are never cut and dried," said Padmini. "People report the numbers they want to report." She moved the vase aside to get a better view of CJ. "I'm glad you decided to study the partition because not many people in America are aware of this great tragedy. This event literally broke India in two and both countries are still bleeding from that wound."

"Did Grandpa and Grandma come over before or after the partition?" asked Nira.

"Years after," Padmini said. "They were children when it happened, but they have vivid memories of it."

"Like what?" asked CJ. "If it's not too personal, I mean."

"They planned on telling Nira their stories when she got older," Padmini said, "but now that you are studying this I don't think they'd mind if I tell you one story." She pushed her bowl aside and asked Nira to refill their water glasses. "Your grandfather was six years old that night when the partition went into effect. His family, all Hindus, lived above the little produce shop that his father owned, and their next-door-neighbors were a Muslim family who owned the blacksmith shop. A little boy from that family was the same age as your grandfather, and they were best friends. They had grown up together, and for all they knew they were brothers because they spent so much time in each other's homes. They wore matching necklaces, little leather strings strung with a single bead, which the Muslim boy's mother had made for them. Grandfather can describe the bead of that necklace today as if he were holding it in his hand."

"Everyone in the families got along?" asked CJ.

"They got along very well," said Padmini. "Just after midnight, when the nation of Pakistan was officially born and the old government disappeared, the riots broke out. Muslims from all over India began moving toward their homeland and Hindus began pouring out of that region into India. Those who saw this as an opportunity to finally lash out at their so-called enemies went completely wild. Towns and neighborhoods and streets where Hindus and Muslims had lived peacefully side by side for centuries suddenly became battlegrounds, including the street where your grandfather lived. He huddled together with his family upstairs and watched from a window as another neighbor, a Hindu man, ran into his friend's house with a pistol. He pulled out the Muslim family members and made them stand against their house with their faces to the wall. They were all screaming and crying, the father, the mother, the two girls and the little boy. The man shot them all in the head, one by one. He ran off into the crowd and left them there. Your grandfather slipped out of his mother's arms and ran outside. They chased after him, but did not catch up in time to prevent him from seeing his friend's body. He placed his necklace on his friend's bloody head, what there was left of it."

Nira embraced her mom with tears running down her face. "I'm sorry, darling," said Padmini, "I shouldn't have told this story during such a nice celebration. How thoughtless of me."

"No," said Nira, "I'm glad you did. I had no idea that Grandpa was part of all this."

CJ put his silverware down. "Your father saw a lot as a little kid."

"My mom did, too," said Padmini.

"But they were OK after that?" he asked.

"They were sad about all the people they lost, but those feelings get less painful over time. It was a tragedy they had to learn to accept."

"Did they ever find the man who killed the neighbor family?"

"Oh, no," Padmini said. "He was long gone. Who knows, he may have met the same fate."

"Do you think Grandpa and Grandma would talk to us for our report?" asked Nira.

"You'll have to ask them," said Padmini. "We can call

them tonight. And if they agree, maybe we can go visit them this weekend. I know they have pictures you may want to see."

As she watched CJ and Nira clear the plates, brush the crumbs from the tablecloth and make tea, she felt like a guest, an old woman in the home of her married daughter. "Let's talk about CJ's swim meet next week," she said. "What do you call it, CJ, when you make a new record for yourself?"

"Personal best," he said.

"That's wonderful. Why did you tell Nira that you think you're going to make that record this time?"

"I came really close at the last meet," he said. "On the last lap I noticed that I couldn't see the second-place guy out of my peripheral vision anymore, which was weird. I knew he was there, but I couldn't see him. That was the first time that ever happened."

"I wish you good luck," Padmini said. "I don't know how you do it, all the practices on top of all your homework."

"It's not so bad," said CJ.

Padmini set out three dessert plates and a covered dish. "Guess," she commanded them, her hands on the cover.

"Have I had it before?" asked Nira.

"Yes, maybe once or twice. You really liked it."

"I have no idea," said CJ.

"Me neither," said Nira. "I give up."

Padmini lifted the cover to reveal a dozen pale yellow balls, ping-pong size, smattered with coconut.

"The pumpkin things!" said Nira, picking one up delicately.

"Angoori petha," said Padmini. "It's made from white pumpkin. I was lucky to find some, and I couldn't resist."

"It doesn't really taste like pumpkin," said CJ, "but it's good."

"I'm glad you like it. Take as many as you wish."

Padmini popped one into her mouth and smiled at the two of them.

Nira volunteered to do the dishes, and Padmini took a cup of tea into the den. CJ joined Nira at the sink with a dish towel.

"She likes you a lot," said Nira.

CJ handled the clean china plates like eggs, slowing stacking one on top of another with fierce concentration. He tapped his fingers against the counter as he waited for Nira to finish washing a bowl. "I wonder how many other moms he's gotten to," he said.

"You can't stop thinking about him."

"Don't you think your mom and dad would be a lot happier if Shepherd never existed?"

"Sure, but thinking like that doesn't do any good. It doesn't even make any sense."

Padmini had come back for another pumpkin ball, but stopped short of the entryway to listen.

"Do you believe in hell?" asked CJ.

"I think we all go somewhere," said Nira, "a nice place, or bad, or in between. And I think we come back, too. They don't believe that in your church, though, do they?"

"Reincarnation?" said CJ. "No." He lined up the clean glasses next to the plates. "I haven't thought about that very much. But if it's true, maybe he'll come back as a rat. Or a worm. A fat white one like the natives eat in the Amazon."

"Gross," Nira said. She turned on the radio and they danced in place as they worked.

Padmini joined them and handed CJ a gift-wrapped box.

"What's this for?" he asked.

"It's something Nira and I picked up in Little India last time we were in New York," said Padmini. "We were going to save it for your birthday, but we thought we'd give it to you now instead. A good luck present for your next meet."

CJ ripped open the package and pulled out a beige tunic trimmed with hand-sewn black piping. He held it up to his shoulders and looked down at the hem, which stopped just below the knee. "This is cool, really cool," he said.

"Try it on," said Padmini.

He took it into the bathroom and returned a few seconds later to stand in front of them, arms self-consciously at his sides. The length and narrow fit of the linen garment made him appear taller.

"It looks wonderful on you," said Padmini.

"Very cool," said Nira, nodding from the sink.

After CJ left on his bike, Nira and Padmini stood out in the front yard in the dark.

"He's a handsome boy," said Padmini. "I'm sure you've noticed that."

"We're just friends," Nira said. "I don't look at him that way."

"I know, I'm sorry. It was just an observation."

TWENTY-FOUR

Clayton Shepherd drove slowly around the maze of buildings in the industrial park until he arrived at the one-story building with the satellite tower in the parking lot. Disappointed in the shabby metal door at the employees' entrance and overweight security guard, he hoped the Mirrorland Communications radio studio would have more class. The guard sat on a stool facing a small TV in the corner of the narrow vestibule.

Clayton showed him his driver's license and told him he had an appointment with WCCM producer Ronnie Dahl. The guard checked him off on his clipboard, made a call and buzzed him in to the lobby. Clayton waited by the empty reception counter and wondered why it wasn't staffed. They had obviously spent a lot on the furnishings, but the walls and floor were bare, as if the place hadn't opened yet.

Ronnie appeared from around the corner. "Sorry to make you wait," he said. "Come on back." He led Clayton down a hallway, past the window of a radio studio where two DJs were one the air, and into his office. "I listened to your demo tape," he said. "It's good."

"Thanks," said Clayton. He handed Ronnie his proposal for a weekly sports psychology call-in show, complete with several eight-by-ten glossies of himself and a resume. "I've got a lot of ideas," he said while hanging his black wool sports jacket on the back of a chair.

Ronnie looked over the proposal and invited Clayton to help himself to a can of soda while he made a few notes. Clayton watched him read, waiting for a smile or nod, and figured him too young for the thick reading glasses on the end of his nose.

"I like your concept," said Ronnie, "but it looks like you have a busy practice and a major speaking schedule. Ever since you emailed me, I've been wondering one thing: How does a child psychiatrist find time to train in a new specialty like sports psychology?"

"I took a course in it designed for professionals with a schedule like mine," Clayton said. "It was a seminar program through the American Board of Sport Psychology, and it earned me certification in the field. A copy of that certification is in the folder. It's from the ABSP."

"I still don't get it. You've got an established practice at Pembroke, but you want to go on sports radio."

Clayton laughed. "For one thing," he said, "I'm a jock. I play tennis and run, and I figured the sports psychology course would teach me a lot about peak performance, and it did. And after years of treating children for anxiety, hyperactivity and depression, I found a pattern among many of them who were in school sports. The pressure they were under to perform and compete added to their anxiety and in some cases was the starting point for bigger psychological problems. A kid who's already getting overextended with homework and some problems at home might have a meltdown, for example, if he joins the track team and adds all that pressure to his life. I wanted to be able to talk to my patients about the specific demands of the sports they're involved in, in order to help alleviate some of that anxiety."

"That makes sense," said Ronnie. He leaned back in his chair and put his hands behind his head. "Tell me how this show would work."

"I'd have one topic per show and start out with about ten minutes introducing that theme. Then I'd have a guest, either in-studio or on the phone, who would talk for a few minutes to add more perspective and expertise. Then we'd open the phone lines, instant messaging and email. I'd bring in a lot of case study material from my own practice and information from all the sources I've collected so that there would always be plenty of substance to work with if the calls get slow—which they won't. Once my audience hears how effective my methods have been with my patients, they're going to call in for advice on everything from how to deal with a hostile little-league coach to what color speedos to buy."

"You sound pretty confident."

"I've got the patient histories to back it up. Their progress has been fantastic. Now that I'm aware of how crucial it is to deal with the sports aspect of these kids' lives, I'm trying to convince a lot of my colleagues to get the same training. Your typical psychiatrist doesn't know a thing about the field of athletic performance and all the issues of competition and anxiety that go along with it. I've got something important to offer your listeners, and I wouldn't be surprised if a lot of them turn out to be counselors and therapists."

"Our sports programming does have a wide demographic."

FATAL REMEDY

"I've looked at the figures," said Clayton, "and that's an understatement. Compared with KJOK, every weekday during the late afternoon time slot there are more listeners with at least one college degree and with incomes higher than $100,000 listening to WCCM sports. At the same time, there are also more listeners in the 14- to 21-year-old age bracket listening to WCCM. That's very impressive."

"We've worked hard developing the sports side at WCCM," said Ronnie. "And that's why I was interested in seeing your proposal. The sports psychology show at KJOK on Fridays is the most popular talk show in that station's history. Dr. Robson is a household name in the Twin Cities. He's a brand, and it's only a matter of time before he gets national syndication. We think there's plenty of room in this market for another sports psychology show, and we've made the decision to produce it. We just need to find the right host."

"You need someone with access to star athletes, on the national as well as local level," said Clayton. "My Blackberry is full of them."

"You've got a picture here of you with Ramirez, right?" asked Ronnie, shuffling through the photographs. He held up a shot of Clayton standing alongside the dreadlocks-toting Boston Red Sox left fielder, who was out of uniform.

"That was taken here in Minneapolis after the Red Sox played Minnesota last year," said Clayton. "Manny and I went out with some friends." He pulled his chair closer to the desk. "Ronnie, you also need someone with stellar credentials. A sports psychology expert with a medical degree makes a bigger impression than one who's just a psychologist, like Robson. He calls himself a doctor, and I realize he has a Ph.D., but when I'm introduced as Dr. Shepherd, the med-school graduate and psychiatrist, I'm going to sound a lot more legit than him."

Ronnie paged through more of the photographs. "Is this John Wooden? He's got to be in his nineties now."

"He's an old friend of mine from my undergrad days when I wrote a paper about him. I interviewed him in person and we're still close friends. Another thing I can bring to this show is a talent for thinking on my feet and a solid, confident radio voice. You heard the tape."

"Do you have any studio experience?" asked Ronnie. "I don't mean being a guest, but actually running a show, using the console equipment?"

"I haven't done that. But I know you offer a crash course, and if I could get through medical school, I can figure out how to run the mikes and answer the phones in a radio studio. No disrespect to your people here, but really, how hard can it be?"

Ronnie chuckled and looked at him over his reading glasses. He thanked Clayton for coming and told him he was their last interview and they would make their decision at a meeting in the morning. "We're moving fast on this," said Ronnie. "The bosses want to launch right away."

On his way out, Clayton slipped through the open doors into the TV news studio, which was lit but empty. He took a seat at the anchor's desk and gazed at himself in a color monitor off to the right. He turned his head left and right and smiled.

"Can I help you?" boomed a voice through the speaker system.

Clayton stepped away and waved at the blacked-out booth at the front of the room. "Sorry," he called out. "I just wanted to check out the set. I watch 'CCM news every night."

He headed out the doors and nearly collided with a young woman wearing headphones, a tight black shirt and ripped jeans. He apologized and shook her hand. "Dr. Clayton Shepherd," he said. "WCCM Radio. What do you do here?"

"I direct the five and six o'clock news," she said.

"You're a *director*?"

She took a step back and frowned behind her glasses. "Yes."

"That's not right," he said.

"Women can vote now and everything," she said.

"That's not what I meant . . . Ashley," he said, moving closer to read her ID tag.

"Nice to meet you," she said. "I have to go."

"I meant you should be on the other side of the camera."

The invisible voice rang out again. "Johnson!"

"I really have to go," she said.

"When are you done working tonight?"

She shook her head and smiled.

"I'm harmless," he said. "Look, I'm a doctor." He popped open his wallet and showed her his hospital ID. "I'll give you an hour's worth of free medical advice over a drink. No strings attached."

She rolled her eyes.

"Come on, Ashley, you know you want to."

A door slammed inside the studio and footsteps clanged down metal steps.

"What time are you done?" he asked.

"Johnson!" a man shouted from inside.

"Eight thirty," she said, and hurried into the studio.

TWENTY-FIVE

Anthony and CJ took their time driving home from the swim meet in Bemidji, taking old highways and stopping at pumpkin stands along the way. They carried two pies and a large pumpkin in the back seat, and CJ's second-place medal hung from the rear-view mirror.

"I think we should bring your medal to the jewelry shop and have something else engraved on the back," said Anthony.

"What?"

"Personal Best: Two minutes and fifteen point sixty-five seconds."

"But maybe I'll have a new personal best by the end of the year."

"That would be great, but what you did today deserves to be etched in that medal. Winning second place in the 200 free was fantastic, but to swim it better than you ever have in any meet is really special. You should never forget it." He grasped the half dollar-sized medal. "There's plenty of room to inscribe something. I'll bring it in to a shop tomorrow on my way to work."

When they turned onto the Interstate at Monticello, the sky ahead looked dark. "It looks like there might be some rain in the city," Anthony said. "Turn on WCCM."

CJ skipped around the radio stations until the call letters showed up on the digital display. *We're going to kick off this new show with some guests that you've never heard live on any other sports show in the Twin Cities, including Ohio State Football Coach Jim Tressel, one of the stars of the Big Ten, and teenage golf superstar Paula Creamer. They're going to shed new light on the art of mental preparation for winning.*

"I don't believe it," said Anthony.

"What?" asked CJ. He stared at the radio and then looked at his dad. "That's Dr. Shepherd."

After the break I'm going to tell you a story about my friend, David Willis, a pitcher who's learned a few things about control and the lack of it—and not just on the mound. In the last half hour we'll be taking your calls.

"What's he doing talking about sports?" said CJ.

This is Dr. Clayton Shepherd, and you're listening to 'Mind Games.'

"'Mind Games?'" said Anthony. He's passing himself off as a sports psychologist now?"

"Can he do that?" CJ asked.

"Maybe he's just sitting in for someone," said Anthony. "I'll call Jack at KJOK. He'll know what's going on." Just as Anthony reached for his phone, it rang.

"Hey," said Camilla. "How did CJ do?"

"He did great. Second place, and the best time he's ever had in the 200 free."

"Tell him congratulations from me. Are you still on the road?"

"We're about forty-five minutes out."

"Listening to WCCM, by any chance?"

"CJ just turned it on because we wanted to hear the weather. Does Shepherd have his own show?"

"As of yesterday, yes. I heard a couple of guys talking about it at the gym, and I called the station. The producer told me they signed him for six months and he faxed me a copy of the press release. You're going to hate this."

"I already do."

"It says that he got his certification in sports psychology from the American Board of Sport Psychology and that he consults for the Vikings, the Twins, Big Ten football and basketball teams."

"I can tell you right now he's lying," said Anthony. "He's making it all up."

"If you can prove that, it will add a lot of ammunition to my case."

"Did you just hear him say that David Willis is his friend?"

"Yes," said Camilla. "Didn't he used to pitch for the Yankees?"

"And Toronto and Boston and Chicago and San Diego. I read his book, and he sure didn't mention anything about his good buddy sports psychologist Clayton Shepherd. There's no way Shepherd is friends with this guy."

"Can you get access to the certification records at the Sport Psychology board?"

"Probably. I know someone there and I'll call him right now. Thanks for asking about CJ. I'll call you back when we get home."

Anthony called his contact and left him a message about checking on Shepherd's certification.

"I changed the channel, Dad," said CJ. "His voice drives me nuts."

Anthony turned off the radio. "Let's forget it. Tell me about the project you're working on with Nira. You're spending a lot of time on it—is it going to be good?"

"I think so." CJ stared out his window.

"Who's going to talk first when you present it to your class?"

CJ shrugged.

"I saw your notes. It looks like you've gone into a lot of detail. And the photos are mind-blowing. Where did you go to get such huge printouts?"

"There's a big printer in the photo lab at school."

"Nice. You're class is going to love it."

"It's no big deal. It's not like I'm ever going to use any of this history stuff again. I won't need it for anything."

Anthony gripped the steering wheel, furious at Shepherd for crashing CJ's mood. "It's not just about the history you're learning," he said, "it's about collaborating and sharing information with a lot of other people. Those are important skills that you'll use for the rest of your life."

CJ put the medal in its box and continued to read the billboards along I-94.

Anthony was relieved to get a call from Susie Bradley, his colleague at the radio station. "Hey, Sue, you'd called at a great time," said Anthony cheerfully. "CJ and I are just driving back from a swim meet and he's got a medal in his pocket."

"That's great," she said. "Congratulate him for me."

"He's had some good private coaching, thanks to you, and it's really paying off. He made a personal best today."

"Anthony, I'm sorry to break in when you're having such a great day," said Susie, "but I've got some bad news."

"What is it?"

"Pete's wife just called me. He had an accident on 169 on his way home from the lab last night and he didn't make it."

Anthony merged into the far right lane and slowed down. "Do you know what happened?" he asked.

"The police said that his brakes went out when he was going down the steep hill along the river valley on Highway 169," said Susie through her tears. "He missed a turn and went over the rail. God, Anthony, she said the car was a black shell. Everything burned up."

Anthony wiped a tear from his cheek with the back of his hand.

"What's the matter, Dad?" CJ asked. Anthony motioned that he'd tell him in a minute.

"How is Laura handling it so far?" asked Anthony.

"Her parents are with her but she's on autopilot."

Anthony thanked her for calling, pulled over to the shoulder and stopped the car. He turned to CJ and reached out his hands until CJ grasped them.

"Uncle Pete died," he said. "He was in a car accident."

CJ hands went slack and then he dropped his head onto his dad's chest. Anthony held him and listened to the traffic rush by until it started to rain. Then he gently moved CJ to the side and drove on.

Just before reaching the city limits, Susie called again.

"I forgot to tell you something," she said. "Laura was in rough shape when she called, but she did make a point that I can't get out of my head. She said she couldn't believe the brakes failed because Pete had just had them replaced about three weeks ago. They were brand new."

TWENTY-SIX

Ronnie Dahl stood in the control room as the engineer cued up calls for the "Baseball Fever" show. The host, seated in the studio on the other side of the window, was taking calls about his guest, retired Twins first baseman Kent Hrbek. The engineer typed in another caller's name and put the call in the queue. "Most of the callers want to ask Hrbek about his old buddy Kirby Puckett, not about his next fundraiser," he told Ronnie. "If this keeps up, he might get ticked off."

"Hrbek doesn't get ticked off," said Ronnie. "I can see why they want to hear about Kirby, though. The guy weighed over three hundred pounds when he got that stroke. I'd like to know myself how an athlete like that could let himself go to such an extreme after he retired."

A production intern knocked on the door and waved at Ronnie through the window. "Corporate has been trying to track you down," he whispered. "They got a call from some pitcher Shepherd talked about on his show. I guess he's real mad. They gave me the guy's name and number and said you should call him right away." Ronnie looked at the message.

FATAL REMEDY

"They said the pitcher is David Willis?"

"Yeah. Who's he?"

Ronnie snapped off his reading glasses. "How did you get this job?"

"I'm a basketball person," said the young man. He turned and jogged down the hallway.

Ronnie called the number from his office and was surprised when Willis himself answered. "Mr. Willis, this is Ronnie Dahl at WCCM in Eden Prairie, Minnesota."

"Did you hire Shepherd, the doctor who hosts one of your shows?"

"Yes, I did. 'Mind Games' premiered a week ago. Clayton Shepherd is a psychiatrist in the Minneapolis area."

"Dr. Shepherd is a goddamned liar," said Willis.

"What do you mean?"

"A friend of mine in Minneapolis heard the show a couple of days ago and told me that Shepherd said, on the air, that I'm a friend of his. He said he's helped me get through some challenges in my career and all kinds of shit. I've never met this guy. I've never even *heard* of this guy. And he's telling people that he's been my shrink."

Ronnie gritted his teeth and threw his pen across the room. "I'm sorry, Mr. Willis."

"You'll be more sorry if he ever mentions my name again. I want him to say on his next show that he made a mistake, that he's never treated me, and that he's never met me in his life, because he hasn't. Who the hell does this guy think he is? What other bullshit is he selling on his show?"

"I'll call him right now."

"If he doesn't make that announcement on his next show, I'm going to sue him and your station. I've got people listening."

"If he doesn't promise to do it, we'll let him go," said Ronnie.

"That's not good enough. If he's out, somebody else has to get the message on the air. The whole message."

"I understand. And I appreciate you giving us the chance to make things right."

"Your man is out of control, if you ask me," said Willis. "My friend out there looked him up on the web and found a picture of him on a singles site. He said the picture was pretty over the top, like the guy was trying to look like a porn star."

"I didn't know about that."

"Now you do."

"I'll take care of it. Thank you. And for what it's worth, I'm a big fan. I was at your perfect game in New York in '96. I'll never forget it."

"Dahl," said Willis.

"What?"

"If Shepherd ever says he's friends with Joe DiMaggio, guess what—he's lying. Just a tip, because you obviously know as little about baseball as you do about shrinks." He hung up.

Ronnie swung around to his computer and typed an Internet search for "David Willis perfect game." He clicked on a site and scanned the first sentence.

"Nineteen ninety-eight," he said. "Shit!"

He called Shepherd and strode out to the second-floor balcony, which looked out over a duck pond that meandered through the industrial park. When the receptionist at Psychiatric Partners told him that Clayton was with a patient, he left a message and told her to mark it "urgent." Back in his office, he emailed the host of "High School Update" to ask

FATAL REMEDY

him to be ready to fill Clayton's time slot in five days, just in case. Then he ran an image search and found the photo Willis had described. He printed it out and put it in an envelope.

Ronnie spent most of the half-hour drive to Pembroke on the phone with the Mirrorland Communications attorney. By the time he turned into Pembroke's cedar-lined driveway, he had explained the situation and also learned that the "High School Update" host could fill in if necessary.

Once inside the Psychiatric Partners office, he asked to see Shepherd, but before the receptionist could answer he heard Clayton's laugh behind the wall. He walked through the door next to the receptionist window and followed Clayton's voice to the kitchen.

"And her suit must have been two sizes too small," Clayton said into his cell phone. When Ronnie walked in, he closed his phone and said, "Hey, Ronnie. Did we have a meeting today?"

"I just got a call from David Willis," said Ronnie, holding up his cell phone. "He's extremely pissed off. He told me he doesn't know you from Adam, and he's going to sue you and the station because you told the entire WCCN listening audience that you and him are pals and that you even treated him at one point."

"Let's go into my office," said Clayton, taking the lead out the door.

"Is he telling the truth?" asked Ronnie. "Did you make up everything you said on the show?"

Clayton gave him an understanding nod.

"Does that mean yes?" snapped Ronnie.

"He's right," Clayton said. "I don't know him. But I know a lot about him. I've followed his career and he's a perfect example of—"

"So you admit that you lied on the air."

"It's a show, right? We're basically entertaining people and selling a lot of advertising."

A vein swelled on Ronnie's forehead. "It's a sports psychology show, hosted by a doctor, designed to give people professional information. It's not a fucking one-act play."

"You could have made that clear when you hired me."

"I was supposed to explain to you that a psychiatrist is expected to tell the truth on live radio?"

"You were ecstatic about the ratings that day."

"The show will be cancelled in a heartbeat if you pull something like that again."

"What do you want me to do?"

"Willis has agreed to forgo suing anybody if you come clean on the air and admit that you never treated him. You also have to make it very clear that you never met him and don't know him."

"All right," said Clayton. "I'll take care of it."

"There's something else he brought up, too." Ronnie handed him the envelope containing the photograph. "What the hell is this?"

Clayton pulled out the photo and laughed. "One of my patients took it and posted it on a web site that about ten people know about. It's just a joke."

"No, it's not. If the execs at Mirrorland find out about this, on top of the Willis fiasco, your show is history. Take it off the site."

"All right."

"Should I be worried about some of the other people you've talked about, some of your other big-name friends?"

"Of course not. The Willis thing was just to shake things up. He's a real character, and people either love him or hate him. He gets people worked up."

Clayton's desk phone buzzed.

"I've got a patient," he said. "I'm sorry you came all the way up here. We could have worked this out on the phone."

"I couldn't reach you. And I had to have your promise that you would make this announcement on your next show."

"Or what?"

"Or I'd fire you."

"Jesus, Ronnie, relax. It's just a misunderstanding. If you react like this to every little hiccup that comes along, maybe we should talk about it. Seriously, do you take anything? I've got a drawer full of samples."

Ronnie strode to the door and squeezed the handle. "I don't need Prozor. I need you to be straight with me and with your audience. Call me when you figure out how you're going to work your statement into the show." He opened the door with such force that Luke Skywalker tipped off the shelf and tumbled to the floor.

TWENTY-SEVEN

Camilla found a parking space on the street in front of the Medical Board offices on University Avenue and fumbled through her purse for quarters for the meter. Louise wanted to meet at the coffee shop on the corner instead of coming up to the office because she needed a break.

Camilla joined Louise at a table in the back and accidentally kicked her gym bag beneath the table. Louise was committed to maintaining a size six by swimming at the club three times a week and religiously following the advice of her son, a nutritionist. Camilla couldn't imagine Louise gaining a pound no matter what because her energy level rivaled that of a hummingbird. The only indulgent calories she had ever seen Louise consume were in the chocolate she sometimes added to her skim latte.

Louise removed her glasses from her short gray hair and sorted through the pages she'd removed from a thick accordion file. "I appreciate you writing up a summary of the Shepherd file so quickly," she said. "I should require all the investigators to create spreadsheets like this."

"I had to organize it like this because there are so many

different complaints against him," Camilla said. "I've never seen anything like it." She took out her own copy and glanced over the categories lined up in the left-hand column: "sexual harassment," "sexual misconduct," "patient abandonment," "unprofessional and unethical conduct," "breach of confidentiality," "fraudulent billing" and, added just that week, "embezzlement." In the next column were the names of those who registered the complaints, including their relationship to Shepherd (patient, office staff, etc.), followed by the dates of the alleged activities and, in the last column, a brief description of the complaint.

"Three sexual harassment complaints," said Louise without looking at the report, "six sexual misconduct complaints, eight patients who claimed abandonment because he left town for weeks at a time, three people submitting for unprofessional and unethical conduct, eight more for fraudulent billing, and last but not least, an embezzlement case from the partner."

"That covers it," said Camilla. "But did you have a chance to read my memo about the previous charges, the ones that have already been settled?"

"I didn't get to the details," said Louise. "But the complainant's name sounded familiar."

"He's a therapist in town. Anthony Robson, the sports psychologist with the radio show."

"That's right," said Louise. "What did Shepherd do to him?"

"Seduced his wife."

"That's a matter for divorce court, not the Medical Board."

"Not if his wife was Shepherd's patient."

"Wow."

"They settled," Camilla said, "and the board, as you may recall, gave Shepherd a slap on the wrist in the form of a notice in the monthly bulletin. That's the cost of unprofessional and unethical conduct these days, for Shepherd, at least."

"Not for long," said Louise.

"Even though that case settled, it didn't end there. Shepherd wanted revenge. He went after Robson by filing a complaint with us stating that Robson was submitting phony insurance claims. Robson was completely exonerated—the investigation proved that he had never done anything wrong. He turned around and charged Shepherd in criminal court for making the bogus claims against him, and Shepherd was convicted. He paid a fine."

Louise tapped her glasses on her palm. "Wait a minute," she said. "I remember reading about Shepherd's reprimand. I was surprised by the board's leniency because the case was strong. This psychologist, Robson, claimed that Shepherd slept with his wife while he was treating her, right?"

"That was it," said Camilla.

"With proof of that kind of sexual misconduct, a doctor usually loses his license. I was confused by that outcome, but I must have gotten too busy with my other cases to follow up on it."

"You're following up on it now," said Camilla. "Like you said, there's a rash of new sexual misconduct complaints against him, along with everything else."

"Whatever happened to Robson?"

"He divorced his wife and, as I wrote up in the memo, he sued Shepherd for unethical conduct. Shepherd settled out of court for one hundred thousand dollars. Robson has a lot of documentation about Shepherd that has been very helpful."

"Have you met him?"

"We've gotten together a couple of times for coffee. I take notes."

"You never do interviews outside the office."

"Sure I do."

Louise smiled. "OK."

"Robson's wasn't the only law suit Shepherd contended with in the last couple of years," said Camilla. She lowered her voice and held up two fingers. "Two sets of parents sued him for wrongful death because they each had a teenager who committed suicide while under his care and Shepherd had not told them about the possible side effects of Prozor. He gave them the meds out of his office and they never saw the label information. Both of those cases were also settled out of court."

"He's been busy," said Louise. "Funny he has time to do so much screwing around."

"What disturbs me the most," said Camilla, "is the fact that he's still treating patients. We messed up by not revoking his license after his last investigation. And if anyone else gets hurt before we finish this one, we'll be responsible."

"That's not true," said Louise. "We don't have the final say on these things. We do our jobs and the board votes and hands down the disciplinary action. You can't take responsibility for that, and you can't expect me to, either."

"He can't get away with it this time," said Camilla. "If all of these complaints get backed up with solid evidence, he'll have his license revoked and a slew of new law suits to deal with. He'll be shut down."

Louise shuffled through her file and pulled out a glossy black-and-white copy of the photograph of Shepherd that had been posted on the Wisconsin website. "I had to bring this along," she said. "I couldn't resist. A picture really is worth a thousand words."

"I saw it," said Camilla. "Look at the veins in his neck—if he holds his stomach in any tighter his head's going to blow off. And if I put that much stuff in my hair I'd be afraid to light a match."

Louise gathered up her papers. "I'm glad you've still got a sense of humor, Camilla," she said. "You're going to need it."

TWENTY-EIGHT

In spite of its location near the University of Minnesota, the Bridgeside Gym didn't claim many student members. Camilla watched throngs of them parade past the window from her perch on the chest press and figured that the ones who worked out probably did so at the university. She had discovered Bridgeside when she was a student herself, and her inclination to be intensely focused drew her to the distraction-free gym. Even if Bridgeside wasn't big, wasn't too clean, didn't have a pool or a smoothie bar, reeked of sweat and the towels felt like sandpaper, she could concentrate on every second of her workout. The whirring ceiling fans and grunts and groans of the guys energized her.

She moved to the leg press, reset the weights and lay on her back. Settling into her rhythm, she thrust the panels toward the ceiling and, between repetitions, replayed that morning's conversation with Cheryl Erlandson at Shepherd's office. She now had a statement about the sexual harassment alleged by former and current staff at the practice as well as Cheryl's detailed report on Shepherd's fraudulent billing. Cheryl also threw in another critical piece that

FATAL REMEDY

hadn't shown up in the file. On several occasions, she told Camilla, she had overhead Shepherd mention that he was having a drink later with a patient. This flagrant violation of ethics had always bothered her. In thirty years of nursing, she had never come across a fraction of such brazen misconduct. As far as she was concerned, Shepherd's offenses not only exposed a lack of respect for his patients' privacy, but also a complete disregard for the practice of medicine. One of Cheryl's last comments still gave her a chill. *Sometimes, Camilla, he doesn't seem human.*

After her last rep, she stretched out her legs and rested them on the floor. She glanced up at the treadmill in the next row, where a red-headed man running at a fast clip was grinning at her. He had only shown up at the gym in the past couple of weeks.

She heaved one final leg crunch and moved on to the abdominal bench, relieved that it faced away from the treadmills. After sixty reps, she looked into the mirror and observed that the redhead had slowed his pace to a cooldown. A minute later he stepped down and grabbed two clean towels from the counter.

"I'm John," he said, handing her a towel.

"Camilla." She wiped her face. "You're new."

"I'm going to buy the place," he said, catching his breath.

She dried off her neck and noticed his freckles. "You better not make it pretty."

He laughed and strolled into the men's locker room, baring his muscular back and runner's calves in her direction. *Nice to meet you, too.*

She stretched her arms and looked around to see if anyone had witnessed their little exchange. The bald firefighter was grimacing at the free weight bench, and Mike

Kelly, the owner, was reading a newspaper at the counter. None of the other guys were facing her direction. She threw her towel in the bin by the front door and asked Mike why he was selling.

"What are you talking about?" he said.

"That new guy said he's buying you out."

"First I heard of it."

"That was a weird thing for him to say, then."

He reached for another section of the paper. "Maybe he was trying to impress you."

She smirked and rested her back against the counter to look out at the floor.

"He's in pretty good shape," said Mike.

"Cross trainer, probably," she said.

"How much should I tell him?"

"About what?"

"When he asks about you, like every other man in this gym has done, what do you want me to say?"

"Tell him you and I are married with six kids."

"We tried that one."

"Save him some time and tell him the truth."

"That he should mind his own business."

"That I've got a wicked mule kick and next time he sees me he can address me as Sergeant Black."

He folded up his paper and wedged it into a mail slot on the wall. "Make up your mind, girl," he said.

"What do you mean?" She caught the trace of a smile on his deadpan face.

"Do you want me to put him off, or break the ice?"

TWENTY-NINE

Anthony and Camilla stood at the floor-to-ceiling window in Isabel Shepherd's penthouse condo and took in the view of downtown. Two years after her divorce from Clayton, she told them, she still relished this part of the settlement, an eighteen hundred square-foot loft in the Mill District. "Every time the elevator doors close I hear the squeeze on Clayton's pocketbook," she said. She adjusted the shades with a remote control to tone down the morning light and invited them to sit by the round fireplace. Camilla turned on her tape recorder.

"So Clayton is being investigated, again," Isabel said. "It didn't lead to much last time."

"We have a big case," Camilla said. "Several women have come forward, and that's only part of it."

"What can I do for you?"

"Let's start with the background on Clayton's brother that you mentioned on the phone," said Camilla.

Isabel opened a photo album and passed it to Anthony. She described Clayton's brother, Sam, as his fraternal, not identical twin, and the son their mother favored from the beginning. "That's Clayton on the left," she said, referring to the ten-year-old boys on matching bicycles. He flipped the page to a photo of the pair at sixteen, wearing matching army fatigues and sitting on top of a cannon with their parents standing behind them. The father was in uniform. "Their dad was a career Army man," said Isabel. "That picture was taken at the base in Leavenworth, Kansas. He died from a heart attack when the boys were in high school. They finally stopped moving around the country after that."

"What was their dad like?" asked Camilla.

"He was pretty tough, I think," said Isabel. "But I never got any details. Clayton didn't talk much about his dad."

The next photo showed the brothers in a restaurant with a crowd around the table toasting Sam, who was wearing a cap and gown. "That was taken at Sam's graduation from medical school in Chicago," said Isabel. "He went into research and landed a spot at the cancer center at Johns Hopkins."

"Did he and Clayton go to medical school at the same time?" asked Camilla.

"He would have if Clayton hadn't flunked the med school entrance exams," said Isabel. "He finally got accepted at an osteopathic medical school. Clayton is a DO, not an MD."

"There's not a lot of difference between the two anymore," said Camilla.

"My cousin is a DO," said Anthony, "and she says DO programs consider students' personalities and attitudes toward medicine almost as seriously as they do their test scores. Maybe that's why it was easier for Clayton to get in—he could have told them exactly what they wanted to hear."

"I didn't know Clayton then," said Isabel, "but you're right. I'm sure he knocked the socks off that admissions committee. If he understood that they were advertising for enthusiastic, compassionate and holistic-oriented healers, I'm sure that's what they got." She said that Clayton applied all over the country for a residency in psychiatry. He finally got accepted at the veteran's hospital in Birmingham, and only with the help of his dad's military connections.

"By that time, his brother was probably doing very well in his residency," said Anthony.

"Right again," said Isabel. "Sam had paired up with a big-name oncology researcher at Massachusetts General in Boston. Both of their names appeared on the study they published in the last year of his residency."

"He must have had his pick of jobs," said Camilla.

"He did. Duke, Sloan-Kettering, Mayo—all the top cancer centers wanted him and it drove Clayton crazy. Sam bought a brownstone in Mount Vernon when he got the job at Johns Hopkins, and years later his wife told me that Clayton showed up for the housewarming party in a brand-new Jaguar that he had driven cross country with a twenty-year-old model. Everyone knew Clayton was earning next to nothing as a resident at that point, and the girl confided in Sam's wife that she had just met Clayton a few days earlier and he had convinced her to ask her dad to borrow his car. It didn't take long for people to figure out most of the story on their own. Clayton looked so ridiculous they felt sorry for him."

"How did you meet Clayton?" asked Camilla.

"I was visiting my uncle in the vet hospital in Birmingham, where he was being treated for depression. He was on suicide watch in Clayton's ward." She blinked from a patch of sun and pressed the remote control to close the blinds further. "Clayton and I had a good time back then. I moved in with him instead of going back to my legal secretary job in St. Paul, and when he finished his residency we moved to Minneapolis where Bill Olson had invited him to join his practice. Olson had done a lot of seminars at Clayton's hospital, and they really hit it off. I have to admit, I never understood why."

"Interesting," said Anthony.

"You need to know," said Isabel, "that Clayton has been obsessed with envy over his brother for as long as I've known him. I'm no doctor, but I think that has a lot to do with the man he's turned out to be. It affects his relationships with his colleagues and everyone else."

"It doesn't excuse his behavior," said Camilla, "but I think my boss will agree that it explains his motivation for it."

"Clayton was, and still is, a very good-looking man," said Isabel. "And he knows how to talk to people. He has an almost supernatural way of saying exactly what you want or need to hear. I couldn't resist him, and evidently a lot of other women haven't been able to, either."

"Evidently not," said Anthony. "My wife is still with him."

"I'm not surprised he went after you," said Isabel. "His brother stayed out East, so he picks high-profile targets close to home that remind him of Sam and turns them into the competition. Then he goes for the kill. Once he decided you had more than he does—more credibility, visibility, success, authenticity—he had to tear your life apart. Your wife didn't have a chance."

Anthony pressed his thumb hard into his opposite palm, a habit he had picked up to keep his anger in check. "Like Camilla said, it explains a lot, but it doesn't excuse anything," he said calmly. The ache in his hand blocked his emotion from reaching his voice. "With all due respect, your ex-husband is a criminal who ought to be locked up. The only question is where. I'm convinced he's a sociopath."

"I don't know about that," said Isabel, "but I do know he can't afford to have boundaries. Clayton is still trying to be loved by his mother, who's been dead for ten years."

Isabel agreed to meet with them again and escorted them out of the building and onto the riverside terrace to enjoy the unusually warm October morning. "As long as I've told you this much, "said Isabel, "I may as well spill some guilt. Maybe it will do me some good."

The terrace gave them a panoramic view of the Mississippi River, its bridges and North Minneapolis.

"I believe we're supposed to learn from our mistakes," Isabel said. "But when I look back, I know I missed that opportunity with Clayton. I would have saved myself a lot of trouble if I would have acted on the warning God gave me in Birmingham. I should have left right then and never looked back."

"What kind of warning was that?" asked Anthony.

"My uncle never made it out of the hospital," she said. "He hung himself in the men's room."

THIRTY

Camilla sat in bed preparing for the next morning's meeting with one of Shepherd's former receptionists. A few minutes past midnight, Cheryl called.

"Do you remember me telling you about Dr. Shepherd's patient, Charlie Saunders?" she asked.

"The one he takes to the bar," said Camilla. "I spoke to his sister last week and just finished typing up my notes on Mr. Saunders."

"His sister just called me. She had my card from the office and tried me when she couldn't reach Dr. Shepherd. Charlie's dead. He shot himself in his car in front of Pembroke an hour ago."

•

Camilla sat in the dark. If they had begun the investigation sooner, Charlie Saunders may still be alive. After a notice went out that Shepherd's hearing was scheduled, Saunders' sister could have learned the facts and pulled her brother out of therapy. *How many of Shepherd's other patients are hanging on by a thread tonight?*

She switched on the lamp beside her bed and opened the Saunders file. On the top was a photo taken four years earlier showing Charlie in a hardhat, smiling broadly. He looked fit in a plaid shirt tucked into jeans as he stood shoulder to shoulder with three other workers. In the photo clipped to it, taken three years later, Charlie looked like a different man. Slouched in his chair at a dining room table with his extended family, he wore a T-shirt stretched over his enormous belly and his hair tied into a stringy ponytail. He stared blankly while the others smiled for the camera.

She turned off the light and called Anthony. When he answered, she started to cry.

"What happened?" he asked.

"Give me a second."

"You've been working all night again."

She sniveled and took a deep breath.

"You've got to give yourself a break. If you burn out, I'll have to do this alone, and then you'll really be in trouble."

She groped around for a tissue and wiped her eyes. "I will?"

"Sure. I'll be in prison for shooting Clayton Shepherd in the groin and you'll have to find a foster home for CJ. You know how long it takes to do all that paperwork. Social services is nothing but red tape. And then you'll be on the road for hours visiting me in St. Cloud for conjugal visits. Think what a bite that will take out of your work week."

"How can I make conjugal visits if we haven't even kissed yet?"

"Exactly. It would all be very awkward."

"I see your point."

"You can avoid the whole thing by getting some rest."

"Thank you."

"So, tell me what happened."

"Cheryl called. Shepherd's patient, Charlie Saunders, whose sister told us all about his happy hours with Shepherd, shot himself tonight. He parked his car in the driveway in front of Pembroke and put a pistol in his mouth."

"Christ."

She took another deep breath. "I could have warned his sister to get him away from Shepherd. I could have given her the number of a good therapist. Instead, I pumped her with questions for my case and didn't tell her a thing about the suicides or fraud or unethical practices that made her brother's psychiatrist a very dangerous man."

"It's not your fault, Camilla."

"I don't believe that. I'm not working fast enough."

"Camilla—"

"Knowing everything I did about Clayton's abuse of Charlie's trust and how lethal it can be to mix antidepressants and alcohol, I still didn't do anything. It's as if he already had the gun to his head and it was only a matter of time, but what did I do? Nothing."

"You're doing everything you possibly can, and once Shepherd is shut down you'll never know how many lives you'll save. You can't trip yourself up with this kind of guilt. We don't have time."

"Charlie was so sick and vulnerable. How many more are there like him?"

"It's another nail in Shepherd's coffin, Camilla. Charlie's family will sue him and the board will have an even stronger case against him. Tell me you understand."

A light from the window flashed against the wall.

"Somebody's in my front yard," Camilla said.

"What?"

"I'll call you back."

She slipped out of bed in the dark and lifted her service pistol from the side table drawer. Crouching down in her bare feet, she descended the stairs and flicked on the porch light. An engine revved and she ran across the yard, but the tail lights were already two blocks away. She grabbed a flashlight from the porch and scanned the outside of the house until she spotted the glint of a staple. She pulled up the rest of the wire that the staple had attached to one of the porch pillars and found a tiny black box dangling at the end of it. A siren sounded from the north and a few seconds later a squad car pulled in front of the house.

Camilla watched the street as she described the night's events to the two officers, and soon Anthony drove up. He grabbed Camilla and held her.

"You hung up," he said, "and I couldn't get back to you." He held her for a moment. "Are you all right?"

"I'm fine. Someone was here, but they drove away before I could see the car."

One of the officers continued to patrol the yard with a flashlight while the rest of them went inside the house.

"I found this stapled to the porch," Camilla said, handing the wire to the officer as they stood in the living room. "I believe it has something to do with an investigation I'm doing for the medical board," she said, "so I'd like to bring it to my director." The officer took another look at the box at the end of the wire and handed it back to her.

Anthony draped his coat over Camilla's thin robe. "We have a good idea who may have done this," he told the officer, "or at least who hired someone to do it. Camilla is investigating an unstable character right now and, from the looks of this, she needs protection." He turned to Camilla. "Have you noticed anyone following you?"

"I already asked her that," said the officer.

"I haven't," said Camilla.

"How do we get her some police protection?" asked Anthony.

"We already covered that, too," said the officer. "Sergeant Black's director at the medical board called the precinct, and they're sending a car over. They should be here within a half hour."

The officer looked at his watch again and made another note on his form. The second patrolman came inside and they asked permission to take a look around. After a walk through every room, upstairs and down, they said it didn't look like anyone had tried to break in.

The officer with the clipboard glanced through the window at the squad car, whose running lights hurled red slashes across the walls.

"Is there anything else, sergeant?" he asked.

Camilla trembled beneath Anthony's coat. "Anthony is part of the same investigation," she said, "and he has a sixteen-year-old son at home. They need protection as much as I do."

Anthony stepped into the kitchen with his phone.

"If your director requests it," said the officer, "they'll put a watch on his house, too." He told her that he and his partner would wait in the squad car until the first detail showed up and that from now on there would be a car out front day and night.

"CJ's fine," said Anthony, returning from the kitchen. "And no one has been near the house since I left."

"You've got security cameras," said the second officer, hitching his flashlight to a clip on his belt. "That's good."

"No," said Anthony. "Something better—a dog."

THIRTY-ONE

Dan McCarthy's transformed appearance kindled Anthony's memory when his friend met him and Camilla at the door. He had worn the same slack posture and dark lines in his face for months after Marie left. They followed Dan into the den and sat around a coffee table covered in newspaper clippings and papers. Camilla placed her small tape recorder on the table and opened her notebook.

"Ellen will be down in a minute," Dan said.

Burning wood crackled behind the sooty glass door of the fireplace, where a dozen framed pictures of Mike and his older sister, Jaclyn, stood on the mantle. Ellen's dark figure came silently down the carpeted steps and Anthony hugged her, startled by her bony figure beneath her black turtleneck. He couldn't think of anything to say. They sat next to each other on a love seat and Ellen drew an afghan around her shoulders.

"The funeral was beautiful," Anthony said.

Dan asked how CJ was doing, and Anthony told him that he and Nira spent a lot of time together working on a project for school.

Ellen asked where they were with the investigation, and Camilla gave her a copy of her spreadsheet listing the complainants. "I appreciate that you're willing to talk about our case at a time like this," Camilla said.

"It's our case, too," said Ellen. "The more we read about the dangers of antidepressants for kids, the more we want to spread the word." She picked up a large envelope from among the papers and gave it to Camilla. "Here's the statement you asked us to type up," she said. "I hope it's helpful."

Camilla thanked her and noticed a brochure on depression on the table. "Were you surprised that Dr. Shepherd prescribed Prozor?" she asked.

"A little," said Dan. "But when he told us that Mike scored above average on the fifteen-minute test for depression he had given him, and then said that drug therapy was standard, we took his word for it. He made it sound like every other teenager in the country was taking it."

"Did you think Mike was depressed?" Anthony asked Dan.

"Not really. We knew he was still hurting from breaking up with his girlfriend and his grades were slipping a bit. We thought a psychiatrist who worked with teenagers might be able to get him to open up." His lifeless hands dangled off the armrests of his chair.

"We thought psychiatrists did talk therapy," Ellen said, "so that little test and short visit Dr. Shepherd had with Mike at his first appointment seemed odd. We had imagined Mike and the doctor sitting across from each other in big, comfortable chairs, talking things over for an hour. We were very naive."

"You did what you thought was best," said Anthony. "You had no way of knowing Shepherd prescribes Prozor like candy."

"We should have followed through and done some research, though, said Ellen. "There was so much we didn't know."

"Like the fact that Prozor's insert carries an FDA black-box warning," said Dan. "We didn't learn about that until we came across it online last week."

Ellen shuffled around the clippings and papers and pulled out a white booklet. "This is what comes in a box of Prozor tablets," she said. "Doctor Shepherd gave us a week's worth of pills at a time himself, in a bottle with a label on it from a local drug store. We never saw one of these inserts until we asked our pharmacist for one a few days ago. The black-box warning is at the top of the first page." She leaned closer to the floor lamp and read aloud:

Antidepressants increased the risk compared to placebo of suicidal thinking and behavior (suicidality) in children, adolescents and young adults in short-term studies of major depressive disorder (MDD) and other psychiatric disorders. Anyone considering the use of Prozor or any other antidepressant in a child, adolescent or young adult must balance this risk with the clinical need.

"The part about 'clinical need' is what bothers us the most," said Dan. "Dr. Shepherd's diagnosis of major depression was awfully quick."

"So you're not convinced Shepherd made the right diagnosis?" asked Camilla.

"With what we know now, absolutely not," said Dan. "We looked up the criteria for major depression in the psychiatric manual, and Mike had shown mild traits of only one of them. In order to make a diagnosis, we learned, the doctor has to identify at least four on the list. Mike did not act depressed all day, every day, and he had not lost interest in everything."

"And he hadn't lost or gained weight," said Ellen, "he wasn't irritable twenty-four hours a day and he wasn't fatigued. The only thing that rang somewhat true was his 'self-reproach,' which we thought was due to his breakup with Patty. We've been racking our brains trying to figure out what Mike may have written on that test."

"Shepherd could have lied about the result," said Anthony.

Ellen and Dan looked at each other.

"We hadn't thought of that," said Ellen.

"The only thing we know for sure," said Dan, "is that Mike didn't start acting up until about two weeks after he started his medication. All of a sudden, he was a different kid. He had never been the angry, nervous type before. It was night and day."

"You probably aren't aware of this," said Camilla, "but it's a matter of public record that two other sets of parents have sued Shepherd for wrongful death because their teenagers committed suicide under his care. They settled out of court."

"That doesn't surprise me," said Ellen. "We've read about many parents who've sued after their child's suicide. They go after the drug company, too."

"Are you considering it?" asked Anthony.

"We're not ready to think about that yet," said Dan.

The front door upstairs closed, and a minute later Jaclyn came down. Anthony gave her a hug and introduced her to Camilla.

"Jaclyn is a freshman at the U," said Ellen.

"Dr. Robson is helping her with a case about Dr. Shepherd at the medical board," Dan told his daughter.

"What kind of case?" Jaclyn asked.

"There are several complaints against him from patients and other people," said Camilla.

Jaclyn sat on the arm of her dad's chair. "I remember when you went through all that with him, Dr. Robson," she said to Anthony.

"That was a case I did on my own, not with the board," he said, "but you're right. I know a lot about him, and that's why I'm helping Camilla. Or at least trying to."

Jaclyn picked up her backpack and said she had to study. "CJ seems OK," she said before heading up the stairs. "He texts me once in awhile."

Dan looked at the fire behind the glass. "Jaclyn is a wonderful writer," he said. "She's majoring in journalism."

"She and Mike were very close," said Ellen. "She comes straight home after her classes these days. She hasn't gone out with any of her friends since the funeral."

Anthony picked up a coaster made from a grade-school portrait of Mike, its thinly laminated top puckered with use. "Mike mentioned to me that he had started seeing a psychiatrist," he said, "but I didn't ask him the doctor's name. I can't tell you how much I regret that."

"You were just being professional," said Dan. "Mike liked the way you always talked to him like an adult."

Anthony figured Mike was about nine years old in the picture, the year their two families went to the Wisconsin Dells over Labor Day weekend in a rented RV. Mike and CJ played Battleship on the little kitchen table most of the way while Jaclyn kept her face in a book about vampires. They canoed past the sandstone cliffs along the Wisconsin River and cooked hot dogs on a campfire every night. The scrapbook of photos, maps, leaves and menus that Marie made after they returned home still sat on CJ's dresser.

He put the coaster back on the table. "We miss him a lot," he said.

THIRTY-TWO

Nira crouched behind a parked car as Clayton walked briskly through the automatic door at Lunds and disappeared. She walked casually to his SUV and shimmied the lock on the passenger-side door with a gadget she'd bought for twenty dollars from a kid at school. Once inside, she opened the storage compartment between the seats and found a silver flask, five bottles of pills with no labels and a plastic bag with a scattering of marijuana seeds inside.

"Weed," she said. "What a hick."

She closed the compartment and turned to the glove box in front of the passenger seat. Digging behind a batch of folded maps, she found a plastic case containing the car's owner's manual and, beneath it, a silver case the size of a tissue box. She removed the case and set it on her lap, then glanced at the doors of the store. She opened the box and whistled as she touched the empty syringe and held up a black rubber tie. Two vials of white powder rolled around in the box. Before closing the box, she held it up to read the florid script etched on the inside of the cover: C SHEPHERD. She slipped the box into her backpack, kicked the glove box closed and jumped out of the car.

THIRTY-THREE

The open layout of the Frye home gave Clayton a clear view of Jill Frye making coffee in the kitchen from his seat on the living room couch. A six-foot-tall portrait of Jill and her three-year-old son, David, dominated the room. Across from the fireplace wall, gold sheers over sliding glass windows filtered out the view of the swimming pool. Jill's husband, Allan, a lawyer in Minneapolis, had hired an architect to design the house on five acres in Wayzata to reflect, as closely as possible, the Frank Lloyd Wright house in Carmel, California, in which the 1959 film *A Summer Place* was set. As Jill had told Clayton in a recent session, Allan thought that she, with her short blond hair and big brown eyes, looked a lot like Sandra Dee, and he had the house built for her as a wedding present.

Clayton watched the light dart around the black marble floor as Jill returned with a tray and set it on an enormous leather ottoman in front of the couch. As she poured the coffee, Clayton inspected her white blouse, low-rise jeans and points of her beaded satin shoes. She sat on a chair adjacent to his corner of the couch.

"I'm a little nervous," Jill said, glancing at the portfolio lying next to Clayton. "I've never heard of having sessions at home. Is this a new trend?"

"You could say that. I've found that it makes a big difference for patients who have a hard time relaxing in an office setting."

"I *like* going to your office," Jill said. "Pembroke is a lovely place."

"I'm glad you like it, but it must be hard to leave here. This is one of the most beautiful houses I've ever been in." He sorted through the portfolio. "You may like our little corner of Pembroke, but I can already see that you're more comfortable right now than you've ever been in my office."

"I'm not sure how I feel about getting longer sessions and a house call. I thought the medications would take another week to start working, but you obviously thought longer sessions were already necessary. I can't help but think that there's something you're not telling me, that my condition is more serious than I thought."

"You're reading too much into it," said Clayton, pulling out a legal pad. "It's all about your comfort level, nothing more than that."

He flipped to a fresh page. "Have you had any nausea or vomiting since I saw you last week?"

"No."

"How about a dry throat or mouth?"

"No."

"Have you had any dizziness, felt a little lightheaded?"

She scratched her head with one finger. "Now *that*, yes. I have felt that."

"When?"

"This morning. I stepped out of the shower and I almost

lost my balance. I thought I was going to faint. It was an awful feeling."

"How long did it last?"

"I sat down and was fine in about ten minutes."

"That's good. You probably won't experience that too much, and it should stop completely after a few more weeks. The adjustment phase can cause this sort of thing, but it's nothing to be afraid of. If it happens again, do exactly what you did this morning." He made a note on his pad. "How about any unusual anxiety? Have you felt overwhelmed by anything in the past couple of days?"

She set her cup on the tray. "That might be a side effect of the Prozor and Wellbotra?"

"It could be. Some people experience slight anxiety on Wellbotra in the first weeks."

"What a relief. I had a bad spell yesterday and I thought my depression was taking a new turn."

"What happened?"

"I was putting groceries away with the news on and they talked about a gas station robbery in North Minneapolis. I got very upset. My heart started pounding and I was frantic. I watch the local news every day and I've never reacted that way before. I kept imagining the clerk lying on the floor, like the robber told him to do, and thinking how terrified he must have been. I couldn't shake it out of my mind. Even after I turned off the TV, my hands were shaking." She began to cry.

"Come here," Clayton said quietly, pulling her by both hands. "Come here by me." She sat next to him and he put his arm around her shoulder. "I'm sorry this happened. It's not surprising at all that a dramatic story like that would trigger some anxiety right now."

She pulled away. "That's quite a side effect. I hope it doesn't happen again. I felt like I was falling apart."

"Most likely it won't happen again. In the majority of patients, the anxiety at the start of Wellbotra treatment, if it's experienced at all, is very short lived."

Jill covered her mouth and yawned. "Excuse me," she said. "That's something new, too. I've been having some trouble sleeping."

"Can you take time for a nap during the day?"

"It just started a couple of days ago, and I've fought off the urge to lie down," she said. "But it hasn't been easy. It's a heavy fatigue that drains me, just like when I was pregnant with David.

"That is a beautiful painting of the two of you," Clayton said, looking up at the portrait.

"It was a gift from Allen. Just before he went to South America for two months."

"He travels a lot?"

"At least twice a year, on long trips. He buys me something special before and after, every time," she said, rubbing one eyelid. "The Chagall print in the dining room came after three weeks in the Cayman Islands where he was helping set up an offshore company."

"How do you feel when he's gone on those extended trips?"

Jill moved back to her chair. "I don't get lonely because I have David. We do a lot together. But sometimes I feel left out. I'd like to go along sometimes, even just to join him for a weekend, but he says he's always too tied up with work and he wouldn't be able to be with me anyway."

"Do the presents make you feel like he's trying to make up for that?"

"The first two or three did, but now it's too predictable. It sounds horrible to say that because these are expensive things that he carefully picked out for me. But they're just things. There's no getting around it. All of this—the incredible house, the pool, the art, the cars—I was never the kind of person who went after these things. Now that I have them, I can't help feeling that people think I'm a different person than before Allen and I met."

"Have you changed?"

"I haven't, but my outer life has. A lot of people look at that and assume things. Some of my old friends got jealous, I think. I can't explain their lack of keeping in touch any other way."

"So your husband is gone for weeks at a time, and when he is in town he probably works long hours."

"He does. He usually gets home around eight at night, sometimes too late to say goodnight to David."

"And your friends have abandoned you because they can't relate to your life in the wealthy suburbs?"

"I thought they were bigger than that. We're all artists, but they think I've sold out because I married a wealthy man. It doesn't make sense. I just had a show of my photography in St. Louis and it went very well. I'm still the same person with the same goals as an artist, but they act as if I'm a big fake."

"I'd be angry about that, too. That photo of the old woman's face in the foyer—is that yours?"

"Yes, I took that in Nepal last year."

"It's wonderful."

"Why should I have to apologize for my good life? I married Allen because I loved him, and I still do. I would have married him no matter how much money he made. And how am I supposed to make new friends out here? I quit my job at the museum because I want to stay home with David until he's in junior high, at least. I don't regret that decision, but I had no idea how alienating it would be. Thank God I can take a quick trip once a year and do some work and meet a few people. But I haven't met anyone around here who I can call a real friend."

"I'm sure you miss your colleagues very much," said Clayton. "They not only speak your language, but they validate who you really are, an artistic soul. Does Allen recognize that in you?"

"I can't speak for Allen." She poured them both more coffee.

"Your creativity sets you apart from most people. I'm sure he realizes that you are a rare woman."

She stretched out her legs. "When I was a little girl my parents always talked about my imagination in hushed tones, as if it were a birth defect. They even sent me to a therapist for a while—I have no idea why."

Clayton made a note on his pad. "I know what your isolation feels like," he said. "I've gone through the same thing."

"When?"

"I've always been a writer, long before I went to medical school, and I take it seriously. I've had a few short stories published. My writer friends thought I sold out when I decided to become a doctor. For some reason, they think the only way to be true to their art is to starve for it. I think that's ridiculous and arrogant. Deep down, I think they're jealous of my ability to do a lot with my life. I miss them, but like you, I don't regret my decision."

Clayton leaned back and looked at her, waiting for her to make eye contact.

"I've been looking for someone like you," he said. "To be perfectly honest, the more I get to know you, the more attracted I become. And I'm not supposed to do that." He made another note in the portfolio and shut it. "I shouldn't have said that, but I couldn't help it. I feel close to you and I want to comfort you, but I'm also aware that I'm physically attracted, too. You're one of the most beautiful women I've ever met. I want to be completely honest, because you deserve that." He drew his hands through his hair and down his face. "I better go."

She put her hand on his arm, but he didn't turn to look at her.

"Is the session over?" she asked.

Clayton looked at his watch. "No, but I should go." He slipped his pad in his portfolio and began to stand up, but she kept pressure on his arm. "We could say that this was a medication follow-up appointment instead of a full session, and then you'd be off duty. In that case, can you stay awhile longer?"

"You shouldn't drink on your medication."

"One small glass isn't going to hurt, is it?"

"I can't stop you, and I would love to stay. But are you sure?"

As she took the tray into the kitchen, Clayton smiled to himself and settled comfortably into the sofa. The combination of Prozor and Wellbotra was creating the desired effect, the Prozor working on the serotonin in her brain to lift her mood and Wellbotra handling another neurotransmitter, dopamine, to ensure the improved mood and kick in some essential side effects. Most precious was Wellbotra's ability to increase a woman's libido, something that Prozor often killed off. And the anxiety attacks and disturbing dreams that sometime accompany Wellbotra conveniently created opportunities to soothe and console. It was a cocktail *par excellence,* and the benefits didn't stop there.

As she became worn down from insomnia by taking her second Wellbotra in the evening (he deliberately failed to mention that if she took this pill in the early afternoon she probably wouldn't suffer from this side effect), she would be even more vulnerable. He would sense when her guard was down enough to coax her into surrendering the big prize, to let him undress her right there on Mr. Frye's big suede couch and have her, all of her, for hours. From there, if all went as planned—and it always did—she would become addicted to the affair, her sex drive revved up from the extra dopamine sloshing around her brain. She would be his, a rich man's wife too dedicated to her son and lifestyle to walk away, but committed to her lover with her entire heart, mind and soul. The perfect mistress.

Jill returned with two glasses of red wine. She sat down next to him and held up her glass.

"To perfect honesty," she said.

They clinked glasses, and Jill did not look away as he stared into her eyes. He took courage in that signal and decided to move up his timing. After taking a drink, Jill sat back and crossed her legs, and Clayton took her glass from her hand. He set it down and pulled her to him with both arms and kissed her. She squeezed his shoulders, then leaned back and lifted her arms above her head so that he could lay her down. He unbuttoned her blouse and pulled it off, then pulled off his shirt and lay on top of her with his full weight. The soft fabric of the couch rubbed against his arm as he pulled off her pants, then his own. She bit his shoulders and ran her tongue along his neck until he pulled her hair and kissed her again. After a half hour of this, just as he was about to come, he managed to spill some semen on the couch before finishing off inside her. Ten minutes later, he picked up her glass from the table and held it to her mouth. After they both finished their wine, still sprawled across the couch, Jill wiped the sweat from Clayton's face.

"Unprotected sex," she said. "Aren't we daring."

"I'm perfectly clean, my love," he said.

"Aren't you curious about me?"

"Not in the least. A creature like you could not have a harmful germ in her body. It would go against all the laws of nature."

"Am I going to fall in love with you?" she asked.

He grabbed the wine bottle, picked her up and walked toward the hallway and staircase.

"Tell me where," he said.

She pointed down a hallway and he took her into the bedroom. The faint smell of men's cologne made him realize that her husband had gotten dressed in this room just hours before, and he immediately got hard. He lay Jill down on the bed and stepped back to sit in the upholstered chair by the door to look at her.

Two hours later, driving back to Minneapolis, Clayton pressed a speed dial code on his cell and stuck a Bluetooth device in his ear. Marie answered.

"Hello, beautiful," Clayton said. "Do you miss me?"

"Yes, I miss you so much. Are we still going out for dinner?"

"Only if you're wearing the dress I bought you yesterday. Without anything underneath."

"I am. I'm all ready."

"And the shoes?"

"Yes."

"I'll be there in fifteen minutes. You better watch for me and come out, because if I come in and see you in that outfit, we won't be going anywhere."

"Did you have a good day?"

"Not really, but that doesn't matter. I'm on my way to you now, and that's all that matters. We're going to have a great time tonight. I reserved that round booth in the back, where everyone can feast their eyes on you."

"You won't get jealous?" she asked.

"I live to watch guys look at you and eat their hearts out. What are you doing right now?"

"Putting on my lipstick."

"What color is it?"

"Chanel Red. It matches my nails."

"I can't wait to feel those nails. Promise me you'll leave marks."

Clayton heard a beep in his ear. "I've got another call, my love. I'll be there in a few minutes." He switched to the other caller. "Dr. Shepherd."

"Pembroke is nice, but I like house calls," said Jill.

"Oh my God," said Clayton. "I've never heard your voice on the phone before. I'm going to drive off the goddamned road."

"I wish you could have stayed longer."

"I'm all yours. Talk to me."

THIRTY-FOUR

Clayton tossed his keys in the air as he strode down the hallway to Ronnie's office. He popped his head in, and Ronnie put his hand over the mouthpiece of his phone. "What is it?"

"I'm taking care of the Willis retraction on today's show," said Clayton.

"Good," said Ronnie. "I'll be listening. And remember, we're sending the tape to Willis right after the show."

"Right," said Clayton. "And there's something else we've got to talk about, boss."

"Clayton, I'm on the phone."

"Just one thing," said Clayton. He swept his hands through his hair and pointed to his left cheek. "I love doing this show, but you've got to admit, this is *not* a face for radio." He laughed and pulled the door closed behind him. Ronnie shook his head.

After slipping on his headphones in studio five, Clayton set up his laptop, leaned back in his chair and put his feet up on the console. He clasped his hands behind his head and watched the muted television in the corner of the ceiling while the clock moved toward the top of the hour.

FATAL REMEDY

Inside the production booth, Burt, the engineer, shook his head. "Good to see you, too, Dr. Shepherd," he said aloud, making sure the mike was not on. "I'm fine—thank you for asking," he continued, punching a series of modules on the computer monitor. "My wife? She's great. So good of you to ask. Do you have any scheduled guests I should know about? You'll just let me know later? Fine, sounds great." He stood up and waved at Clayton through the glass, then held up the one-minute signal with one finger.

Clayton swung his feet to the floor and rolled up to the microphone. An instant message popped up on his laptop screen. "Where are you?"

The initials identified the sender as Leslie Doyle, with whom he had just spent the last two hours in a king suite at the Marriott.

"I'm on the air in ten seconds," he wrote.

"I'm listening in the tub. I love this room."

"It's ours for twenty-four hours."

"Happy birthday to me, xxx."

"Have you got your phone?"

"Yes, don't worry," she wrote.

Burt's fingers counted down.

Clayton pulled the mike boom toward him, sat back and crossed his arms. *Good afternoon and welcome to 'Mind Games.' This is Dr. Clayton Shepherd. Thank you for joining me today. I'm going to start the show with a confession. Do we have some confessional music, Burt?* Two seconds later the soft swell of a church organ filled Clayton's headphones. *Perfect. Two weeks ago I talked to you about my friend David Willis. I shared what most people would consider intimate details of his inner challenges as a major league pitcher and, as I'm sure you'll recall, my work with*

218

him on anger management and other personal issues. I confess to you now that I've never had a session with David Willis.

Clayton looked up at Burt and gestured for an increase in the music volume. Burt pushed a lever on the board and quickly brought it back down. *In all truth, I have never even met David Willis.* He raised a finger and Burt produced another swell. *My intentions were not to deceive, but to teach a lesson.* Another dramatic swell. *By the look of all the emails we received here at the station after that show, filled with more of your questions about Willis and the pressures of the big leagues and the nuts and bolts of psychotherapy, it appears that all of you believed every word I said. I am, after all, a doctor and a voice on one of Minnesota's oldest and most respected radio stations, discussing important issues of health and well-being and sportsmanship. Of course you believed me.*

He scribbled a lightning bolt on a piece of paper and held it up to Burt. *But it was just a mind game, my friends.* He flicked open the fingers of one hand and Burt sent a crack of thunder over the airwaves. *It is important to understand how easily we are deceived, how effortlessly we put our trust in professionals and people in authority. But, you say, that's the job of someone on the radio, of those in the media, to talk straight and tell the truth. You say the same thing about your doctor, your child's math teacher and the golf pro who's charging you two hundred dollars an hour. But these are just people, like everyone else, who can sometimes become distracted and leave out an important piece of information or, to pursue an agenda of their own, misconstrue the facts.*

He pushed the mike toward the console and sat forward to open an email on his laptop. Keeping his eyes on the screen, he continued: *Think about it. The tennis coach you hire to work with your teenage daughter five days a week gives you a rundown of her progress every Friday afternoon, praising her extraordinary talent, the vast improvement she's made in her serve. You don't really see it yourself, but you believe him. Maybe he's putting himself through college and he needs this job for the whole summer and if he really told you what he thought, he knows you'd send him packing. Maybe your daughter doesn't have quick reflexes or strong wrists and she'd be happier spending those three hours every day playing the piano or walking the dog. But you're paying good money for this coach, so you're going to believe him. I advise you to trust your instincts. Ask questions. Don't put people on such a pedestal that they can easily take advantage of you.*

He glanced up and caught Burt's puzzled expression.

Don't get me wrong—I'm not promoting that everyone become paranoid and distrustful. I think it's important, however, that you understand how easily someone—even a doctor on the radio—can mislead you. The vast majority of people are honest and have good intentions toward their fellow human beings. I truly believe that. But that doesn't mean you may not cross the path of someone in the minority. If anyone is offended by my little experiment, I apologize. I did not intend to harm or offend any of you, including Mr. Willis, who has been a very good sport about the whole thing.

He looked over at Ronnie standing stiffly in the hallway watching through the studio window.

After the break, I'll take your calls about this and anything else you'd like to bring up today. Burt gradually increased the volume of Clayton's favorite bumper music, a rousing march played by the U.S. Army Band. *In the last half of the hour, we'll be talking to my special guest, a therapist who specializes in compulsive gambling and who will shed light on the world of sports betting. This comes with a warning: his horror stories about people who have destroyed their lives through online betting may make you find another hobby . . . so stay tuned. This is Dr. Clayton Shepherd with 'Mind Games' on WCCM.*

Ronnie stepped in and closed the door behind him. Burt switched on the intercom so he could listen in.

"That was *it*?" he asked. "That was your retraction?"

"I did everything you asked me to do," said Clayton, shutting his laptop. "I admitted that I never worked with Willis and never even met him."

"But you made it sound like you had this all worked out from the beginning," said Ronnie. "There was no real apology in that at all."

"I did apologize," said Clayton, turning to the production booth window. "Burt, you heard me, didn't you? I said that I apologized to anyone who was offended."

Burt shrugged and nodded at Ronnie.

"I heard that part," said Ronnie, "but I don't think this is what corporate or Willis had in mind. You got yourself completely off the hook."

"If I look better, WCCM looks better," said Clayton. He swung his feet up on the console. "Just wait for the calls. I promise you that a lot of people are going to be blown away by this little experiment. They're going to thank me for opening their eyes and for taking such a risk for their benefit."

"That's what you think?"

"I guarantee it," said Clayton. "I know people, Ronnie. That's what I do. Just relax. It's going to be fine."

Burt held up two fingers, and Clayton pulled his headphones from a hook next to the microphone and hung them around his neck.

"We'll see how your listeners take this," said Ronnie. "If they're pissed off because they've been lied to, we'll be back to square one."

"Trust me," said Clayton. "You won't be sorry."

Ronnie walked out and stopped at the production booth. "Any calls?" he asked Burt.

Burt rolled away from the computer monitor to reveal a screen filled with blinking caller ID's. "They're stacked to the hilt."

"How did they sound?" asked Ronnie.

"Positive, most of them. They started as soon as he said he'd never had a session with Willis."

"I'll be damned." Ronnie pulled the door shut and returned to his office to listen to the rest of the show.

At the start of Clayton's show, eight listeners scattered throughout the metropolitan area listened closely to the radio with their phones and a few notes at hand. As soon as Clayton made his confession, Leslie Doyle stretched her arm out of her tub and dialed the studio. Once Burt took her information and put her on hold, she turned on the speakerphone. In a shopping mall south of town, Jill Frye was also on hold with WCCN, her cell phone wedged between her shoulder and ear as she picked through a rack of dresses at Nordstrom's. In a boardroom on the forty-ninth floor of the IDS Building downtown, Emily Carter's Blackberry waited on hold while she ate lunch alone and listened to the online stream of the show on her laptop. In the fourth-floor break room at Hennepin Metro, three male orderlies pinned their phone to their shoulders, waiting in the studio queue. At the nurse's station down the hall, Regan Moyers leaned against the drug closet door with her phone to her ear, waiting to tell Dr. Shepherd exactly what he had instructed her to say. In a downtown warehouse near the riverfront, a man in white overalls sat on a forklift and lit up a cigarette while waiting for his turn on the air.

When they came up in the queue, each of Clayton's callers heaped praise, shared their own stories of learning to trust the hard way and thanked him for reminding him of those lessons. With only two minutes until the guest slot, the last caller to get through was one of the orderlies from Clayton's ward at Hennepin Metro.

Hey, man, I agree with everybody else. I think you're great. My brother's spending his life savings on his kid's golf trainer, some preppie guy that got all talked up at his country club, and I can tell he's not doing the kid any good. My brother won't listen to me, but now I can tell him what you said and have him listen to the show online if he doesn't believe me. Maybe he'll fire this guy's ass and hire somebody who knows what he's doing.

Thanks for that, Frank. Do you think I crossed a line when I made up that story about knowing David Willis?

Hell no, that's why I keep listening. I can't wait to hear what kind of freaky thing you come up with next.

On that note, it's time for a news and weather break. When we come back we'll talk with my guest and take your calls on your experiences with sports gambling. This is Dr. Clayton Shepherd with 'Mind Games' on WCCN.

Clayton hung up his headphones and met Ronnie in the booth.

"The people have spoken," said Clayton. "Just like I knew they would."

"It sounds that way," said Ronnie. "But don't ever pull something like that again."

"You're the boss."

Holding the door open for Ronnie, Clayton asked him to send someone into the studio with an espresso from the machine and a bottle of water, because he would be too busy to run around during the break. He returned to his mike to check his notes for his phone guest, and a couple of minutes later a young woman in a short skirt and jean jacket knocked lightly on the bottom of the door with her shoe. He rolled his chair toward the door and opened it.

"Jackie, come in!" he said. "Did you bring those for me?"

"Mr. Dahl said you asked for them," she said, setting the coffee and water on the console. "Sounds like you've had a great show so far," she said.

"Did Mr. Dahl tell you that?"

"No, I've been listening."

Clayton sipped the espresso from the small paper cup. "Would you like to stay in here with me for the rest of the show?"

"In the studio?"

"Sure. You could keep me company. It's kind of weird being in here by myself."

"I don't know if Mr. Dahl—"

"Don't worry, he won't mind."

"What will I do?"

"Just sit here and listen, and during the breaks I'll ask for your feedback. It'll help me a lot."

"Sure!" She rolled a chair to the other side of the console.

"You're a communications major, right?" he asked, facing her.

"I was. I just graduated from the U."

"Why did you take a job as an assistant?"

"It's is a great place to start," she said. "I want to learn everything from the ground up, and Mr. Dahl has already taught me a lot. I'm going to have my own show someday, a liberal talk show for the under thirty market with guests like rock stars and actors and activists."

Clayton glimpsed a swerving green line on her wrist that disappeared beneath the sleeve of her sweater. "You could do that on TV," he said. "Ronnie probably has the connections to help you shoot a demo here at the station."

"It's a lot harder to get on TV," she said. "Most people get their start on radio."

"Not anymore. Look at all the young women on CNN and Fox—do you think they spent ten years on the radio before launching into TV? No way. They started at affiliates in cities this size." He looked at her wrist. "Is that a tattoo?"

She pulled up her sleeve to reveal a stem-like figure that wound into a triangular Gaellic knot just below the crook of her arm." He traced the line with his fingers. "I've got a good friend who's a producer on MTV. We should talk about this."

Her eyes widened, and Clayton handed her a pair of earphones. "We're on in one minute," he said as he pulled on his own set. "Let's have dinner one night this week."

THIRTY-FIVE

Cheryl pulled up Clayton's speaking schedule on her computer and wrote down the place and time of his upcoming appearance at a Brown-Dixon seminar. Not until Bill Olson intervened did Clayton finally forward the schedule to her, and the day she received it in an email she called Ted Elliot and described the dozens of engagements filled in over the next six months. Clayton could not bury his extracurricular time or income from the practice any longer. "Party's over," she said.

Thanks to Cheryl, Camilla learned that Clayton was booked to speak at the seminar on a Saturday in Rochester, Minnesota, home of the Mayo Clinic. She convinced Louise to order a temporary state medical board ID for Anthony that would allow him to attend the event with her, and they planned to bring CJ and Nira along. A friend of Anthony's would take them to the Rochester Museum and Science Center while he and Camilla were at the seminar.

Camilla drove, and Anthony reviewed the newest contents of Clayton's file along the way. He pulled a hand-addressed envelope from his pocket to add to the file and held it for a moment, staring at the familiar handwriting. Peter Roland had mailed him his lab report on the pill Anthony had brought to him, and the envelope was postmarked the day of Peter's accident. Just as CJ's recording of Shepherd and Terry Strick revealed, the drug Shepherd had been giving Mike McCarthy was not Prozor but an unknown compound that looked very similar to other SSRIs but contained an unfamiliar and, according to a comparison of similar drugs, seemingly unrelated enzyme. After listening to CJ's recording and obtaining the lab analysis, which Anthony had scanned and emailed to Louise and Camilla, Louise assigned an additional investigator to work solely on that part of the case.

He carefully tucked the envelope to a folder pocket and looked at the papers in the front of the file. According to the tax returns Cheryl had given Camilla, Shepherd had been on Brown-Dixon's payroll for almost four years. "Shepherd probably knows Brown and Dixon personally by now," he told Camilla as they rolled by another field of sheared, dry cornstalks.

"They each must be getting something out of the relationship," said Camilla, "something that continues to be valuable."

"Money is always valuable," said Anthony.

"And a charismatic doctor on your PR circuit is a hot commodity, too," said Camilla. She pulled Anthony's ID card and a neck cord from her purse. "When we get to the hotel," she said, "our IDs will get us in the door. Clayton Shepherd has no idea who I am, but if he sees you, he may suspect you're up to something. We can't afford to scare him off. How can you manage to avoid him?"

Anthony faced his window, fumbled in his pants pocket

and spun back around wearing a black mustache. "I'll fool them all," he said, raising his eyebrows up and down and slipping on a tweed cap and black-framed glasses.

"Please, Anthony," said Camilla, laughing. "I'm serious. If he sees you snooping around he might—"

CJ reached over the seat, peeled off the mustache and stuck it to his own upper lip.

"He might figure out that something's up and skip town," Camilla said. "We can't hold a hearing if we can't find him."

"Right," said Anthony. "You're absolutely right. I need to keep out of his line of sight, and I'll do that. But the mustache won't hurt—I think it looks natural. Show her, CJ."

CJ popped his head over the front seat.

"Not bad," said Camilla.

CJ pressed the mustache back onto his dad's face and looked him over. "I think it'll work," he said.

After dropping CJ and Nira off at the museum with Anthony's friend, they drove another half mile to the hotel. Anthony waited at the newspaper stand in the lobby while Camilla took the elevator up to the ballroom floor. She signed in at the table, entered the opulent room where Clayton would be speaking and spotted him already seated at a dais at the front. Half of the crowd was seated at the twenty or so formally set dining tables and the others milled around them or at the bar at the back of the room. She called Anthony and suggested he find a place to observe near one of the doors rather than inside, just to be safe.

She took the only open seat at a table near the main door, and a tuxedoed waiter swept in and poured her a glass of Chardonnay. She glanced at her watch, which read 11:05. *A tad early for alcohol.* The waiter refilled the wine glasses of a few others at the table, and they all turned to the front of the room when someone tapped a microphone.

A Brown-Dixon vice president stood at the lectern on the dais and invited everyone to be seated. He introduced the guests at his left and right, most of them executives at the company, and saved Shepherd for last, describing him as the keynote speaker and "one of the foremost child psychiatrists in the country." Clayton shook hands with the VP and took his place behind the lectern. He pulled a pair of reading glasses from his snugly tailored Armani suit and glanced at his notes. His wore his white shirt, with a European straight collar, open at the throat without a tie. The effect was a casual, expensive elegance that struck Camilla, all the way in the back of the room, as utterly phony.

Thank you for taking time from your busy schedules to join us today. You are all aware that the horizons of child-adolescent psychiatry have broadened exponentially over the past fifteen years, on a parallel course with adult psychiatry, thanks to the ever-developing sophistication of psychotropics that alleviate both the rare and the most widespread diagnoses. Millions of children and juveniles have regained normal, happy, and full lives with medications that erase the problems associated with attention deficit disorder and depression, and these treatments not only halt the advance of these disorders, but prevent the development of more serious problems that can predictably arise from them in later years.

He took off his glasses and gripped the sides of the lectern.

A friend of mine recently described children's psychopharmaceuticals as a modern miracle that can fix everything from a child's mood to his bad taste in music.

Laughter erupted from the tables. Camilla shot a glance

at Anthony, who was partially hidden from view by one of the plants flanking the doorway. He rolled his eyes at her.

She scanned the tables as Clayton continued his talk. A familiar profile prompted her to put on her glasses for a closer look. She recognized the man at the far side of the next table as a member of the Minnesota Medical Board. When he leaned forward slightly, she observed that the man at the table behind him was also a member. She picked up her wine glass and casually walked out to the foyer.

"There are at least two members of the medical board here," she told Anthony when he caught up with her. "Dr. McCallum and Dr. Redfield."

"Is that unusual?"

"Not really, I guess," she said. "But they're general practitioners, not psychiatrists."

"A lot of GPs prescribe antidepressants," said Anthony. "They probably come to a lot of these for the free drinks."

"We'll see." She handed him a cube of white cheese she had lifted from her table and returned to her seat.

. . . and of course, the ultimate discovery would be an antidepressant designed specifically for children and adolescents. I predict that this will be the new breakthrough in psychiatry . . .

Just as Camilla finished her chicken Kiev, a flock of waiters breezed through the room to collect the plates. A moment later they returned with shiny metal carts filled with dishes of crème brûlée. Clayton finished his speech to robust applause, and the guests at the dais stood up and chatted with each other, signaling that the formal portion of the event was over. Clayton strode toward the back of the room, and Camilla instinctively turned the other way. She set her compact mirror on the table and watched Clayton shake hands with the two board members near the next table. All three laughed loudly at something Clayton said and then moved away from the foot traffic, stopping just inches from her. Camilla stuck a pair of headphones loosely in her ears, attached them to her media player and opened a small notebook. She pushed away her dessert plate and strained her attention on the conversation behind her.

"The figures are very low," said Clayton, "but of course, the public thinks that two or three percent is still too high."

"It's a small price to pay for the drastic decrease in teen suicides over the past decade, though," said McCallum. "I just read that the rate is down twenty-five percent."

"You won't see that quoted in a lot of public literature," said Clayton. "They usually talk about the number of suicides per year, which always sounds bad. They don't go into the details about how those numbers have decreased, per capita, thanks to psychopharmacology."

Camilla kept her eyes on her mirror and watched the two board members nod in agreement. "I've been coming to a lot of your talks for years now," said Redfield, "and I prescribe a lot of Prozor, but there's one thing I'm still waiting for you to say."

"What's that?" said Clayton, smiling and lifting a glass of white wine from a waiter's tray.

"We're all scientists here. We've read the fine print and watched the drug help a lot of people. But after all this time, we still don't know how these antidepressants actually work, do we?"

Clayton slipped his reading glasses off his head and stashed them in his breast pocket. "We don't know how aspirin actually reduces inflammation, either," he said, "but that hasn't slowed down its use."

Camilla watched Clayton's face brighten when the man

who had been seated at the dais and wearing an ID tag labeled "Terry Strick, Regional Sales" joined the three men.

"Great job," he said to Clayton. "Did you ply these gentlemen with a trunkful of samples yet, or should I?" They laughed again, and Clayton introduced Terry to the board members.

"We're all going golfing next weekend in Pebble Beach," Clayton told Terry. "You should come along."

"Thanks," he said. "Maybe I can. I'll let you know."

"We're going to drop into the presentation next door," McCallum told Clayton, "So we'll see you later." Clayton reminded them that he'd meet them at the airport the following Friday. After they left, Terry pulled an envelope out of his jacket and handed it to Clayton.

"Thanks, boss," said Clayton.

"When they start throwing around checks after we go to market, I'll be the one thanking you."

"I'm almost finished with my summary," said Clayton. "I'll have a first draft to bring to headquarters next week when I meet with the boys."

"How does it sound?"

"Like a dream come true," said Clayton. "No suicidal ideation, much less initial aggressiveness, exactly what the doctor ordered, right down the line."

Terry leaned in and put his hand on Clayton's back. "Is any of it true?"

They burst into laughter and walked out of the room.

Camilla yanked out her headphones and called Anthony.

"He just left—did you see him?"

"Yes," said Anthony, looking at her from the doorway across the room. "And I'm sure he didn't see me."

"I got a real earful," said Camilla. "I'm sure Shepherd is tight with those two members of the board. Strick is here, too—we can put a face to the name. He and Shepherd talked about a drug trial, just like they did on CJ's recording."

"Let's get out of here," said Anthony. "I'm starving, and after listening to Shepherd for a half hour, I need some fresh air." They walked out to the car and headed toward the museum and science center block. Nearing the entrance to the city park, Anthony suggested they take a minute to drive through. They had only been at the hotel for an hour, and the kids probably had more to see. They drove slowly beneath the park's dazzling canopy of orange and red maples and stopped near one of the stone bridges that crossed the narrows of the pond. Strolling across the bridge, Anthony asked Camilla to stop for a picture. "That's nice, with the willows behind you," he said. "Smile."

Camilla leaned against the gently arched sandstone bridge. "You're smiling like you just landed in the dentist chair," said Anthony. "Go ahead, smile like you just smacked Shepherd on the head with your kendo stick." She laughed and he caught it.

They walked on, and he showed her the photo in his camera. "I'm glad I can make you laugh," he said. He clasped her hand as they continued strolling. He wanted to kiss her, but snapped a picture of the pond instead. She stopped, kissed him lightly and then rested her chin on his shoulder. He put his arms around her and watched a whirlwind of leaves near the bridge grow taller as it gathered strength. "I'm glad you did that," he said into her ear. "I think I'm falling in love with you."

She rocked gently and closed her eyes. "You make me very happy," she said.

A flock of Canadian geese appeared above the tree line across the pond and glided over their heads, honking gossip.

"Let's go get the kids," Anthony said.

THIRTY-SIX

Padmini set a glass jar of Indian shortbread cookies on the kitchen table between CJ and Nira's laptops. She told them to finish up because Nira's tutor would arrive soon.

"Do you like her?" asked CJ.

"I call her my writing coach," said Nira, "and yes, she's great. My reports are going to be better this year, and she's helping me with a short story, too. Wait until you hear her accent. She came here from Ireland to go to law school."

"You must read her short story, CJ," said Padmini. "Maybe you can get an autograph before she becomes a famous writer and is too busy for all of us." She answered the doorbell and returned to the kitchen with Jan, who heaved her messenger bag onto a chair. After Padmini left to run some errands, Nira and CJ sat across from Jan at the kitchen table and pushed their laptops aside.

"You're going to law school, right?" Nira asked.

"Yes, you know that," Jan answered. "Why?"

Nira looked at CJ. "We need to talk to you about something," he said.

"What is it with you two?" asked Jan.

"Show her," said CJ.

Nira unzipped her backpack, pulled out a silver box and placed it in front of Jan. "Open it," she told her.

Jan put both hands on the box and lifted the lid. "Where did you get this?" she asked. "Did you open this vial?"

"No, we didn't touch it," said Nira.

"Nira found it in the car of the psychiatrist that turned my mom against my dad and messed up Nira's mom, too. That's why my parents got divorced and Nira's parents are separated. He's done a lot of other real bad stuff, too."

"What were you doing in his car?" Jan asked Nira.

"Looking for something that would get him in trouble."

"I've been in law school long enough to know that that could get *you* into trouble," she said.

"This guy stole my mom, wrecked our families and killed our best friend, but he's still free," said CJ. "Breaking into his car is nothing. He should get arrested and thrown in jail and sent to the gas chamber."

"What do you mean he killed your best friend?" Jan asked.

"He put Mike McCarthy on some drug, and two weeks later he hung himself," said Nira. "Before he started taking those pills, he never even raised his voice let alone went nuts like he did at school that last week."

"He's not the only patient of Dr. Shepherd's who's killed himself," said CJ. "There were—"

"Did you say Shepherd?" asked Jan. "Dr. Clayton Shepherd?"

"That's him," said Nira. "Do you know him?"

"I know who he is," she said, resting her forehead in her hand. "This is amazing."

"What?" asked CJ.

"It's a mad coincidence," Jan said. "He comes to the restaurant I work at a couple nights a week."

"Can you show this to somebody," said Nira, pointing at the box, "and get him arrested? It makes him a drug user, right?"

"It's not quite that easy," said Jan. "We have to prove that it belongs to him."

"No problem," said CJ. "Look at the inside of the cover."

Jan lifted the cover again and read Shepherd's name inscribed in the silver. "Holy Mary," she said.

"What are you going to do?" asked Nira. "Are you going to help us get him arrested?"

"I'll take it to one of my professors and get his advice," said Jan. "He'll know what to do." She put the box in her bag and took out her laptop. "But now we've got to get to work, young lady," she said.

"I'll go," said CJ. He slung his bag over his back, grabbed two cookies from the jar and left through the kitchen door.

"What are those?" asked Jan.

"Some kind of Indian cookie my mom makes. They're good." She slid the jar to Jan.

Nira clumsily dug through her backpack and finally pulled out a three-ring binder.

"Nira," said Jan. "Are you OK?"

"I'm fine," she said. "I finished my short story and two more worksheets."

"Fantastic," said Jan. "Let's start with the story—why don't you read it to me?"

Nira tapped the pages on the table to straighten them, then began to read:

The two little boys who lived next door to each other looked very much alike. They wore leather strings with matching blue beads around their necks and washed their brown faces at the same well at the end of the dirt street. Jalal's father was a Muslim and Gopal's father was a Hindu, and they were friends, too . . .

THIRTY-SEVEN

CJ was so confident in Clayton's routine that he no longer rode his bike to the Pembroke entrance but waited for him near the parking ramp behind the Uptown Mall. Just on time, a few minutes past five thirty in the afternoon, the black SUV drove into the ramp and Clayton appeared a minute later, striding into the Loon Bar with his phone at his ear. CJ rode into the ramp and pedaled up to the second level where Clayton had parked. Without getting off his bike, he unfolded his three-inch knife blade and stabbed the right back tire twice. That side of the car slowly tilted downward. He moved over to the left tire and stuck it twice, and then rode off. Before turning down the ramp, he looked back at the SUV's sinking back end and laughed.

Fifteen minutes later, Clayton walked back to his car, tossing his keys up into the air and catching them. "Shit!" he said when he came in sight of his car. Inspecting the tires, he found two gashes in each. "God *damn* it!"

He called the garage that serviced his cars, explained what had happened and insisted that he was in a hurry to get to a hospital and needed two new tires immediately.

When the mechanic suggested he use their loaner car or rent a car at the agency just down the block, Clayton angrily replied that he had to drive himself and he didn't have time to explain why. "Fortunately, Dr. Shepherd," the mechanic said, "I've got one guy still here and we've got those tires in stock. Gary will be there in ten minutes."

Clayton leaned against the side of the car and read his email on his phone while he waited. A white van soon arrived, and a young man in a blue denim work shirt with "Gary" embroidered on the pocket hopped out. He looked at the back end of the SUV and scratched his head. "What happened here?"

"Someone slashed my tires, obviously," said Clayton. "I told your boss that I'm running late to get to my hospital, so I need these replaced *toute suite*."

"Yes, sir," said the mechanic. He opened up the back doors of the van and rolled out two tires, then went back for the heavy-duty jack. Clayton handed him a piece of paper with his cell phone number on it and told him to call him when he was finished. He walked out of the ramp and across the street to a Greek restaurant and ordered a glass of white wine at the bar. He cursed himself for missing a call while the phone was in his pants pocket and checked the alert for the number. Logged into his contacts as "Herbie," the caller was his rush appointment that evening. Just after he set down the phone and grabbed a handful of popcorn from the bar, Herbie called again.

"I'm on my way," said Clayton. "I had car trouble." A cry belted through the receiver, forcing Clayton to move it away from his ear, and he hung up. He chatted with the bartender about the restaurant soon losing its lease and, ten minutes later, got the call that the car was ready. He sprinted across the street and up the ramp just as the mechanic was shutting the van's back doors.

"Those were some nasty cuts," Gary said, chuckling and wiping his forehead with a shop rag. "Somebody must be pretty mad at you." Clayton took the clipboard from Gary's other hand and signed the charge account form. "Thanks for working so fast. I really appreciate it."

"People usually call the police—" Gary began to say, but Clayton ignored him and jumped into the car. He drove off without looking back and, after paying his ticket, headed north on Hennepin Avenue. He drove through the city, across the bridge into North Minneapolis and continued on Hennepin as it veered eastward. Turning north on a residential street, he headed for a block on Filmore and turned into the driveway of small white house with a sagging porch and a backyard just a few yards from the railroad tracks. He reached over to open the glove box and dug beneath the maps. When his fingers couldn't find the familiar smooth surface of the box, he pulled out the contents onto the floor and peered inside. "Fuck!" He ran out to the other side of the car, opened the passenger door and searched beneath the seat. Running back to the driver's side, he searched beneath that seat, too, and found nothing but loose change and a pen. He ran his hands through his hair, thinking about the last time he had delivered Herbie a fix. He remembered distinctly putting the box back in the car where he always kept it. Someone was on to him.

He drove back downtown to Hennepin Metro, calling in an order for a vial of methadone and a syringe pack along the way. After parking outside the front door with the hazard lights flashing, he sprinted up the stairs and rushed to the nurse's desk. Carolyn stood up and handed him a white bag. "I've got the federal form up for you to approve," she said, swiveling her computer monitor toward him. Clayton punched a code into a blinking box and walked briskly to the stairs without saying a word. "Do you need any help?" Carolyn called after him, but he was already in the stairwell.

Back in North Minneapolis, he parked in Herbie's driveway and walked in the front door without knocking. The front room was dark except for the glare from the TV, and the large, white-haired woman wearing an apron over her sweatshirt and stretch pants did not move from her chair. Clayton knew where to go. He found Herbie on the floor in the corner of his room, crunched up against the wall and shaking violently. "What took you . . . so long, doc?" he whimpered. "What happened to your guy? You haven't come up yourself in a long time . . . " Clayton didn't answer, but tied a rubber strap above Herbie's elbow. Herbie closed his eyes and rested his head against the wall. Clayton pierced the syringe into the vial and drew in the drug, pulled out the needle and tapped the syringe. Holding Herbie's bony wrist, he swabbed the inside bend of his arm with an alcohol pad, felt the skin for the vein, and stuck the needle in. He untied the armband while emptying the syringe. "You're almost there," Clayton said as he checked for messages on his cell phone with his free hand.

Five minutes later, Herbie's shaking had stopped. He looked up at Shepherd, bewildered. "What did you give me, doc? What's happening?"

"Nothing's happening. I gave you methadone. You won't get high, but you won't get sick, either. Somebody will bring you the real shit tomorrow night."

"Methadone!" Herbie drawled. "Fucking methadone!

I'm going to call Hal and tell him you stopped helping me out, doc—"

Clayton crouched down and grabbed the grimy collar of Herbie'sTt-shirt. "You won't tell Hal anything because if you do you'll never see me again. Understand?"

"But I thought you were bringing the shit . . . " Herbie said tearfully.

"If you tell Hal, I might come back with something else in my bag that you won't like at all. Something that will relieve you of your misery for good. Would you rather have that? You know, I might just have some out in my trunk. Should I get something to make you go away?"

"No, doc, no," said Herbie, trying to squirm out of his grasp. Clayton dropped him against the wall and left.

Driving across the bridge back into downtown, Clayton called his connection and set up a meeting to replenish his supply. The scent of roasting barbecue wafted through the open windows as he passed over a row of restaurants on the riverfront, making him suddenly hungry. Finished with his call, he tossed his phone into the passenger seat and rummaged through the glove compartment one more time. "Whoever is fucking with me is going to be fucked," he said, pounding the steering wheel with his fist.

THIRTY-EIGHT

By eight o'clock on a Saturday night, the only sign of life in downtown Seaward, Minnesota, was the red neon "Open" sign of Angie's Grocery. The bar across the street was open, too, but no one but locals would know it. The gas station on one corner closed at five on weekends, forcing townspeople to drive fifteen miles to the truck stop on the Interstate if they needed to fill up. Camilla parked in front of the grocery store at dusk and bought a can of soda from the machine on the porch. She walked in and let the screen door slam behind her. The woman behind the counter finished selling cigarettes and a lottery ticket to a couple who looked like they belonged to the Harley parked out front. She saw Camilla at the door and beamed.

"Cam! What a wonderful surprise!"

Camilla stepped around the counter and hugged her. "I hope you don't mind me popping in on you like this."

"Of course not. I'm so glad to see you. I'm about to close up, and we can go home and have the beef stew I've had in the slow cooker all day."

"That sounds great."

"Is everything OK, honey?" Angie asked, stroking Camilla's hair down both sides of her face.

"Yes," said Camilla, "I'm working on a tough case right now and I just need to clear my head."

"I'm glad you came." Angie walked to the corner where two teenage boys were playing pinball at her vintage machine. "Sorry boys, I'm closing up."

"OK, Angie," they said, and left to collect their bicycles on the porch.

"They're good kids," Angie said. "I feel bad that they don't have anything else to do in the evenings now that the movie theater closed down." She flicked off the neon sign, threw her keys at Camilla and asked her to lock the back door. She emptied the contents of the cash register into a zippered bag and locked it in a small safe beneath the counter. Camilla went out the front, and Angie locked the door behind them.

"I'll follow you, Mom," said Camilla. They drove fourteen miles west of town and turned onto a gravel road marked with nothing but a "No Trespassing" sign and Angie's house number on a small metal sign nailed to a tree. The road wound through the woods for a half mile to Angie's small log home. Camilla pulled her duffel bag out of the back seat and followed her mother into the house.

Angie took two bottles of beer out of the refrigerator, grabbed a can of mosquito repellant and led them out to the porch facing the lake. They sprayed themselves down and sat in wicker rocking chairs. The sun had just set, leaving a frail orange line along the lake's horizon.

"God, this is nice," said Camilla.

"You look tired," Angie said. "Can you talk about it?"

Camilla took a long swig of beer. "We're working on

a long list of complaints made against a child psychiatrist in Minneapolis. I've never seen such a vile combination of ethical and criminal violations by a physician in my entire career at the board. This guy sleeps with his patients' mothers, takes his depressed and medicated patients out drinking, talks about and denigrates his patients in front of the staff—he breaks every boundary rule in the book. I don't understand how someone that sick can function well enough to get through medical school let alone make a career." She stopped when a loon began its eerie cry out on the lake.

They listened to the bird's repeated calls, which echoed off the banks of the lake. "Remember how Thoreau described that?" asked Angie.

"Like 'a long-drawn unearthly howl,'" said Camilla quietly. She went inside and came back with two more beers.

"On top of everything else," Camilla continued, "this doctor is on the payroll of one of the drug companies. He makes out very well on their speakers' circuit. Unfortunately, he's supposed to put those earnings back in his partnership, and his partner just found out he's been withholding thousands of dollars a year. So he doesn't play nice on the business end, either. And there are so many other things." She pulled over a nearby footstool, and the floorboards continued to creak beneath their chairs.

"He's sloppy about his child and adolescent diagnoses," Camilla said. "Three kids whom he listed as depressed and put on Prozor have killed themselves in the past two years. The parents weren't convinced their kids were depressed, and he settled two negligence cases out of court. I wouldn't doubt it if the latest family who lost their son sues him, too. And he just started parading himself as a sports psychologist with his own radio show."

"Can he do that?" asked Angie. "Doesn't he need to have special training to call himself that?"

"He claims he did a licensed program, but a friend of mine who is a real sports psychologist thinks he's lying. He's checking it out."

"Why would he want to do sports psychology on the radio, I wonder?" asked Angie. "I would think a child psychiatrist would be kept pretty busy with all these hyperactive kids popping pills every day."

"That's an interesting part of all this," said Camilla. "I've gotten to know one of the guys who's sued him in the past—not for his kid's suicide, but for seducing his wife while she was under his care—and it looks like the psychiatrist is trying to copy this man's life. He's the *real* sports psychologist I know. It all adds up in a strange way. First, the doctor stole the guy's wife and gloats about it to his face whenever he can. Then he got a radio show just like the sports psychologist's. It looks to me like he's obsessed with trying to outdo him. After we talked to the psychiatrist's ex-wife, it all made sense. She said he has a twin brother with whom he's been pathologically competitive his entire life. Now he competes with not only his brother, the world-famous research scientist, but every professional who crosses his path. He's constantly trying to make himself feel superior."

"How did you meet the sports psychologist?" Angie asked.

"I interviewed him for this case. I thought he'd have some insights into the doctor that would be helpful. And he's turned out to be a good friend."

"That's nice," said Angie.

"I feel better already, Mom," said Camilla. "It helps to talk about this instead of facing it down by myself every day.

The pile of bad news on this doctor gets worse and worse the deeper I dig into it, and I had to come up for air. He's hurt so many people."

"Sounds like you're going to stop all that," said Angie. She picked up their empty bottles. "I'm going to set the table, and I'll call you when it's ready." Camilla put her hand on her arm as she walked past. "Thanks." Angie kissed her on the forehead and went inside.

They bundled up in sweaters and ate in the kitchen with the doors open to the porch in order to listen to the loons, geese and frogs. After dinner, they cleared the table and played rummy, Angie's favorite card game. Camilla kept score with a short, chewed-up pencil that she remembered using at that very table as a child. After playing for a couple of hours, Camilla told her mother that she was going down to the dock for a while before going to bed. Angie went to her room to sleep, and Camilla turned off all the lights so she could get a good look at the sky.

She walked down the worn wooden steps to the shore, stopping once to smell the thick evergreen shrubs that surrounded them, and stepped out on the dock her father and grandfather had built before she was born. With just a sliver of a moon, no clouds, and no artificial lights polluting the view, she lay down to watch for falling stars. Waves sloshed up on the wooden fishing boat tied to the dock, lulling her into a serene wakefulness. She imagined ancient Greeks looking up at the same sky, making forms out of random specks of light.

As her eyes grew accustomed to the darkness, Camilla saw greater numbers of stars and the Milky Way became a thick band of light. She lay there for an hour, trying to make out the half-man, half-horse in Sagittarius.

As she stood up, she startled a flock that had settled near the dock, and they moved out in a rush of wings and splashing. She walked slowly to the shore and brushed the soft pine needles with the palms of her hands as she ascended the stairs.

When she reached the top, a blur of darker black moved against the trees to her right, but she saw it too late—an arm grabbed her around the throat and a hand covered her mouth. She raised her right leg and stomped down on the attacker's right foot, jolting him from his grip. She spun around and freed herself, then, as the attacker reeled from the shock, she raised her right leg parallel to the ground, bent it for momentum and kicked him in the chest. With a loud crack, the blow hurled the attacker to the ground with a broken sternum. He put his hands on his chest and cried out in pain, then tried to sit up. "You're going to pay for that, you bitch," he said breathlessly. She positioned herself next to his left leg and stomped down on his knee, shattering it. His scream echoed off the lake, and a few seconds later the lights came on in the house. Angie ran out to the porch, and Camilla yelled at her above the man's screams to bring a flashlight.

Angie illuminated the ground before her as she ran to them. "Point it as his face," said Camilla as she pulled off the man's black stocking cap, exposing a shock of red hair. She tore off her T-shirt and began rubbing the black camouflage grease from his face. He looked familiar, but she couldn't place him. She unzipped his black athletic jacket to reveal his thin, muscular build and looked once again at his face, which was littered with freckles.

"The guy from the gym."

The man continued to shriek in pain, motionless but for his shaking hands.

"Who is he?" Angie cried out.

"I'll tell you in a minute," said Camilla. "We need to drag him to the porch and secure him. Bring me the yellow cord from the toolbox." Angie ran back into the house and came out with the cord as Camilla dragged the man toward the porch. He was silent, passed out from the pain. She tied his hands to a post, ran inside and called 911.

By the time the two police cars arrived, Camilla had fished out the man's wallet and cell phone from his pockets. When the three officers came in, they found Camilla sitting at the kitchen table holding an ice pack to her neck and the man's driver's license and other cards strewn on the table.

The oldest officer walked over to Angie, who was clutching her robe with both hands. "Angie," he said, "are you all right?"

"I'm fine, Ed. He didn't touch me. But he hurt Cam's throat real bad."

The second officer sat down next to Camilla and gently took the ice pack from her hand. Deep red blotches covered the front of her neck.

"He grabbed me from behind," she said hoarsely, "just as I came up from the lake."

"The ambulance will be here any second now," said Ed. He pulled a notebook out of his back pants pocket. "Did you recognize him?"

"I saw him at my gym once, about a week ago," she whispered. "I'd never seen him before. We barely said two words to each other."

"What did you talk about?"

"He said he was buying the gym, which I thought was weird. That's all."

The ambulance siren pierced the air from a mile away,

and the other two officers went outside to untie the attacker. When the ambulance arrived, the driver and another paramedic jumped out of the cab, and the officers helped them put the man on a stretcher and into the truck.

Ed instructed the officers to follow the ambulance to the hospital and take a statement from the man when he revived. Back inside, he gathered the wallet and loose contents into a plastic bag. "I'm going to take you in to the hospital," he told Camilla. "You've got to have that throat looked at."

Angie stood behind her. "He's right."

"In the dojo, they always wore chest guards," said Camilla, looking straight ahead.

"What's she talking about?" Ed asked Angie.

"I don't know," she said. "Cammie, what do you mean?"

"I kicked him just like I've kicked my opponents for years, but I never heard that sound before. I could feel his breastbone break beneath my foot." A wet film covered her face.

"She does Kendo," said Angie. "She must have kicked him hard, just like she does in class."

"You did quite a number on his knee, too," said Ed. "I'm sure never going to sneak up on you in the dark."

"He's trained, too," said Camilla, not breaking her gaze. "He was ready to crush my windpipe in a snap. He knew exactly what he was doing."

"You're clearly the better fighter, though," said Ed. "Or you wouldn't be sitting here."

Angie stroked Camilla's hair. "She's the best fighter in the world."

While Angie got dressed, Ed led Camilla to the back seat of his cruiser, and in a couple of minutes Angie slipped in beside her.

"I'm sorry to bring this out here," said Camilla. She leaned her head on Angie's shoulder and cried, and winced from the pain of constricting her throat. Angie held her and supported the arm with which Camilla held the ice pack to her neck.

"If I get groggy, Mom, don't let them take them off," Camilla whispered.

"Take what off?"

She moved Angie's fingers to the dog tags hanging from her neck. Angie pulled her closer. "I won't," she said. "I promise."

THIRTY-NINE

Early on a Friday morning, the First Precinct in downtown Minneapolis was relatively quiet. The sergeant manning the intake desk on the third floor was reading a newspaper, and a half dozen detectives sitting at their desks were either staring at their computers or drinking coffee. Outside the windows, the bare branches of aspen trees jerked around in the cold wind.

Louise and Camilla, who wore a black turtleneck to hide her bruised neck, approached the tall counter and asked the sergeant for Detective Williams. He made a call, and Bo Williams soon strode through the precinct room.

"We're interviewing the defendant in room three," he told them. "I'll show you where you can observe." He ushered them down a long hallway and into a dimly lit room separated from an interrogation room by a two-way mirror. Camilla stood near the glass for a front-on view of Hal Richards. His loose denim shirt covered the white bandages wound around his torso, and his left leg, in a white cast from mid-thigh to mid-shin, extended forward and was propped up by a pole attached to his wheelchair.

"So far," said Williams, "we know he's got a record for theft and assault and he's on parole. He'll be going to jail no matter what, so he's aware that cooperating will be in his best interest. I think he'll tell us very soon who hired him to attack you last night."

Louise asked Williams to turn up the volume on the one-way intercom.

"The sooner you give us a name," the first detective in the other room said, "the lighter we'll go on the assault. You're already guaranteed five years for violating parole, so the rest of the sentence is up to you." The second detective sat adjacent to Richards at the table. "You beat up an ex-cop who works for the state," he said calmly. "Her pals at the courthouse next door are ready to string you up, so the quicker you get this over with, the sooner we can put in a request to move your trial."

The man looked glumly at the mirror and moved his shackled hands from his lap to the top of the table. "Terry Strick," he said. "He's a sales rep for Brown-Dixon, the drug company."

"Why would a pill salesman want to beat up Ms. Black?" asked the first detective.

"It's something about a doctor she's investigating," Richards said. "They want her to lay off."

"That's very good," said the second detective. "How do you get in touch with Strick?"

"His cell number's in my phone."

"Good," said detective one. "We'll go get your phone so you can give him a call." He glanced at the mirror, and Williams left the room. A minute later Williams stepped into the interrogation room with a cell phone.

"What's Strick paying you for this?" the second detective asked.

"Nothing."

"Right," said the detective. "You're the Robin Hood of assault and battery. What's the story? We don't have time for this crap!"

"He's doing me a favor, and I have to do what he wants or his doctor friend will stop helping me out."

"What's the doc doing for you?"

"My brother's in bad shape, and he keeps him fixed up."

"Your brother's a junkie?" yelled number two. "What's his name?"

"Herbie. He's been through treatment once, but he couldn't keep clean. He's my kid brother and his life is shit. I've been taking care of him since we were in high school."

"What does this doctor get for Herbie?" asked Williams.

"He hires some guy to bring him smack twice a day. Herbie hasn't left his house in a year. He's in tough shape."

Camilla recalled the bravado Richards had shown in the gym, making a cool spectacle of himself. *He's just a punk doing Shepherd's dirty work.*

Williams placed the phone on the desk.

"Tell Strick you did the job and you need to meet him in an hour," said the first detective. "Convince him, or if this falls apart, you're back to square one. Tell him to meet you in the lobby at Hennepin Metro." He held up the phone to let Richards punch a key and then held the phone by Richards' face.

"I did the assignment last night," Richards said, "but we've got a problem. I'm downtown and I have to see you. I can't talk about it on the phone." He paused to listen and his face turned red. "I can't talk about it! I've got to see you now or you're going to be sorry you made me touch that bitch. You've got to come to me. I'm in the lobby at Hennepin Metro." Another pause. "Because I like the *coffee*. Just get here." He jerked his head aside and the detective stepped back. "He'll be there in an hour."

Williams returned to the observation room. "Do you know what investigation he's referring to?" he asked Camilla.

"We've got a pretty good idea," she said, looking at Louise.

"You need to find out the name of the doctor who's giving drugs to Herbie," Louise told Williams. "If you bring in Strick and get him to confirm it, our case will be air tight."

Williams left and talked to the first detective in the interrogation room through a crack in the door, then returned. "They'll get the name. Let's go to the conference room and wait," he said. "They're writing up an arrest warrant for Terry Strick right now, so if he shows up to meet Richards, they'll be bringing him in soon."

•

The detectives taped a wire to Richards' shoulder as they rode the three blocks to the hospital in a van with a lift for the wheelchair. "Remember," said one, "if we get a clean recording and a good arrest, we'll take care of your brother."

"You'll put him in Hazelton, right?" said Richards. "Where the movie stars go?"

"We'll put him in Hazelton. It's only an hour away—hell, we can drive him up there ourselves."

"Don't worry," Richards said. "I'll make sure Terry talks loud and clear. His buddy who's been taking care of Herbie hasn't been taking care of him so good."

"What do you mean?"

"Herbie called me last night, real pissed off, complaining that the doc had given him methadone. He was supposed to get the real shit, every day."

"Has he ever given you the doctor's name?"

"No, I don't think he knows. But whoever he is, he's tight with Terry." He grimaced when the truck hit a pothole. "He's the doctor that bitch is investigating, the one who got me into this fucking chair. He made Terry order *me* to follow her, bug her house and scare her off."

A half hour before Terry was due to show up, they wheeled Richards into Hennepin Metro and parked him at a table in the lobby next to the gift shop. While one bought him a coffee, the other checked the sound of his wire with the police in the van parked out front and on their own headsets hidden in their ears. Detective Williams showed up a few minutes later with another plainclothes detective and they took positions on chairs near the information desk, where they had a clear view of Richards.

Fifteen minutes later Richards sat alone at the table, fidgeting with the cup, scratching his leg around his cast and glaring at people who interrupted his view of the glass entryway doors.

"Here he comes," he finally said. Terry glanced around nervously as he strode across the lobby.

"What the hell happened to you?" he asked. "And why are we meeting out here in front of the whole city?"

"Sit down, for Christ sakes," said Richards. "I think somebody might be on to me. The bitch had her phone on when I grabbed her. Somebody could have heard my voice."

"That's the emergency you pulled me out of a two hundred dollar breakfast for?"

"You didn't tell me she was a fucking *judo* master," said Richards. People turned to look at them.

"Keep it down," hissed Terry.

"She kicked my chest open and smashed the hell out of my knee. I almost lost my goddamned leg."

"If you're looking for sympathy, forget it. You told me you're a prize fighter. What do you fight, cats?"

"Forget it," said Richards. "I just thought you'd want to know about the phone. You told me you wanted details."

"The only details I need to know are whether or not you scared the shit out of her."

Williams nodded at the detectives on the other side of the room. "That's it," he said. "Let's pick him up." The four detectives walked toward the table, and one pulled Terry's hands behind his back and bound them in plasticuffs. Terry shot Richards a bewildered look as a detective read him his rights.

"Call the precinct," Williams told the detective at his side, "and tell them Strick's on his way. Then call the county attorney."

FORTY

Anyone looking through Padmini's kitchen window would have thought the woman and her daughter had just learned that missiles were headed toward North America.

After the break, Dr. Clayton Shepherd will be back for more of "Mind Games," the sports show that's got the Twin Cities talking . . .

Padmini stared at the radio. Nira slumped down in her chair and sent a text to CJ. Then she began to cry.

"What is it, Nira?"

"Everybody knows he's so bad, but they don't do anything about it."

Padmini held her and waited for her to calm down.

"I hate it, Mom," she said, grasping for breath. "He hurt you so bad, he hurt Dad. He killed Mike, and he's getting away with all of it." She put her arms around her mother's shoulders. Padmini forced back her own tears and gently rocked Nira back and forth. The sensation of her daughter's frail body convulsing with tears reignited her rage. She had finally made peace with her own actions, forgiving herself for being taken in by Clayton when she was weak and vulnerable, but she could not forgive him for exploiting her, crossing the line and never looking back until her entire family was shattered.

"We all got hurt, darling," she said softly, "but we're all healing, too. Nothing he did can destroy me or you or Dad. We're strong, and this has made us even stronger." She put Nira's face in her hands. "You can't carry this by yourself, Nira. You aren't the only one who wants this man to pay for his crimes. Many people are working hard to make sure that happens, especially CJ's dad. This is not a war you have to fight. Do you understand?"

Nira wiped her face, leaned into her mother's arms and rested her head on her shoulder.

"I love you more than anything in the world," said Padmini.

FORTY-ONE

Terry Strick stared at the cinderblock wall in the First Precinct's basement holding cell, his suit jacket folded neatly beside him on the bench. He shared the room with three others, each sitting as evenly spaced as possible on the cold concrete benches that lined the walls. The sergeant who processed Terry's belongings traded one of his premium cigars for a newspaper, which Terry held up to avoid eye contact with his cellmates. The two sitting in the corners of the opposite bench snored loudly, and from the smell emanating from them Terry figured they had been drinking for the past week at least. The other man had taken off one shoe and was intently picking the calluses on his foot.

An officer tromped down the stairs and opened the barred door. "Strick, you can make your phone call." Terry picked up his jacket and followed him to the room next to the cell, which contained one chair and a black telephone sitting on a folding table. The officer picked up the receiver and handed it to Terry. "Dial nine to get an outside line," he said. "You've got six minutes. I'll be outside." He left and closed the door.

Terry dialed Clayton's cell phone.

"It's Terry. You're my one call, so listen—"

"Where are you? This connection is terrible. Why don't I call—"

"Clay, shut up! I'm in jail."

"Jesus!" He swept a medicine bottle and envelope of pills into the top drawer of his desk.

"Richards set me up. He asked me to meet him downtown and there were cops all over the place. He's all beat up with a broken leg—when he tracked down that investigator up at her mom's place, she practically killed him."

"Shit!" said Clayton. He closed the blinds and paced around the room. "What have you told the police?"

"I've been sitting in the holding cell since this morning and haven't talked to anybody. Clayton, listen to me. You have to call Brown and tell him to get a lawyer down here. Tell the assistant who answers his phone that it's an emergency and that you must get through to him, no matter where he is."

"All right," said Clayton.

"If this goes to trial, I'm going to be in deep shit," said Terry.

"It's never going to trial—don't worry," said Clayton.

Terry undid another button on his white oxford shirt. "How can you say that?"

"The lawyer will cut down Richards so quick the D.A. will never have a case. Do you think a judge will take the word of a hood who's willing to do anything to score heroin for his junkie brother over the word of a Yale-educated executive from one of the biggest pharmaceuticals in the world? Not in a million years. We've been over this, Terry. Brown's lawyer will have you out of there tonight."

"Just get him down here." He glanced at the window

in the door and lowered his voice. "I'm worried about what Richards might say."

"You can't do anything about that, so don't get yourself all worked up."

"Worked up? That little creep's got my life in his hands!"

"Terry, slow down. Brown and Dixon aren't going to let anything happen to you. They can't afford to. You know how many cases they've settled out of court. If those two can keep negligence cases from going to trial and invent new loopholes in drug patent law, I think they can get rid of the statement of an ex-con from Chaska."

The officer knocked on the door and held up one finger.

"I've only got one more minute," said Terry. "Call Brown right now. And then call Frank at Wheatland Health. I'm supposed to be speaking at his banquet in two hours and I don't want him to find out why I can't make it. Make something up."

"OK. Anything else? I've got a patient waiting."

"Clay! Aren't you worried that all this might get back to you?"

"I've had my share of close calls, but Brown-Dixon has always been there for me. I'm also covered at the medical board. You remember that what happened last time over there—after all the commotion over an investigation all they did was bury a disciplinary notice in a newsletter that no one reads. I've got my ass covered in this state, and so do you, so don't worry. And be nice to the cops. Crack a joke once in awhile. They like that."

The officer opened the door. "I've got to go," said Terry. He hung up and reached into his pants pocket.

"I'd give you a dime for the call," he told the officer, "but the sergeant took all my change."

"Ha, ha," said the officer, walking him back to the cell. "You can mail it to me in a Christmas card."

Terry stepped into the cell and returned to his spot. The man with one bare foot had confiscated his newspaper and was absorbed in the sports section, and one of the drunks lay in his own vomit on the floor. The other drunk was huddled in the corner, laughing to himself with his eyes closed and flinging out his hands as if trying to keep someone away.

Terry pressed his back into the wall and clutched his jacket. The officer smiled at him. "Have a nice day," he said, locking the barred door.

FORTY-TWO

Clayton eyed his reflection in the glass behind the bar, moving his head to get a view between two bottles of vodka. He ran a hand through his hair and began to unbutton the cuffs of his sleeves when John the bartender breezed over with a cosmopolitan.

"Where's Jan?" asked Clayton. "I saw her when I walked in."

"She'll be right back. Can I get you anything else?"

"This is perfect, thanks," said Clayton. He swung around to look out at Lake Calhoun and absently pushed around the cherry in his glass until a light touch on his arm made him turn back to the bar.

"Hey, doc," said Jan. "John took care of you, I see."

"The Celtic goddess!" said Clayton. "Now that I've seen that face, all's well with the world."

"You keep that up and you might become my friend one day," said Jan, leaning her elbows on the bar to show her décolletage.

Clayton seized the moment. "Tell me about your perfect man," he said.

Jan stared into his eyes for a few seconds. "He's very smart, he's knows a good thing when he sees it and he's got to have a history."

"What do you mean, history?"

"He has to have a few stories, if you get my meaning," she said. She ignored the rest of the bar while John moved swiftly to keep up.

"You want a bad boy," said Clayton. "I knew it."

"You Americans are so clean," she said, sliding her finger along his white cuff, "so careful, so predictable. I need a man who will surprise me."

"You have no idea," said Clayton. "I've got stories that will make your head spin."

"I'm not talking about stealing from the church plate or cheating on your taxes," she said.

"I'm serious," said Clayton. "Doctors have access to a lot of things that can turn them into bad boys real quick."

"Do they, now." She scratched her rib where a piece of tape was holding the wire that the female detective had fitted to her in the back room. "So tell me something fast, or I'm going to get fired for gabbing to a customer so long," she said. "Tell me something you can do that nobody else in this place can do."

He leaned in toward her cleavage and felt the warmth of her skin. "I've got a list of guys who will do anything for me. I could have someone kick the shit out of John's brother, say, or rough up one of your professors who's not giving you a decent grade." Jan raised her eyebrows with interest.

"I can get my hands on all kinds of mind-altering substances that would have a creature like you walking hand-in-hand with Jesus himself for a few hours."

"Could you, now."

"I've got real connections, and I can get you anything you want."

"I'm not into the hard stuff myself," said Jan. "But I do like the idea of the payoff on your end. It must help the bank account a little."

"I don't sell, darling, I use it to keep the help in line," said Clayton.

"Exactly what kind of stuff are you talking about? Mushrooms from Momma's garden?"

Clayton laughed. "No, the real thing. The shit that gets boys into so much trouble. Mexican horse, p-funk, poppy, Hazel, Rambo, or, as they probably call it at law school, smack."

"That is the dark side, all right," said Jan. "I hope you're nice to them."

"You do?"

"After you get them to do their business, of course, whatever that is," she said.

"We are going to be such good friends," said Clayton. Jan smiled as she picked up his empty glass and walked over to the far end of the bar to wash it in the sink. John immediately stepped in with a fresh drink, and Jan began serving other customers.

"Whew," said Clayton as he watched her. He took a sip of his drink and read a text message from the nurse's desk at Hennepin Metro, which alerted him that a patient had just stabbed his neck with a broken pen. "Shit," he said, popping the cherry into his mouth. He washed it down with half of his drink, set a fifty dollar bill on the bar and left.

FORTY-THREE

Two maids in black uniforms with white aprons whisked out of the conference room and past Clayton as he waited in the lobby on the penthouse floor of Brown-Dixon's New York headquarters. The young receptionist in pearls and an updo hairstyle, upon whose desk he had halfway perched himself, answered the phone.

"They're on their way," she told Clayton.

A door open somewhere around the corner, and a trio of male voices grew louder as they walked toward the lobby. When they turned the corner, Clayton put out his hand to greet Robert Brown, CEO of Brown-Dixon Labs; Leonard Dixon, Executive Vice President and Co-CEO; and Terry Strick. The receptionist held open the conference room door for them.

Brown stood behind the high-back executive chair at one end of the table and gestured for Clayton to sit to his right, while Dixon and Strick took seats at his left. Clayton faced a wall of drawn curtains that had previously, when he glanced into the room a half hour earlier, displayed a view of Midtown looking west, with the Hudson River sparkling in the background. Although the room and the gleaming walnut table were extravagantly large, the dim lighting created intimacy and cast a series of soft splashes down the center of the table. The receptionist pushed a button on the wall, and a cabinet door slid open to reveal a full bar. She arranged a tray with scotch and bourbon bottles, crystal highball glasses and an ice bucket, and set it on the table next to Brown.

"Thank you, Lacy," he said, and she left the room.

"Terry already mentioned what we've got in mind to compensate you for your help with our study," Brown said to Clayton. "We wanted to bring you out to talk about that plan in person and personally congratulate you on your work." He opened a worn manila folder containing a stapled set of papers. "We've read your first draft of the study summary and—"

"We're very pleased," Dixon broke in. He reached over for the report, flipped through a few pages until finding a highlighted passage and read aloud:

While fluoxetine (Prozor) has been approved for depression in non-adults, it was not specifically developed for that population and remains a controversial treatment due to the life-threatening aggressiveness and suicidal ideation that occurs in a small percentage of young patients. Nine years of patient trials with Zema (flexoradine), the first selective serotonin reuptake inhibitor designed for ages 4 to 25, the age span in which the human brain continues to develop, revealed none of the side effects associated with fluoxetine.

Dixon had emphasized "none" in the last sentence and glanced up at Clayton when he said it. He continued:

This breakthrough drug ushers in a new era in medicine by addressing the unique demands of serotonin-affecting chemistry on the developing brain. Flexoradine answers the critical need for a child and adolescent antidepressive that not only eliminates traditional debilitating side effects but lays the foundation for a new age of psychiatric pharmacology.

Brown set the paper on the table. "Very good," he said. "This should be copied word for word into the press release."

Clayton rolled back his chair and rested his foot on his knee. "I appreciate your confidence in me. It was a challenge, but I received very clear direction and I think I followed it to the letter."

"You did," said Dixon. "We realize how much work goes into extrapolating nine years of data into a summary that so brilliantly downplays the side effect numbers."

"The independent trials will take at least two years from the launch of Zema to be published," said Terry, "and we'll have more time to refute those with a new study of our own. That will give us at least four years of sales of a product that promises everything the market is looking for."

"One out of five children in this country is prescribed an SSRI for either an attention disorder or depression," said Brown. When Zema goes to market, we believe that most doctors dispensing to juveniles will make the switch, based on our results."

"And our two-billion-dollar advertising campaign," said Dixon.

"That means we'll have about nine million users from the outset. Doctors have been increasing the amount of psychotropic prescriptions they write for children exponentially in the last several years, so there is every indication that they will be even more apt to prescribe Zema to children. We foresee a dramatic upsurge in prescriptions."

"That's a very big point," said Dixon. "Even though more and more doctors are prescribing Prozor to kids, they know that the side effects are a real concern. The only reason the FDA finally approved it for kids was that it determined that the benefits usually outweighed the negatives. We've done a formidable job in keeping some of the worst bad press at bay about Prozor's history with suicidal ideation, but in spite of that, doctors have been more reluctant to prescribe it to kids than we predicted."

"Zema will make Prozor's youth numbers look like small change," said Terry. "Especially after we establish Zema as a safe new class of drug in our print campaign, associating the Columbine shootings with the 'old school' drugs."

"That sounds convincing," said Clayton.

"Not if it scares parents away from all psychotropics, though," said Brown, pouring himself a bourbon. "We haven't made a final decision on that yet."

"We are moving on a campaign for the journals that focuses on the structure of Zema's breakthrough chemistry, though," said Dixon.

"The miracle?" asked Clayton.

"Right," said Dixon. "We knew we had a hit when our flyboy in research synthesized a mild opiate that cancels out the negative effect of the SSRI and figured out how to cloak it," said Dixon. "Parents wouldn't take well to giving their kids what is basically Prozor, Zalift or Wellbotra laced with heroin, so he created a structure that makes the opiate look like a harmless enzyme."

"What about the opiate's addictive effect?" asked Clayton.

The three men looked at him until he fully understood what he had just asked.

"Jesus, that's brilliant," said Clayton.

"Zema is a two-edged sword," said Brown. "It creates enough euphoria to offset the aggressive potential of the SSRI and also carries just enough opiate to develop an addiction. Just when a parent thinks that the child has outgrown the drug, little Johnny will stop taking it and become hell on wheels. Mom will have no choice but to get him back on the horse, so to speak."

"If this is true," said Clayton, "if this drug really works the way you've described, you can't fail."

The three men chuckled. "That's why we're already working on our little compensation package for you," said Dixon. "Zema is going to be the biggest product in the history of Brown-Dixon, and we decided to commemorate its release with a reward for one of the physicians who helped with the trial. As Terry will tell you, we spent months shortening a list of several people who have contributed to the trial in various ways. In the end, the remaining name on that list was yours."

Clayton straightened up and put both feet on the floor. "Thank you," he said.

"We read your articles about your success with a therapeutic style that develops a more pliable doctor-patient boundary," said Brown, "and we were impressed with that kind of innovation, especially as it applies to child psychiatry. Your field has worked on the strict border model for a hundred years, and it took courage to step out of that box. You've made psychiatry more relatable."

"Thank you," said Clayton.

Brown and Dixon stood on either side of an easel with a cloth draped over it. "First," said Brown, "we're giving you a piece of the profits. You're signed on for one percent of Zema's earnings."

Terry, who had helped the men design Clayton's compensation, smiled at his friend. "If Zema follows even a fraction of Prozor's early performance," he said, "that will produce a multi-million dollar figure in the first year."

"We also decided," said Dixon, "that a psychiatrist who practices his own style of therapy should have his own clinic." He pulled away the cloth to reveal an architect's drawing of a white two-story building with silver lettering at the entrance that read, THE SHEPHERD CENTER.

Clayton stared at the drawing with his mouth open. "I don't know what to say." He walked over to the easel and inspected the drawing. "Is that the Johns Hopkins research complex in the background?" he asked. "You know that my brother works at Johns Hopkins, don't you?"

"We thought you'd be pleased to have your own shingle in his neighborhood," said Brown.

Terry exchanged satisfied looks with Brown and Dixon.

"I don't want to sound greedy," said Clayton, "but when will it be ready?"

"We'll break ground in the spring for a November opening next year," said Dixon. He pointed at a section of the building. "Your office will take up a third of the first floor, and the upstairs will have nine offices for psychiatric nurses and psychiatric interns."

"It's only five thousand square feet," said Brown, "but it's a beautifully outfitted space. All the interiors will be done by the designer who did the Dior Building in Manhattan. The electronic records and communication systems are all wireless, state of the art."

"This," said Terry, pointing to a circular space on the blueprint in one corner of the drawing, "is a media room for lectures and films."

Clayton stepped back and shook his head.

"We'll celebrate tonight," said Brown, "but there's one more thing. Another token of our appreciation that you can enjoy right away." He handed a letter-sized envelope to Clayton.

"Thank you," said Clayton. He opened his jacket to slide the envelope in a pocket. "Go ahead," said Dixon, "open it."

"Now?" said Clayton, looking at Brown.

"Sure," he said.

Clayton pulled a slim gold pen from his pocket and wedged the tip into a corner of the envelope. Ripping it open neatly, he looked inside to find a check in the amount of two hundred fifty thousand dollars. He stared at Brown in astonishment.

"You've earned it," said Brown.

Clayton shook their hands and dropped into the nearest chair. "It's a real pleasure doing business with you, gentlemen," he said. "I really don't know what else to say."

Dixon ushered everyone out to the lobby, where the receptionist was waiting to congratulate Clayton. She stood alertly just outside the conference room with her feet together, as if ready to salute. Clayton held her face and gave her a kiss, which left her with smeared lipstick and a flush of red creeping up her neck. The men discussed where they'd have dinner later on. "Le Bernardin?" suggested Dixon. "Bobby Flay's?" asked Terry.

"Anything special you'd like?" Brown asked, turning to Clayton.

"I don't care where we go," Clayton said, "as long as Lacy can come along."

FORTY-FOUR

The columned, federalist style Aitkin County courthouse had remained the tallest building in town since it was built in the late 1920s. Since Camilla's attack occurred in the county, Hal Richards' attempted murder trial would be held at the courthouse and prosecuted by Aitkin County Attorney Dan Peterson, who had filed the charges. Camilla brought a suitcase and two boxes of work to her mother's house when the trial started so she wouldn't have to commute, like Anthony, who rescheduled his patients for a week so he could drive up every morning and return home to CJ in the evening.

Richards had the best legal team Brown-Dixon could buy. Four lawyers from the company's New York firm sat at the defense table and a team of fifteen more sat in the benches behind them. Six other members of the firm, impeccably dressed young male and female assistants and interns, took up additional space in the first three rows of benches. On the other side of the aisle, Louise Sunderland, Camilla, her mother and Anthony sat in the front row behind the prosecutor's table, and five other observers, including a reporter for the local paper, scattered themselves in the benches behind them. Dan Peterson, the county attorney, and his assistant made up the prosecution.

On the third day of the trial, the court officer watched dispassionately as Hal Richards lumbered up the steps to the witness box on his crutches. Wincing with every turn of his torso, which pulled on the bandaging that protected his healing sternum, he reached the top and stood in front of the chair. The officer stepped closer and held up the Bible, and Richards swore to tell the whole, honest truth. He transferred one crutch to the other hand and leaned back on the arm of the chair to carefully lower himself, pushing the chair back to make room for his extended leg. Once seated, he leaned one crutch on the side of the judge's bench and used the other for support, resting both hands on the metal bar to help him sit upright. His defense attorney had selected a dark, well-cut suit with a white shirt and red tie to accentuate Richards' good looks and provide a stark contrast to his bandages. With one pant leg rolled up to expose most of the cast, Richards looked every inch the victim.

In the back of the room, Jill Frye slipped through the double doors and took a seat in the last row. When Clayton told her about the trial, in which the defendant had made up a wild story about drug running between Clayton's friend and Brown-Dixon rep, Terry Strick, and himself, she decided to attend the trial and report back to Clayton. She hired a live-in nanny to look after her son for a week, or however long the trial would last, and checked into a motel in Aitkin. As she had recently told Clayton in a letter, she had begun to look for her own place in Minneapolis and a kind way to tell her husband that she was leaving him. She wanted a new life on her own but with Clayton as her equal partner. She wanted another chance at her career and, even more, another child. She flipped open a notebook and sat up as tall as possible to see the front of the packed courtroom.

When signaled by the judge, the lead defense attorney stood up and walked to the witness box. "What were you doing on Angie Black's property on the night of November fourth?" he asked Richards.

"I was looking for a way down to the lake to get my fishing rod," he answered. "I'd left it near the shore earlier that day, and I'm not very familiar with that lake, so I drove down a road in the dark and started looking for a path."

"Why were you fishing there in the first place, if you weren't familiar with the area?"

"My friends in Chaska told me that Mille Lacs is the best lake for walleyes in the state, probably the country," he said. A few chuckles sprang from the crowd.

"Why do you think Camilla Black attacked you that night?"

"I probably scared her, because I was just about to go down the steps and all of a sudden she was right there."

"Sergeant Black claims that she had already cleared the stairs and that you grabbed her from behind," said the attorney. Richards cleared his throat to respond, but was stopped by the prosecutor.

"Objection, your honor," said Peterson. "The defense has not asked a question."

"Objection sustained," said the judge. "We've heard Sergeant Black's testimony, Mr. Grant, and we don't need a lecture on it."

"I'm sorry, your honor," said the attorney. His team at the table whispered to each other. "Mr. Richards," he continued, "what happened when Sergeant Black reached the top of the stairs?"

"She jumped because I surprised, her, like I said," said Richards. "Before I had a chance to explain that I was just trying to find the lake, she pulled up her hands in like this"—he swept up his fists to his ribs—"and swung around in a karate-like move and kicked me square in the chest. I heard a crack and flew about a yard before I fell to the ground."

Camilla's mother shook her head angrily.

"Did you try to explain to her what you were doing after she kicked you?" the attorney asked.

"I started to yell out, but she was already on me again. She stomped down on my knee and smashed it. I passed out after that."

"Why do you think Sergeant Black took such violent action?" Grant asked.

"She's obviously an expert in the martial arts," said Richards. "They're trained to strike first and ask questions later." He pulled a white handkerchief out of his jacket and wiped his forehead.

Peterson stood up. "Objection, your honor. The defendant has not been identified as an expert in the martial arts."

"Objection sustained," said the judge. "Members of the jury, you will ignore the defendant's last remark."

"No further questions, your honor," said Grant. He stepped back to his table and sat down.

"Mr. Peterson," said the judge.

The county attorney closed the folder in which he'd been writing notes and stood up. "Mr. Richards, why did you visit the Bridgeside Gym in Minneapolis for the first and only time in your life, on October twenty-sixth of this year?" he asked from the table.

"I was scoping out the property as a possible investment," Richards said. "There are no other health clubs in that part of town, just next to the university, and anybody that's seen the gym knows why students never go near the place. It's a real rat hole."

Flutters of laughter spread throughout the room again.

"In your statement to the police," said Peterson, "you described yourself as a real estate agent and contractor. You even gave them this business card, which you pass around and which lists your title as the owner and president of Lake Country Real Estate." He held up a transparent plastic folder containing a business card and introduced it as evidence. "But we looked into the records, and the state agency that licenses real estate agents has never heard of you. It turns out that you're not licensed in any other state, either. And there is no company by the name of Lake Country Real Estate filed as a business in the state of Minnesota. So, Mr. Richards, what exactly do you do for a living?"

Richards looked at Grant and shifted painfully in his chair. "Lake Country is the company I'm just launching. I haven't filed the papers yet. I'm studying right now for my agent exam and I'm scheduled to take it next month. There's no law that says I can't look at properties in the meantime."

Peterson leaned down to say something to his assistant and she typed a note on her laptop. "That's exactly right," he said, "but there are laws against lying to the police, fraudulently identifying yourself as a licensed professional in a regulated trade, trespassing, attempted murder and lying under oath in this courtroom. We'll call the exam site at recess and verify that you're on that schedule," he said. Half of the jurors jotted in their notebooks, and Richards shot a worried look at Grant.

"Objection, your honor," said Grant, remaining in his seat as two lawyers at the table passed him sheets of paper. "The defendant is being tried by this jury for one offense. The prosecutor has permanently and unfairly imprinted a multitude of other unofficial allegations against Mr. Richards' in the minds of the jury members during the course of his presentation of this evidence." He stood up and continued, "I therefore move that this evidence be discarded on the grounds that the prosecutor has inappropriately burdened it with illegitimate allegations that have irreparably tainted the jury's view of the evidence."

Peterson smiled slightly and kept his eyes on the notebook at his desk.

"Mr. Peterson did not contaminate evidence but merely summarized the implications of Mr. Richards' words under oath," the judge said to Grant. "Motion is denied. And if you attempt to throw any more ornately improvised and clearly unsubstantial arguments around in my courtroom, I'll have you thrown out for contempt."

"Yes, your honor," said Grant, taking his seat. The lawyer at his side shoved a piece of paper beneath his hands, which he ignored. The judge's ruling confirmed what Grant had suspected from the opening moments of the trial—rather than being intimidated by the small army of East Coast lawyers descending upon his small-town courthouse with the cornfield murals on the walls, the judge apparently resented the fact that they were so openly trying to intimidate him. Grant had not only miscalculated, but offended. He decided to drop his casual stance, which he played in order to project overwhelming confidence, and to send all but three lawyers back to the hotel during recess.

"You may proceed, Mr. Peterson," said the judge.

"Mr. Richards," Peterson said, "please point to the person in this room who was working out at the Bridgeside Gym on the day that you just happened to stop in, and to whom you introduced yourself."

Richards took one hand off the crutch and pointed at Camilla, seated just behind Peterson's aide. The room erupted with hushed voices.

"Did you speak to anyone else at the gym that day?" asked Peterson. "You should be aware that the gym owner, who was in the workout room the entire time, is in the courtroom today and on the witness list." Camilla turned around and made eye contact with Mike Kelly, who was seated two rows behind her with his thick arms folded across his chest. He nodded at her.

"No, I didn't," said Richards.

"Had you ever met Sergeant Black before that day?"

"No, I had not," said Richards flatly.

"Why did you approach her?"

"She was the only woman in the gym, she was staring at me and she was hot." Tongues clicked in the jury box, and Grant watched a brick wall descend between Richards and the four women jurors.

At the moment, Grant thought the jury members could not have disliked Richards more if they knew how close he had come to practically getting away with attacking Angie Black's daughter in the middle of the night. They would go after him with pitchforks if they knew he had originally confessed and made a deal with the Hennepin County Attorney to serve a short sentence in return for helping arrest Terry Strick. Minneapolis was more interested in pursuing the pharmaceutical executive who ordered the attack on a government investigator than in bringing Richards to trial. But when Terry made bail and disappeared, Hennepin County's case against him ground to a halt. With Terry out of the picture, Richards' deal was cancelled, and Peterson was free to prosecute him in his own court, knowing full well that Brown-Dixon would hit town with everything it had.

In the seconds following Richards' remarks about Camilla, Peterson saw Grant's pained expression and knew what he was thinking. Grant had marched into Aitkin with a paper-thin self-defense case and full knowledge that the community loved the victim's elderly mother and drove a few miles out of town with their kids to buy candy at her charming little store, just as their parents had done. No matter how hard he tried, Grant could not find one citizen in the jury pool who had a sliver of suspicion about the Black family. He knew he was in for a challenge when he walked by a memorial to Camilla's fallen soldier husband on his way up the courthouse steps. Not even a slick crew like Grant's with the unlimited backing of a Fortune 500 company could break down loyalty with roots that deep.

After letting Richards' comment sink in, Peterson asked, "Why were you wearing a black wool stocking cap with eyeholes over your head when you approached Ms. Black that night?"

Grant pursed his lips but quickly regained himself. "Objection, your honor," he said, standing up. "A black stocking cap has not been brought into evidence."

"It was added last night," said Peterson, "and the updated evidence list was sent to your hotel."

The lawyers at the prosecution desk dug through their briefcases, and a male intern in the row behind them turned pale. He flipped open his leather portfolio and quickly leaned forward to hand Grant a piece of paper.

"May we have a moment to review this updated document, your honor?" asked Grant.

"No, you may not," said the judge. "Your inability to manage your associates is not this court's concern, and I will not allow it to interfere with this trial."

"Yes, your—"

"And you just brought another question to the bench without waiting for my ruling on your objection," the judge continued, "which is going to cost you a ten-thousand-dollar fine. It's not this court's fault that you are unprepared, and I will not allow you to waste this jury's time. Objection denied."

Grant sat down, and the partner seated next to him turned to glare at the intern with the portfolio.

At the back of the room, Jill sent Clayton a text, "Richards is crashing."

Peterson brought the tagged stocking cap to the clerk, who entered it in the log, and then held it up to Richards. "Is this the stocking cap you were wearing that night?"

"I'm not sure."

"Are you aware that your DNA is on record with the authorities in this state?" Peterson asked without revealing Richards' prior record.

Richards took a few seconds to figure this out.

"Yes, that's my stocking cap," he said impatiently.

Grant knew they hit a dead end with the new evidence. And Richards' stupid sexist remark about the girl next door had already cinched his conviction, anyway. The day had quickly careened off the tracks, and he had to put a stop to it. He stood up. "Your honor, may I approach the bench?"

The judge gestured him and Peterson forward.

"The defense would like to request a meeting with the

prosecution to discuss a deal." Peterson nodded at the judge.

"This case is adjourned until further notice," said the judge, pounding his gavel on the block. "Warden, please sequester the jury."

The room burst into activity, and Jill Frye rushed out to the lobby to call Clayton. When his voicemail kicked in, she told him that Richards made such a fool of himself on the stand that his attorney gave up and asked for a deal. "The three-piece-suit from New York looked so humiliated, I think he'll leave the courthouse through the back door," she said.

Behind the courtroom, Peterson and Grant stood in front of the judge's desk. "The maximum for felony assault is seven years in a federal penitentiary," said Peterson, "but Mr. Grant's client was also on parole, so he's also up for a big fine."

"I'm aware of that," said Grant. "But when you find Terry Strick, Richards will be valuable to you again. It would be a shame if anything happened to him in the penitentiary in the meantime."

"What are you requesting?" asked Peterson.

"Two years at the minimum facility in Faribault and four years' probation," said Grant.

"I could arrest Richards today for perjury and trespassing and make him serve consecutive sentences," said Peterson. "He's going back to prison for a crime he's already been convicted of twice, and this time he attacked a state employee who's very tied in with law enforcement. Nobody wants to see him walk out in two years. Minimum six years in level-four close security at Stillwater and six years probation. That still keeps him out of the federal penitentiary, and he can learn how to build rocking chairs."

It was a stiff sentence but better than Richards would get if the men and women of the jury found him guilty, which Grant knew they would. "What about a reduction if he cooperates in the Strick case again?" he asked.

"You can discuss that with the Hennepin County attorney, if it ever comes to that," said Peterson.

It was a bad or worse scenario, Grant thought, but the prime directive was to avoid a conviction, even in a county court in God-knows-where Minnesota, which would risk bringing too much visibility to the case. Brown-Dixon expected Grant to keep Strick and the company's name out of this mess and paid him well to do it. He had no choice but to accept the deal, and he shook Peterson's hand.

The judge returned to the courtroom through his private door, and Peterson and Grant rushed out the same way they had come in. Grant stopped Peterson at the courtroom door and asked him why the judge was so testy toward him. "It almost seems personal," he said.

"He knows you're the lead counsel for Brown-Dixon Labs," Peterson answered. "Everybody who reads the Law Review at least once a year knows that, Mr. Grant."

"What's he got against us?"

"His wife sued a big pharmaceutical a few years ago after she had a heart attack while on their arthritis drug. The drug was recalled shortly after that and she won a multi-million-dollar settlement, but she died of a second heart attack a week later."

"I see," said Grant.

Peterson flung open the thick oak door, and they filed back into the courtroom.

FORTY-FOUR

The morning after Clayton returned from New York, he woke to the revving engine of a city bus as it pulled away from a stop below his bedroom window. He opened his eyes and looked at Marie's sleeping face, then switched off the alarm before it rang. They had celebrated his Brown-Dixon bonus the night before with a late dinner in the neighborhood and an escapade in the parking lot of the Minneapolis Women's Club, two blocks away from his condominium. Just as he had done about three weeks after they met, he drove her to the parking lot next to the imposing old building, slipped off her dress, pulled her onto his lap and had sex.

They had done the same in many parking lots and back streets all over town since then, but they had not returned to the Women's Club until that night. Clayton talked into her ear about how excited their noises made the young live-in maintenance man whose bedroom light shown through the window and how he was probably watching them. That kind of talk drove both of them crazy, and when lights flicked on in some of the windows upstairs Clayton pushed

Marie away, sped out of the lot and headed around the block toward his building. He drove slowly to point out the young men who stood on the corner of Oak Grove and 15th Street most nights, waiting for johns. Marie, still tipsy from dinner, gawked and waved at them.

Smiling at the memory of Marie hanging out the car window half naked, Clayton got dressed for his nine o'clock meeting with Bill in a lawyer's office downtown. Bill usually called meetings like this to talk about a new tax issue that would affect the partnership, an investment opportunity or some other topic that Clayton found painfully boring. He would not give either of them the benefit of showing up looking like a buttoned-down drone, so he wore a sports jacket, jeans and suede loafers. After leaving a fresh pot of coffee and note for Marie asking her to meet him for lunch, he drove downtown.

In a conference room at the law firm, where they sat around a bulky 70s-era table in faded chairs, Bill introduced Clayton to a lawyer named John Whittacker. "We've asked you here today to try to clarify something that's come up in the office records," said Bill.

"We could have met at Pembroke," Clayton said. "We need to get some use out of our redecorated conference room, which, no offense, Mr. Whittacker, is much more comfortable."

Bill ignored him and held up some papers. "There's a discrepancy between your bank deposits and your Brown-Dixon speaking schedule," he said. "According to your calendar, you should have deposited at least thirty thousand more in speaker's fees into the partnership account in the last year. Do you have some kind of an explanation for why these don't match up?"

Clayton maintained his casual pose, elbows resting on

the arms of his chair and hands folded loosely. He shrugged slightly. "I guess you've got me, Bill."

Bill frowned and glanced at the lawyer, then turned back to Clayton. "You mean you admit it?"

"It looks like you've got the hard evidence—it would be pretty hard to deny it." He tapped his thumbs together.

"This is a serious offense, Clayton," said Bill, raising his voice. "You've broken the contract of the partnership. Technically, this is embezzlement, and that's a felony. Do you know what that means?"

"Why don't we ask the lawyer, so he can earn his fee," said Clayton.

"Sentencing is restitution and up to ten years in prison," said John.

Clayton crossed his legs and sighed. "I can pay it all back, Bill," he said. "We don't need to go to court and make a big mess out of it."

"How do I know you won't leave town and I'll never see you, or the money, again?" asked Bill.

"It was never your money," said Clayton with a smirk. "I earned it and I poured a lot of my fees into the partnership. Just because it's not as much as you put in from your book royalties doesn't mean it's not a fair portion."

"We had a solid agreement about your speaker's fees," said Bill. "There is no vague language about fair portions in our partnership contract. All of your speaker's fees and twenty percent of my royalties go into the practice. That's it, no gray area at all. You can't just change the rules as you go along."

"Bill has got every legal right to sue you for the missing amount as well as for damages," said John. "Or, he could turn you in and let the state deal with it."

"Or," said Clayton, "we can deal with it like adults and let me write you a check right now. I'll leave the practice, and you won't hear from me again."

"You'll give me thirty thousand dollars plus damages today?" asked Bill.

"What kind of damages?"

"Lost interest and legal fees," said John, "about thirty-five hundred dollars."

"Fine." Clayton pulled his wallet from his jacket pocket and took out a blank check. He slid forward in his chair to write on the desk.

Bill grabbed his arm. "Don't you have an explanation or at least some regret over committing a felony against your partner?" Clayton pulled his sleeve out of Bill's grip and returned to his check.

Bill stood up. "I don't get it," he said. "I could get you hauled off to prison and make the state revoke your license, and you sit there writing a check! Do you have a conscience, Clayton?"

Clayton stood up and handed the check to Bill. "You can take this to the bank downstairs and validate it," he said, "and we'll be done. Or you can plan on spending a lot more money suing me for the same outcome, or haul yourself in front of the media by calling the cops and making a state case out of it. What will people think about you when they hear about our long partnership and how I managed to do this right under your nose? Do you really want to risk your own reputation?"

"I don't believe this," Bill shouted. "You're giving me ultimatums, and you're the one who committed the goddamn felony!" He turned to his lawyer. "What the hell is going on here, John?"

"He's actually got a point, Bill," he said. "I can keep him here while you validate the check and you'll have the full restitution. You just won't have the satisfaction of giving him a criminal record and taking away his medical license."

Bill glared at Clayton and breathed heavily. He snatched the check from his hand and held it in front of Clayton's face. "I wouldn't settle here and now with you for a million dollars. You're a pathological liar and a sociopath, and if I let you walk away from this and continue practicing medicine I'll be just as guilty as you." He ripped the check into pieces. "Find a good lawyer. An officer from the state will be calling on you soon."

Clayton shook his head and looked at his wallet sitting on the desk. "Do you feel better, now?" he asked Bill. "Now that you've gotten that off your chest? Good." He pulled another blank check out of his wallet.

"Don't you dare," said Bill. "Get out of here."

Clayton shrugged, gathered his scarf and gloves and left.

Bill and John gazed at the door. "Did you see his reaction?" Bill asked. "He doesn't think he did anything wrong. He was just pissed off that he got caught!"

John pulled two bottles of water from a small refrigerator and handed one to Bill. "Have you ever treated anyone like him?" he asked. "A sociopath, as you called him?"

Bill shook his head. "I've never met anyone like Clayton Shepherd," he said. "And I thank God for that."

FORTY-SIX

Two women peeled off their scuba diving suits on the beach near the open-air bar where Terry Strick sat drinking scotch and puffing on a hand-rolled cigar. The bartender turned to see what Terry was looking at.

"*Muy bonitas*," he said to Terry. "Pretty women from all over the world come to Belize to dive in the reef."

"Very nice," said Terry. The bartender refilled his drink and dropped in two fresh ice cubes. Terry ambled across the white sand to a blue-and-white striped lounge chair and adjusted the umbrella to block the midday sun before lying down. He sunk into the warm canvas and called Clayton.

"*Buonas díaz.*"

"Let me guess," said Clayton. "You're lying under an umbrella with a scotch in your hand, looking out over the blue sea while a lovely young thing with an orchid in her hair massages your feet."

"Pretty close," said Terry.

"Bet you had a nice trip, too," said Clayton.

"You were right. They boarded me on a private jet about two hours after the lawyer walked me out of jail. He told me everything would be cleared up in a few weeks and I should just enjoy myself. That won't be hard in the condo they put me in and all the free time I've got. My only job is to take in the mail, put it in an envelope and mail it to Brown-Dixon headquarters once a week. It helps them keep up the appearance of an actual offshore operation running from down here."

"I know the drill," said Clayton. "I spent a couple of weeks in that condo last winter with a friend. We had a blast. I don't think she wore more than a bikini for thirteen out of the fourteen days we were there."

"It's an incredible setup," said Terry.

"No one is going to find you, my friend," said Clayton. "Even if someone tracks down Brown-Dixon's Belize address, they've got people watching all the flights. If anyone even remotely connected to law enforcement in Minnesota heads your way, they'll warn you and make you invisible until the coast is clear."

"Good. I'm going to visit a marina about a mile down the beach tomorrow and check out a boat I read about in the paper."

"You've already got a boat."

"I know, but I'd like to sail back to the U.S., go up the coast and take the lakes all the way to Lake Michigan. I've always wanted to make that trip. I can sell that boat or my old one when I get home."

The two women divers, now dressed in bikinis with bright scarves wrapped around their hips, stood at Terry's feet. The blonde sprayed his legs by shaking out her wet hair, and the brunette helped herself to his scotch.

"Who would you take with you?"

"I'm making some new friends who might be fun."

"Good man. I'm tempted to get on a plane and join you."

"You don't have time. The boys are almost ready to file for FDA approval and things are going to move very fast once headquarters get your documentation."

"I'm working on it," said Clayton.

The women took off their scarves and bikinis and stretched out along either side of Terry. He rolled over on his side and began rubbing tanning oil along the entire length of the brunette's backside, from her neck to the soles of her feet.

"You've got a bright future ahead of you, Dr. Shepherd," said Terry, his cigar flopping along one side of his mouth. "Just don't screw anything up."

"OK, captain."

The blonde reached around and began rubbing tanning oil on Terry's chest. He reached over the brunette to stick his cigar in the white sand.

FORTY-SEVEN

Clayton stood at the seafood counter at Lunds with his hands clasped behind his back. A woman eyeing the scallops glanced at him repeatedly and finally said, "I'm sorry, but don't you work at Hennepin Metro?"

"Yes, I do," he answered, smiling.

"I'm a nurse in the ER, and I thought I recognized you." She held out her hand and said, "I'm Carly."

"I'm Clayton," he said. "I work up in the psychiatric ward." His eyes wandered over her fitted leather coat and stiletto heel boots. "Those are some boots," he said.

She laughed. "I got them in Italy last summer. I took my son—he's twelve—as a present." The butcher called out a number, and while she turned to wave him down Clayton glanced into her cart to read the label inside her purse.

"Was it his birthday?"

"No." She ordered a pound of salmon. "He was a good sport about our divorce, and he deserved a reward. Something memorable. Have you ever been to Italy?"

"Yes," said Clayton. "Many times. I've got a little place in Lucca, actually."

"You're kidding!" she said. "That's where we stayed on our trip!"

"No, really?"

"What a coincidence," she said, shaking her head.

"I'll bet you had a great time."

"Oh, yes, wonderful." The butcher handed her a white package, and she dropped it in her cart.

The butcher called out Clayton's number and he ordered a pound of jumbo shrimp. A boy in black jeans, tennis shoes and a pea coat appeared next to Carly and held up a six-pack of a high energy drink. "No way, honey," she said. "You know how fast your heart races when you drink that stuff." She turned the boy toward Clayton. "This is Leland."

"Hi, Leland, I'm Dr. Shepherd. I see that you and your mom match today."

The boy looked at his mom's coat and his. "No we don't."

"Just kidding," said Clayton. "I like your Pumas."

"Thanks." He turned to his mom. "Do I really have to put these back?" She looked at him, and he walked away. "He's a great kid," she said.

Clayton collected his package from the butcher and tucked it under his arm. "You're lucky he's handling things so well. As far as you can tell."

"What do you mean?"

"Boys can be tricky about their responses at that age. Some are brilliant at putting up a good front, especially if they're protective of their moms."

"Oh."

He jotted something on the back of his business card and handed it to her. "If you ever want to talk about it, call my office and make an appointment to come and see me. I'd be happy to give you a free consult."

"That's very generous of you," she said.

He slowly removed the sunglasses from the top of her head while loosening a strand of long blond hair entangled around them. "I would really like you to call me," he said, placing the glasses in her hands and holding them there. "I can't believe our paths haven't crossed. I know I haven't seen you at the hospital because you're not a woman I would forget." He placed the glasses back on her head and stroked the two strands of hair falling along the sides of her face. "My cell number is on the back of that card."

In an adjacent aisle, Jill Frye pulled her knit cap further down to cover her hair and backed her cart a few inches closer to the lane in which Shepherd stood, keeping her back to him. She had stopped a few minutes earlier at the sound of Clayton's voice and, hearing the woman, did not turn around. She listened to the entire conversation while glancing at the ceiling from time to view their small, curved reflections in a round mirror. Her hands trembled on the bar of her cart.

Leland came back with a box of cereal and Carly stepped back from Clayton.

"How about this?" Leland asked, holding up the cereal with doughnuts and fudge in the name.

"Sure, honey," Carly said cheerfully. She threw the package in the cart.

FORTY-EIGHT

Even *Clayton's hired thugs couldn't slow Camilla down*, thought Anthony as he read an article about the Hal Richards trial on his laptop at the kitchen table. The county attorney was quoted as saying that the "incontrovertible evidence" brought to trial compelled Richards' defense to approach him about a deal. Although Peterson could not give the details of the arrangement, he assured the reporter that Richards would serve a sentence. Angie was also quoted giving glowing praise to Peterson and the county's entire law enforcement system. Since the trial, she had hung a framed photograph of Camilla by the cash register, a studio shot in which Camilla, dressed in her kendo robes and gear, stood poised in an attack position gripping her bamboo kendo stick. Kids stood in front of it every day to imitate her pose and lunge at each other.

He put a bag of popcorn in the microwave and was about to turn on the TV when Camilla called.

"I was just looking at your Miss Kick-Ass picture in the *Aitkin Courier*," he said.

"Someone broke into my house tonight, Anthony," she

said. "I'm at a hotel and the police are here taking my statement."

"Are you all right?"

"I'm fine. They were gone by the time I got home tonight, but they tore up everything. My furniture is slashed, the dishes are all broken, the refrigerator is lying on the floor, and upstairs . . . I got back just in time."

"What happened upstairs?"

"The bed was smoldering. They had tried to set it on fire from the bottom but the fireproof fabric didn't ignite. The smell is awful."

"What the hell happened to the cop who was watching your place?" Anthony asked, pacing back and forth in the kitchen.

"Whoever did it broke into the back door during the shift change. There was about a five-minute gap before the relief cop pulled up, and by then they'd done all the damage. They figure there were at least two of them."

"What about your files?"

"I lock them up in a safe behind the water heater every time I leave the house, and they haven't been touched. The TV and stereo system in the living room are smashed to pieces, though. It's going to take an army to get the place cleaned up."

Anthony stood beside the counter and pressed his knee into the wall until the drywall cracked. *What if she had been home during that shift change?*

"Are you sure you're all right?" he asked.

"I'll be fine. Louise is on the way over."

"I'll call you back," said Anthony. CJ was at Nira's watching a movie and Padmini was not due to drive him home for another couple of hours, so he grabbed his keys and left.

"Wait!" said Camilla.

"I'm still here," he said.

"Where are you going?"

"Nowhere. I have to take something out of the oven."

"You're upset. CJ is at Padmini's, and you're going to do something," she said.

"I can't stand around here while Clayton is plotting his next attack on you."

"Come over here. I'm at the Westin by Southdale."

"I have to find him, Camilla. The wheels of justice are running too slowly for all of us."

"Find him and do what? We're so close to scheduling the hearing—don't do Shepherd a favor by giving him a chance to turn this against you. Come over here and let's talk about it."

"The hearing," he said, kicking the dented spot in the wall. "He'll burn down the building before he'll let the board conduct another hearing."

"You're scaring me now, Anthony. I'm the one who's supposed to be upset tonight."

"I need to see him, Camilla. I need to tell him how I feel to his face. That's all I'm going to do. I'm sorry."

Winding through the south Minneapolis streets toward downtown, he rolled through stop signs and drove dangerously close to each car that made its way in front of him. He had no reason to assume Clayton would be home at nine o'clock on a Wednesday night, but he gut told him to look there first. His mind raced with images of Camilla's ransacked house, the bruise on her neck that still hadn't disappeared and CJ's thin, sad figure placing a rose on Mike McCarthy's coffin.

Driving along Loring Park he glanced up to see Clayton's well-lit building towering over the naked trees. He turned onto Oak Grove and parked in the circular drive in front of the condominium. Standing by the door, he waited for a tenant to arrive and pretended to be fumbling for his keys in his coat. He followed the man in, checked Clayton's unit number on the directory and rode the elevator up to the twelfth floor. He pulled out the emergency stop button, then called the other elevator up and halted that one, too.

Leaning against Shepherd's door, he felt the rhythmic thud of a stereo bass. He pounded on the door.

A few seconds later the music stopped.

Anthony knocked again.

Shepherd opened the door as far as the chain lock would allow.

"What the hell are you doing here?" he asked.

"Open the door or I'll open it for you," Anthony said, breathing hard. His pulse throbbed in his eyes and throat.

"Fuck you," said Shepherd. He began to close the door, but Anthony heaved himself against it and broke the chain, throwing Clayton to the floor. Anthony swept in, locked the door and walked over Shepherd.

"Do you really think you can get away with terrorizing a state board investigator?" Anthony said, backing into the living room.

"What the hell are you talking about?" said Clayton. He picked up a piece of mangled chain from the floor. "You just wrecked my door—are you nuts?"

"This is a friendly warning, Clayton. I came over here so I can see your face when you get a dose of reality. That investigator who beat your hired stooge to a pulp has so much on you that you'll never practice medicine again. And the police have a case so tight you'll be off the streets for a long time. You've been lucky so far, but your run is over. You're a menace, and you're going away."

"You can't just break in here, you crazy son of a bitch," said Clayton, rubbing his head. He tied his black silk robe shut and boldly walked past Anthony to stand by the white leather couch. "My neighbors have called the police by now, and you're the one who will be going away." He rubbed his neck and laughed.

"It's hilarious to you, isn't it? You don't think anyone can touch you. But your luck just ran out."

"Are you threatening me, Dr. Robson?"

Anthony glanced at the coffee table where an open box spilling over with newspaper clippings stood next to a familiar-looking glass paperweight. He focused on the object and made out his name in gold lettering beneath the University of Minnesota logo. Sirens sounded in the distance.

"Where did you get that?" he asked Clayton, motioning to the coffee table with his head. Clayton kept his eyes on Anthony.

Moving closer to the table, Anthony saw within the clippings an autographed black-and-white photograph of him with Minnesota Governor Jessie Ventura.

"You took these things from my house," he said, unable to hide his astonishment. "We have a mutual friend who brought some things over," said Shepherd.

"I don't think so. Do you have a shrine for me in your bedroom, too, maybe with some candles and a copy of my diploma from graduate school? What else have you stolen? If you really love me, I'll bet you're wearing my underwear under that Victoria's Secret outfit right now. Am I right?"

"Love you?" said Clayton. "You're all mixed up. I'm in love with your wife, remember?"

"Right," said Anthony. "When are you going to get tired of Marie, too, and toss her out like the others? I've read their testimonies—you've left such a long trail of furious women

I'm surprised one of them hasn't gotten to you yet. Are you watching your back, Clayton?"

"You just can't stand the fact that your wife hopped out of your sack and into mine. That's got to hurt."

"One day Marie will get tired of taking your pills and it won't take her long to see you for who you really are. One insecure little prick."

Clayton laughed and stuck his hands in his pockets. "Are you about done?"

"No," said Anthony. "You better take a last look at your nice digs, because once the county attorney gets done with you, you won't be coming back. If the sexual misconduct part of your case doesn't shut you down, the secret drug trial will. We know all about it."

"You're crazy," said Clayton.

"No, you were crazy to think Terry Strick would just disappear. He's sitting in a holding cell in the federal building as we speak, coughing up more details to the FBI."

Clayton frowned in disbelief.

"They picked him up on some Caribbean beach, easiest thing in the world," said Anthony. "Two undercover cops in bikinis."

"You're full of shit," said Clayton.

"I am? Then how do I know that he's been delivering experimental drugs to you, little green pills cooked up at Brown-Dixon Labs that look just like Prozor? Pills laced with enough opiates to make kids forget their names let alone their self-destructive thoughts? Pills that Brown-Dixon plans to pass off as harmless SSRIs? How do I know that Brown and Dixon themselves just handed you a check for a quarter million dollars and hired a contractor to start plotting the site for the Shepherd Clinic in Baltimore? How would I know all that, Clayton, if Terry Strick wasn't spilling his guts?"

Clayton put his hand on the knob of a drawer in the console table behind him.

"And that's not all we've got," said Anthony. "Remember your last conversation with your favorite bartender by Lake Calhoun? When you bragged to her about how you could buy heroin and hire thugs to beat people up? She was kind enough to wear a wire that night, and it's all on tape."

"Jan?"

The sirens grew louder and red and white lights strobed faintly on the walls.

"There's another tape, too," said Anthony, "recorded outside your car window when you were talking to Strick about the drug trials. You boys were having a real good time with your rolled joint, remember?"

"This is all crap," said Clayton. "You're trying to scare me to make me give your wife back, but it's not going to work. You're a broken little man. It took me six months to get everything you worked a lifetime for, and you can't take it."

Anthony strained to calculate how much longer it may take the police to climb the stairs to the twelfth floor. "So this is what it's all about," he said, "trying to copy my life? Little Clayton couldn't measure up to his brilliant brother, so he has to prove himself by cutting me down? They're going to have a field day writing you up in psychiatric journals, the narcissistic freak who paraded as one of their own."

"Shut up!" said Clayton, sweat running into his eyes. He pulled open the drawer and grabbed a pistol. "I can shoot you right now for breaking in here," he said, stepping toward Anthony and pointing the gun at his chest. "You've given me the perfect opportunity to finish what I've started. I got your wife and you're so-called career, and now I can get rid of you."

Anthony backed up against the wall next to the kitchen entryway. "The cops are in the building, Clayton," he said.

"And you're the one who broke down my door like a maniac. I've got every right to blow your face off."

Anthony forced himself to not look at the pistol. *What would he say if I were standing here with a gun?*

"I came to warn you, remember?" said Anthony. "I gave you a chance to flee the country tonight, or stay here and take your chances with all of Brown-Dixon's support behind you. You were right—I wanted to scare you so you would run away. I thought you'd leave so fast you wouldn't bother to track down Marie tonight and wait for her to get ready to go with you. Then she would be rid of you, and I could get her back. That was my plan. So let me go, and do what you need to do."

Clayton smiled. "You must think I'm—"

The front door crashed open and four officers streamed into the room. Clayton was too stunned to lower his pistol, so the two men in front aimed their revolvers at him. Anthony raised his arms, and an officer pulled him out into the hall.

•

At the precinct, Detective Bo Williams sat across from Anthony in a meeting room without a two-way mirror and windows opening to the hallway. Anthony assured him, again, that he did not want to call a lawyer. "Clayton Shepherd won't file charges against me for breaking down his door because his lawyers know they can't prove I intended to steal anything. More than that, they don't want a statement on record from me about the reason I went to see Shepherd tonight. I had a lot to say to him and statements like that can get into the wrong hands."

"He could have shot you," said Williams. "You don't need a permit to have a pistol in your house."

"And the broken door and bump on his head would have made it easy for him to prove self-defense," said Anthony. "I know. I'm a lucky guy."

Williams stepped out to talk to another detective. When he returned, he kept the door open.

"You know this man well," he told Anthony. "Shepherd didn't file charges. You're free to go."

FORTY-NINE

A waiter refilled Jill Frye's water glass as she waited for Clayton in their favorite downtown restaurant near her new apartment. Settled into a corner banquette, she recalled it was here that Clayton initiated his gift-giving ritual. The first was a diamond tennis bracelet, followed the next week by a large amber cocktail ring in a Tiffany box. The week after that came pearl earrings, then a card containing two tickets to the Chicago Philharmonic, on tour at Minneapolis' Orchestra Hall. She counted off the gifts by pressing her fingers against the stem of her martini glass. His fifth present, an outrageously expensive French handbag presented in a pink hatbox that Clayton had carried into the restaurant with both hands, sat at her side. Then came the Ansel Adams coffee table book, in which he had slipped a round-trip ticket to New York to see a new photography exhibit at the Museum of Modern Art and the address of a chic Midtown hotel where he'd made her reservations.

The night he gave her the New York trip, she sat in that very corner and insisted that he didn't need to compete with Allan (who, she reflected with a pang of conscience, had probably just arrived home from a trip and was sitting alone in front of the fireplace instead of cradling David in his arms as he watched TV) and that she preferred he stop giving her gifts. She told Clayton that she didn't need material signs of his love because their connection, their indescribable physical and spiritual bond, transcended any relationship she had ever had. She still believed that then, just like she believed he considered her the most precious, enlightened woman he had ever known and the soul mate he had been searching for his entire life.

The shock of his betrayal—no, more than betrayal, his bludgeoning revelation that his every touch and word was a lie and vulgarity—first led to sadness and then anger. She berated herself again for being so dense that it took a ridiculous scene at the Lunds meat counter to wake her up to his true nature. She left the grocery store that day with a broken heart, but her anguish had gradually burned itself down to a fluid, simmering rage.

She kept her eye on the door and glanced from time to time at the men looking at her in the brown, strapless chiffon dress she'd bought in New York on orders from Clayton, who had asked her to buy something that matched her eyes. She smiled when Clayton came through the door and walked toward her. He kissed her before sitting down.

"You wore it," he said. "I've been waiting all day to see that dress."

The waiter brought them menus and returned a minute later with two glasses of wine.

"A weekend in New York would have been a lot more fun if you had come along," she said. "But thank you. I had a marvelous time." She lifted her glass. "To our happy reunion."

Clayton clinked her glass and kissed her bare shoulder.

"May I?" Jill asked, holding up the small white box he had set on her plate.

"Of course," said Clayton.

She opened it and lifted out a gray velvet box containing a delicate, leaf-pattern pinky ring in Black Hill's gold. The coppery metal sparkled in the soft light and she slipped it on her finger. "I love it."

He kissed her fingers and gently tugged at the ring with his teeth. The waiter arrived and Clayton ordered the special for both of them, but Jill handed the menus to the waiter and, after apologizing to Clayton, told him she would like the duck.

Throughout dinner, Clayton talked about the chaos on the ward after his patient stabbed himself, the bloody mess he made all over their clothes when they restrained him and the nurse's aide who fainted at the sight of the blood-soaked bed. The ER doctor who picked out the bits of broken plastic from his neck and cleaned the wound before surgery did a good job, he said, but he was surprised that she could be so deft with her instruments when she had such grossly fat fingers and hands. "The woman is huge," he said. "The residents call her Darth Vader because she breathes so hard."

They skipped dessert and finished with apricot liqueur. "Do the nurses in the ER do a good job?" Jill asked innocently.

"They're all right, as far as I know," he said.

"I'll bet nurses on every ward have their eye on you," she said, running her hand along his forearm. "If I worked there, I wouldn't be able to take my hands off you."

"You're a funny little minx," he said. "How thoughtless of me to talk about work when I've missed you so much. Let's get out of here and take a walk."

Jill said she would love to go to Loring Park, where they had walked before spending their first night together at her new place. They drove toward the basilica, its ashen dome glowing on the black horizon of west downtown, and stopped on the north side of the park. Once they started on the winding pathway they passed a male couple walking hand in hand. "Don't mind the boys," Clayton said. They walked arm in arm, and Jill looked westward at the art museum where Allan had thrown her a birthday party the previous year. Clayton's arm felt like a rod of cold steel through her coat. *Wait for me, Allan. I'll make it all up to you.*

Her muscles stiffened as they strolled beneath another dim pool of light cast by and old street lamp.

"Are you too warm?" Clayton said, tugging her wool scarf. "Your face is getting red. I think we need to get you out of that dress."

She wrapped her arms around his neck and kissed him. "Let's go to the hot spot you showed me," she said, "where it's dark and cozy." She kissed him again and then clutched his arm to lead him toward a stand of spruce trees mixed with bare lilac bushes.

"It was warmer that night," said Clayton, as she pulled him into the trees.

She took off her shoes and stood on a metal grate that emitted a foul-smelling steam. After throwing her coat and purse in a heap, she pulled off his leather jacket.

"My God," said Clayton. "I'll have to send you off on cultural weekends more often." He unzipped the side of her dress and dropped his pants. She tossed his sweater and undershirt on the ground and kicked his shoes aside.

They stood on top of the grate and kissed, and when he tried to pull off her dress she pulled his hands away and finished pulling off his jockey shorts with her toes.

"You really missed me, didn't you, baby," he said, rubbing his hands against her bare back beneath her dress. He shook from the cold, and she told him to turn around so she could warm him up. She held him with her face pressed against his back and slowly slid down until she could reach into her purse. After rising back up, she scratched his naked chest with her free hand while adjusting her grip on a wire garrote with the other.

"I know who you are," she whispered into the back of his neck.

"Jill, this is fun, but I'm fucking *freezing*."

"I'm sorry," she said. She looped the garote over his head and twisted the handle. He scratched at the wire and broke free from her, falling on his knees a few feet away in front of the trees. She leapt behind him, covered his head with his coat and tightened the wire again.

"I spent the afternoon with the police," she said, hunching over his covered head. "They're talking to all your patients—did you know that?"

She leaned closer and felt the garote compress as it cut through another layer of flesh. As his weight pulled against her grip, the wire penetrated deeper.

"You thought you could treat me like all the others," she whispered, "all your pretty little friends. I threw away my life, but it was just a *game* to you!" She jerked back his head and his arms dropped to his sides. "No more games, Clayton."

She held him and watched her breath shoot out in foggy pulses that vanished a few inches from her face. All of his weight pressed against her, motionless, while the rumble of traffic from Hennepin Avenue on the other side of the park floated over her.

"No more games and no more lies."

His body twitched and she released the garote, dropping his body face down onto the grass. She pressed his wrist to feel for his pulse and lifted the coat to stare at the dark, glistening ribbon where the wire disappeared into his neck. She loosened the garote, worked the wire free from the gash and dragged the loop over his head.

Grabbing the coat, she sprang up and glanced at his long, naked body before running back into the trees. She pulled on her coat and shoes, swept up his things and walked up Willow Street with the bundle under her arm.

FIFTY

Bill Olson got the call from Detective Williams at 9:00 a.m. as he was driving to Pembroke. Fifteen minutes later, after a slight change of route, he pulled into the underground parking ramp at Hennepin Metro. The hospital entrance on that level led directly to the basement, where Williams was waiting in the morgue with Anthony, Camilla and Louise.

The detective knocked on the window, and a woman in a white doctor's coat waved them in. "Are you ready for us?" Williams asked her as they crowded behind the counter that separated the front area from the main room.

"Sure," she said. "He's right over here."

They followed her to the far side of the room where a body, covered by a sheet, lay on a metal shelf that had been pulled out of the wall. Williams introduced them to the medical examiner, Liz Carlson, whose name tag was hidden behind by the pair of elbow-length vinyl gloves hanging around her neck.

"It wasn't a quick, painless death, I can tell you that," said Carlson. "The metal wire cut through his spinal cord pretty deep before he suffocated. Whoever did this placed the handles slightly off to the side of the back of his neck so that the wire could cut between two vertebra and get to the cord." She folded back the sheet to expose the upper third of the body.

"Jesus," said Anthony.

"Do you have any leads yet?" Bill asked Williams, his eyes fixed on Shepherd's neck.

"First things first," said Camilla. "There's a lot to sort out, including the evidence from this morning." She turned to Williams. "Did they find the weapon?"

"No," he answered. "But a garrote is not a common gadget. They're calling shops to track down everyone who's bought one in the past couple of years."

"Anything else come up at the scene?" asked Louise.

"They're still working it," said Williams.

"How strong do you have to be to kill someone with a garrote?" Camilla asked.

"Not very," said Carlson. "Once the attacker makes the first twist, the victim is powerless, especially if the attack comes from behind."

"Like it did here."

"Right."

"So, a woman easily could have done it," Camilla said.

"Even a small woman, as long as she was quick enough to take him by surprise."

They all stared at the white sheet.

"If it's one of Shepherd's patients or someone he worked with," said Williams, "we'll know soon. The lab is running DNA tests on a few strands of hair they found on the body. We got subpoenas to run DNA on everyone we questioned, and the turnaround on those is pretty fast right now. We might get a match."

"Did anyone seem ruffled over the DNA test?" asked Louise.

"Not that I heard about," said Williams.

A young couple accompanied by a female uniformed officer entered the morgue and stood behind the counter.

"Anything else?" Carlson asked.

"No, we're done," said Williams.

They headed back to the door, and Carlson followed until she got to her desk. "Wait," she said, reaching into a drawer. She dug around, pulled out a garrote with aluminum handles and tossed it to Williams.

"What's this for?" he said.

"A sample, so your green recruits know what they're looking for."

Williams led them out, and Camilla and Anthony turned back before closing the door. They watched as Carlson pushed the metal slab holding Shepherd's body into its slot, slowly at first, then with a quick final shove to secure the door latch with a click.

•

Two days later, Detective Williams showed up at Jill Frye's apartment with an assistant district attorney, two uniformed officers, Allan Frye and his attorney. She let them in without a word and watched Allan collect David out of his booster chair in the kitchen while Williams informed her that she was under arrest for the murder of Clayton Shepherd and recited her Miranda rights.

FIFTY-ONE

Camilla threw a duffel bag on her new mattress, still covered in plastic, and began to fill it with clothes. She glanced around the room for her hair dryer—which her mom told her to bring because she dropped hers in a bowl of cereal and it hadn't worked since—and caught her reflection in the freestanding mirror. She stepped over to it and peered at her face and the hint of chain above the collar of her T-shirt. She pulled the dog tags over her head and placed them in a glass box by the bed.

Anthony's car horn sounded, and she yelled from the window that she would be down in a minute. CJ, Nira and Padmini were waiting with him, their bags piled in the back of his SUV for a long weekend at the lake.

As she brushed out her hair, she noticed a live breaking news report on the cable news and turned up the volume on the TV. The reporter stood in a crowd of other journalists and cameras.

Officials from Brown-Dixon Labs have finally released a statement confirming that both Robert Brown, the CEO of Brown-Dixon Labs, and Leonard Dixon, the company's

Executive Vice President and Co-CEO, have been arrested by state authorities in their headquarters, which you see behind me.

According to our sources, Brown and Dixon have been accused of overseeing an unauthorized human drug trial in an undisclosed state. A sales executive for Brown-Dixon Labs blew the lid off the secret trial after he was arrested in Belize last week. Unconfirmed reports state that Brown-Dixon integrated data from the disputed drug trial into the large database of the authorized trial they had been running on the drug over the past nine years. They did this, according to our sources, in order to bypass a time-consuming period of seeking a pool of human subjects and receiving their approval to participate in the study. In a shocking twist to the story, we learned a few minutes ago that the psychiatrist from that undisclosed state who gave the experimental drugs to his patients was recently murdered.

Camilla zipped up her duffel bag, switched off the TV, kicked a cardboard box of case files into a corner and bounded down the stairs.

FATAL REMEDY